C000259527

Paperback ISBN: 978-1-7398220-3-3

First published June 2022

The Burning of Mary Channing

Haines Gritton

Chapter One

'No, no, no, *NO*! I will *NOT* marry *THAT*!' Mary pointed at the squat man sat in a wing back chair, a determined expression on her face. She stood, legs apart, one hand on her hip, a look of defiance in her eyes while her cheeks were flushed red with anger.

Richard Brookes was exasperated. 'You will do as you are told, young lady!' He shook his head in bewilderment. Her mother, who was sat in a corner of the room watching proceedings unfold, stifled a smile and turned her head to one side to avoid it being seen.

The object of Mary's derision stood to leave. 'Sit down, young man!' Richard ordered and Thomas Channing immediately did as he was told, dropping back into the chair, gripping tightly on to the rim of his hat.

Mary made to push her way past her father but he refused to move, putting his arm across her chest and forcing her to take a backward step. 'Father, I have no intention of doing what you tell me to do. I shall do as I please and there is nothing you can do about it.'

1

'Do as you please? We shall see about that. You have a straight choice, Mary. Marry Mister Channing and do as you are told. Or leave this house and see how you prosper without my financial support.'

Mary pouted. "Fine! I will leave!'

She pushed past her father once more and he let her go this time. Richard listened to her stomp up the stairs and slam the door shut on her bedroom. He shook his head in frustration, looking to his wife. 'Go to her and explain that my mind is set. I shall conclude my business with Mr Thomas and begin making the arrangements. Inform her that she has no choice in the matter.' He turned to Thomas Channing. 'Sir, I must apologise for the behaviour of my daughter. She may be sixteen, but she has much growing up to do.'

Thomas stood up. 'But sir, it would appear she has no intention of marrying me and it is not in my nature to force her.'

Richard gestured for him to sit down once more. 'She will be fine. She will soon come round to the idea. Indeed, she has no alternative. It is either marry you, or go to the poor house. She will see sense.' He went to the side table and picked up a crystal decanter. 'Brandy?' Thomas nodded and Richard poured two glasses. Replacing the heavy lid, he handed the younger man a glass and sat down on the chair opposite him. 'I fear it is my fault, for I have been far too lenient on her. She is a sweet girl, but headstrong, a trait I suspect she gets from me.' He chuckled to himself. 'Also, with six brothers to look after her, she has been indulged to the point where I have turned a blind eye to many of her activities, much to my cost.'

'So I have heard.' Thomas looked away and took a large swig of the brandy for fear of saying something that would put the proposed arrangement in danger. He need not have worried. A long line of potential suitors had come and gone, all put off by Mary's reputation as a girl without virtue who played hard and fast and had an eye for the boys. As far as Richard Brookes was concerned, Thomas was the last man standing and he was keen to conclude proceedings as soon as possible so that she would no longer be his responsibility.

Richard waved his hand, as if swatting a fly. 'There is nothing to worry about. Her mother assures me she still has her virtue. It is just her manners that need repairing. Now, we must set a date.' He arose and walked over to a wooden bureau. Pulling down the front, he retrieved a leather bound book and returned to his seat. Opening it up, he flicked through the pages. Arriving at a suitable page, he ran his hand down his scribblings and settled on a date. 'I propose it takes place early next year. This looks like a convenient day. Three weeks, this Sunday. January the fourteenth, 1705. What say you?'

Thomas was taken aback. 'Why so soon? There are many arrangements to be made!'

Richard laughed. 'Don't worry about that! I will take care of all the arrangements, along with my wife. All you need do is let me know who you wish to be there and I will arrange for the invitations to be sent.'

Thomas shook his head. 'It is too short notice for my family. I will let them know in due course. I have a few friends here in Dorchester who may be able to attend. I will let you have their details.'

'Splendid!' Richard stood up and gently squeezed Thomas's shoulder. 'I shall pay the dowry after the wedding as agreed. All you have to do is turn up at the church!'

The two men clinked their brandy glasses together to seal their pact before knocking the fiery liquid back in one.

Meanwhile, upstairs, Mary was sobbing into her mother's shoulder. 'I don't want to be married. Why would father make me do such a thing?'

Elizabeth Brookes stroked her daughter's long hair as she embraced her. 'It is for your own good, Mary. You know you cannot go on forever like this. Besides, Thomas seems a kind, considerate man. A gentleman.'

Mary pulled back, wiping at her eyes. 'A gentleman? He is a monster! You have seen him! He looks like a troll! And he is old! Why would father want me to marry someone like him?'

'Shush, child.' Elizabeth forced Mary's head back into her shoulder and she started sobbing again. 'Of course you will marry him. And he is not that old. He is just twenty-five! That is a good age for a husband to be. Your father will make the arrangements and you will become a respectable, married woman. Besides, how do you think I married your father? Do you think I had any say in it?'

Mary sobbed in response. Elizabeth carried on. 'It was arranged without my knowledge. I barely knew of him until I met him just a few weeks before our wedding day, and even then I was chaperoned so I could never be alone with him.'

'Yes, but you love father. I could never love *him*.' Her voice was muffled as her face remained smothered in her mother's shoulder.

'Not at first. It took time. But love grows in the strangest of places and I am sure you will grow to love Mister Channing. Besides, he is respectable, comes from a good family and has his own property and business. You are lucky. Few of your friends will be so fortunate in being given such a match.'

Mary's sobs were subsiding now and her mother sat her up straight, grabbing her by the arms. 'It will be fine, I promise. Just do this for your father and you will be free of his tyranny. After that, whatever takes place between your husband is none of your father's business.'

Mary wiped her face once more, the beginnings of a smile on her face. 'I suppose you are right. Once I am married, what I do is up to me.'

Elizabeth frowned, wondering what her daughter was thinking. 'And your husband.'

'Yes, of course,' Mary nodded. 'It will be up to me. And my husband.'

Chapter Two

The bell of the shop tinkled as the door to Thomas Channing's grocery shop was pushed open. Thomas looked up and smiled as he saw the woman enter. 'Good morning, Eliza. How are you?'

'I am well. I have bought some fruit cheese for us.' She held up a small piece of cloth for him to see.

'Thank you. You are too kind.' He indicated for her to carry on through to the back room where she took a seat at the small, wooden table. He followed her in and put a pot on the stove. 'I shall make us some ginger tea.'

Eliza placed the small package on the table and carefully opened the cloth out into a square, revealing four small chunks of orange coloured cheese. 'Two each,' she announced as she picked up one piece and put it in her mouth.

Thomas leant over and picked one up, putting it in his mouth and chewing slowly, letting the flavours fill his mouth. 'Mmmm, delicious.' He took two cups from the dresser and placed them on the table alongside the cheese. Taking a teapot from the cupboard, he said 'I shall just go and get some ginger.

I won't be long.'

He returned promptly and checked the water in the pot on the stove. It was beginning to come to the boil. Lifting it up with a cloth, he carefully tipped the water into the teapot. After setting the larger pot to one side, he sat down alongside her. 'Just give it a minute or two to brew. This cheese is delicious.' He picked up a second piece and put it in his mouth. Still chewing, he said 'Now tell me about your day.'

'I went back to see Mrs Arkle. She's the lady with the sores on her legs.'

'Is she any better?'

Eliza nodded. 'Yes, there is much improvement. I applied some more ointment, though. I think another couple of days and she will be better.'

'Good. Weren't you also seeing the blacksmith's father today as well?'

Eliza grimaced. 'Unfortunately he passed during the night.'

'Oh. I'm sorry.'

'It was not unexpected. Although I like to think I gave him some comfort in his final days.

'I am sure you did.' Thomas picked up the pot and swirled it round. 'I think this will be ready.' Placing some gauze over the cup, he poured the sweet smelling tea into the two cups and pushed one over to Eliza. 'Did you want that last piece?' He looked at the last chunk of cheese on the cloth.

Eliza smiled. 'No. You can have it.'

Thomas picked it up and quickly popped it in his mouth before she could change her mind. 'Thank you.'

'What of your day? You said yesterday that you might have important news to tell me.'

Thomas looked down at his cup as he picked it up and sipped at it carefully so as not to burn his lips. He slowly placed it back on the table, leant forward and grabbed both of Eliza's hands in his own. 'I'm afraid I do. And please do not think unkindly of me.'

Eliza smiled sweetly at him. 'Why would I do that?'

'Because I fear you will not like it.'

Eliza frowned. 'What is it? Are you going away on business again?'

Thomas shook his head and withdrew his hands from hers. 'No, nothing like that.' He sat back in his chair and took another sip of tea. Steeling himself, he took a deep breath. 'I am to be married.'

'Married?' Eliza's face dropped. 'Oh. I see. I must confess, I did not expect that.'

Thomas shrugged, not knowing what else to say.

Eliza gathered herself. 'So who is this lucky lady?' The news had been totally unexpected and she was struggling to maintain her composure.

'I'm not sure she is a lady!' he responded, a wide grin on his ruddy face.

She raised an eyebrow, questioning him further without saying a word.

Thomas's face turned serious again. 'She is a local girl, of good stock, born to a wealthy family. Her father owns much of Dorchester and I believe he also has business interests in Honiton and Exeter. He is keen to see her married.'

'But why you? How do you know her?'

He shook his head as he took another sip of the sweet ginger tea. 'I don't, really. I mean, I know of her. Everybody around these parts does. She has a certain, erm, reputation.'

'Reputation for what exactly?'

'My dear Eliza, I didn't realise you would be so interested in my personal affairs!'

Eliza tried to make light of it, although inside her stomach was twisting. 'Well, I suppose I shouldn't be. But I want to know all about the woman who is taking my Thomas away from me.' She rested her hand on his arm and he didn't move it away.

He stared deeply into her eyes.

'To be honest, if it wasn't for the money that comes with taking her hand in marriage, I would not be interested. I believe her family would like to see her attain respectability as she has gained a reputation for spending her life in "pleasure." Her father recently requested that potential suitors make themselves known to him and I met with him last week. It has now been decided that she is to marry me.'

A pang of jealousy struck at Eliza's heart. She promptly removed her hand from his arm and he looked at her sadly. 'I am sorry. To be honest this has come out of the blue for me as well. But it is simply too good an opportunity to turn down. Having just finished my apprenticeship and opened the store, the money that will come from marrying her will set me up for life and will enable me to open up more stores without having to rely on my father. Fiscally speaking, it makes sense and I am keen to prove I can do it without him. Besides,' he looked into her eyes once more, 'it isn't as if I have lots of suitable young women falling at my feet, is it?' He looked ruefully down at his foot. 'I will soon be twenty-five years of age and it will be prudent to marry sooner rather than later as my options for choosing a wife are beginning to thin out.'

Eliza thought about declaring her own interest in him but decided against it for fear of embarrassment. 'I see. And she is attractive, this girl?'

Thomas nodded. 'She is easy on the eye, but this is just a fortunate coincidence. She could look like an old nag and I would still be set to marry her!'

'Well, it's not as if you are a Greek statue!' Eliza snapped, regretting it immediately as he looked away. 'I'm sorry,' she added. 'Forgive me. That was uncalled for.'

Thomas smiled weakly at her. 'You are right though. With my deformed foot, I should be lucky that anybody would want to even look at me, let alone marry me.'

'So when is to be the happy day?' Eliza tried to sound happy for him, but there was a slight tremor in her voice.

'It is to happen quickly. Within just a few weeks. January fourteenth next year has been decided upon. Her father is making the arrangements. All I need do is turn up and do the honourable thing. It has been requested that a child follows quickly. Preferably a son.'

'And what does your father think of this?'

Thomas shook his head. 'He does not know.'

'Pardon?'

'My father, indeed my family, they do not know.' He looked up at her, his eyes pleading. 'And neither are they to find out.'

Eliza placed her hands in her lap, her fingers tightly interlocked. The look on her face said it all and Thomas knew that he had hurt her. 'I am sorry.'

Eliza blinked quickly, as if holding back tears. She gathered herself. The silence fell between them again and they both drank their tea. Finally, she spoke. 'So tell me all about her. Your wife to be.'

Thomas's face brightened. 'Her name is Mary. She has been well educated and appears to be quite bright. She is also very well connected, which bodes well for my business. But she is quite young.'

'Young? What age is she?'

'She turns seventeen in May. I understand it is a good age to bear children, however.'

'I see.' Eliza was older than Thomas and the news that he was to be married to a woman far younger than herself felt like a punch to the stomach. She stood up to leave. 'Then I should go, for it is not right for me to be alone here with you.'

Thomas grabbed at her hand but she snatched it away before he could grip it. 'Eliza, please!' he implored her. 'Surely we can remain friends?'

Eliza shook her head. 'It is not right, for you know I have feelings for you.'

Thomas had known that she had grown fond of him in the few months they had known each other. 'I am sorry. But you know it is impossible for me.'

'But why is it impossible? Don't you have feelings for me as well?'

Thomas shook his head sadly. 'You know I care deeply for you. But you have been married once before.'

'My husband is dead! I am free to do as I please.'

'I know that. But you are a widow. My father would never countenance such an arrangement.'

'Why not?' Eliza demanded angrily. 'Is your father so immune to affairs of the heart?'

'It is not practical!' he snapped. 'You know it isn't. Society frowns upon such arrangements.' Thomas looked out of the window, regretting his outburst, but unwilling to apologise for it.

'So you are doing this to keep society and your father happy, are you? Are you really so weak?' Her words were bitter.

Thomas shook his head, sadly. 'It is the right thing to do. I have no choice. Regardless of what I feel about you, my father would never agree to us getting married. I must do what is right.'

'And yet you are prepared to enter into a marriage with this girl without even informing your father for fear of his reaction.' Eliza turned on her heel and headed for the door. She half turned as she reached for the handle on the door. 'Well I suppose this is goodbye.'

Thomas said nothing, maintaining his gaze as he stared out of the window, looking at nothing in particular. He heard the bell tinkle once more as the door opened, then closed. Only when he was sure she had gone did he rise from the chair, gathering up the two cups and sighing deeply as he dropped them both in the bucket of water next to the stove.

Chapter Three

Thomas waited patiently in the ante-room. He could hear muffled voices on the other side of the closed door. Even though he could not hear what was being said, he sensed the urgency. He heard footsteps disappearing down the hallway and looked up as the door finally opened. Elizabeth Brookes entered the room. 'I am sorry for the delay. We are not quite sure where Mary is at the moment. But I am sure she won't be long. Would you like to come through to the drawing room?'

Thomas stood up and followed her through to the same room where Richard Brookes had accepted his offer to marry Mary. He sat down in the same chair he had occupied just one week earlier and wondered what he was doing there. Mrs Brookes sat apart from him, looking down at the polished floor, seeking out flaws and patterns in the wooden planks. An awkward silence fell between them and Thomas found himself listening to the wind gusting strongly outside. His gaze fell upon a skeletal oak tree in the garden, its heavy branches swaying to and fro as the wind forced its way through it.

'I think it will be quite some storm tonight,' he said. His

voice sounded louder than he had expected and he quietly chastised himself, feeling stupid.

'I fear you may be right.' Elizabeth Brookes followed Thomas's gaze and looked out at the tree. The dark clouds were rushing past and even though it was early afternoon, the sky was already darkening. With winter solstice taking place the previous week, it would not be long before night fell. She wondered once more where her daughter had gone, conscious that Thomas would wish to return to his home before nightfall. Mary had known that Thomas was coming and Elizabeth was annoyed that she had trusted her daughter to present herself when Thomas had arrived.

Thomas was also wondering where his bride to be was. He pulled his pocket watch out of his waistcoat and gathered the time. 'Is Mr Brookes here?'

Elizabeth shook her head. 'No, he is in Honiton on business. He left last week.'

'I see. When is he to return?'

'I am not sure. He should be back in time for the Christmas celebrations. Perhaps you can come to our party on Christmas night.' Elizabeth looked up. 'It is always quite an event.'

'That would be nice. I must check with my father to see what his plans are first, but if I can, I will.'

Elizabeth suspected he would not come to her party and felt disappointed. She started slightly as the door suddenly flung open. The servant looked harassed, his cheeks red. 'I have found her mistress. But she wishes to speak with you first.'

Elizabeth got to her feet. 'Please excuse me Mr Channing. I shall return shortly.'

Thomas stared out of the window again, trying once more to hear the hushed conversation the other side of the door but the words were indistinct and the wind was now rattling the windows. His stomach rumbled and he wished he had eaten something before setting off on horseback to the Brookes' residence.

His thoughts turned to his soon-to-be wife. She was

attractive and shapely and he had never believed he would be so fortunate to get such a bride. But he had heard that she was also a handful and he wondered if he would every truly be able to exert any form of control over her. There were many rumours about her. Her house parties were well known and there was talk of her having a man friend, close to her own age. Which was why he had been so surprised when he had heard that she was available to be married should someone wish to do so.

It had taken several days to pluck up the courage to visit Mr Brookes to see if he would consider him as a suitable husband for his daughter. But, when he had presented himself, he had received a warm welcome. Mr Brookes knew of his father and had been full of praise for the Channing name. Indeed, he had embraced the idea of joining the two families together. But Mary's reaction upon meeting him that first time had shocked him. Instead of being respectful and warm towards him, she had put on a display of such petulance that Thomas had pushed the thought of ever marrying her out of his mind. It was only the reassuring words of Mr Brookes that had brought him back to the notion of taking Mary for his wife.

The purpose of his visit today was to meet with Mary in order for them to get to know each other. Protocol determined that she would be chaperoned and it was Mrs Brookes who was to oversee the encounter. He felt his foot throbbing and he rubbed at it, wishing he could remove his boot and put his foot up to ease the pain. His splayed foot had caused him problems throughout his life and the deformity troubled him. What would Mary think when she saw it for the first time? Would she be afraid? Or would she mock him? He feared it would be the latter. He was stirred from his thoughts as the door opened once more.

'Thomas?' Mary entered the room and curtsied before him, her mother close behind her. Her dress was adorned with ribbons and her hair was loose, cascading down onto her delicate shoulders. He stood up and took her hand when it was offered, gently brushing the back of it with his lips. As soon as he released it, she snatched it away and sauntered to the chair opposite him. Her mother took her seat in the corner of the room, close enough to hear the conversation, but far enough away to be ignored.

'Miss Brookes. You look lovely.' Thomas half murmured, taking her appearance in, still standing.

Mary beamed up at him. 'Thank you, Mister Channing. Are you going to sit down or are you going to stand there gawping at me all afternoon?'

'Mary!' Elizabeth admonished her.

A demure smile returned to Mary's face. 'Please, Mr Channing, do sit down.' Thomas did as he was told. 'Would you care for some refreshment?' Without waiting for an answer, Mary stood and went to the gold coloured rope hanging behind her. She pulled at it and Thomas heard the faint sound of a bell ringing. As Mary retook her seat, the door opened and the servant entered carrying a tray. He deposited it on the table before retreating.

Elizabeth Brookes rose and went to the table. 'Coffee, Mr Channing?'

Thomas nodded and waited in silence as Elizabeth poured him a cup and handed it to him. Thomas perched the cup on his knee, his stomach still rumbling. He had hoped there would be some food, but there was none on the tray that had been brought in. Once again, he regretted not eating prior to setting out.

Elizabeth poured a cup for Mary and handed it to her. 'Thank you mother.' Mary turned to Thomas as her mother poured a third cup and returned to her seat. 'So, Mr Channing, tell me about yourself.'

Thomas shrugged, then cleared his throat. 'Where to begin? I am Thomas, I am twenty five years of age and I have lived in these parts all of my life. My father is a merchant and I have just finished my apprenticeship as a grocer, which is my chosen profession.'

'Oh, how exciting! A grocer!' Mary clapped her hands in delight, her eyes sparkling, a big smile on her face.

Thomas suspected he was being mocked, but chose to ignore it. 'Yes, a grocer. I have just opened my first shop in Dorchester, on East High Street. You may know of it. Hopefully, it will be the first of many. I deal in exotic spices, herbs, sugar, coffee beans and we have recently started trading in chocolate. It is proving to be quite a successful venture. Now, tell me about yourself.'

'I am Mary. I am sixteen years of age. And my father tells me I am to be married to you. Apart from that, there is not much to tell for there is little point in what I am and what I think.'

Thomas heard Elizabeth Brookes' cup and saucer tinkle as she moved in her seat. 'Mary, I am warning you.'

Mary gave her a sideways glance. 'Sorry, mother. My apologies, Mr Channing. Please permit me to begin again. I am Mary. I am sixteen years of age. I am educated to a high standard and I can speak and write in Latin. I have six brothers of varying ages, my father is a respected businessman and is currently away in Devon. I cannot cook, but I can sew. I can also dance, when the occasion presents itself, and I love to attend balls and parties. Do you love parties, Mr Channing?'

Thomas shook his head. 'I haven't been to a party in years, I'm afraid.'

'Shame.' Mary's eyes glanced down at his foot. 'Do you dance?'

'No, not really.' Thomas crossed his legs, placing his good foot on top of the other as if to hide it.

'Then I must teach you.'

'That would be nice. I would like that very much.'

'I am sure you would. I assume you ride.'

With no table close by, Thomas put the cup of coffee down at his feet. 'I do. I find it most pleasurable.'

'And do you hunt?' Once more, Thomas sensed a mocking

tone in her voice.

'On occasion, when I get the opportunity and if my foot allows me to.'

'Your foot?'

'Yes. I have a condition called splayfoot. It flares up on occasion making riding uncomfortable, particularly across terrain.' He was now sure that she already had knowledge of his condition.

'Splayfoot? What is it, exactly?' Mary glanced at her mother and Thomas noticed Elizabeth glowering at her.

'It is a condition where my toes and the bones in my foot are spread. I have had it since birth.'

'I see. Is there anything else I should know about before I am to wed you?'

Thomas narrowed his eyes. 'Not that I can think of. It does not affect me as a man.'

Mary giggled. 'No, of course it doesn't. But I feel as if I am making all of the conversation. Do you have anything you would like to ask of me?'

Thomas thought for few seconds, before asking 'What are your thoughts about children?'

Mary giggled again. 'I should like to have them one day, although I know my parents would like me to have them as soon as I am wed. But I believe there is plenty of time for that.' She changed the subject. 'Tell me about the home which we are to share. Is it big?'

Thomas looked around the room they were in. 'Nowhere near as big as this, but it is large enough. It is located in Dorchester, close to my shop and the centre of the town with all of its facilities. I am sure you will have seen it before.'

'And do you have servants?'

'Yes,' Thomas nodded. 'Just the one. A young girl called Molly.'

'How long has she been with you?'

'For just over a year now. She is a fairly good cook and an adequate cleaner. She looks after me very well and I am sure you will like her.'

'How did you come by her?'

'Her father works for my father. He approached him saying that the girl was requiring work and lodgings so he sent her along to me.'

'What does she look like?' Mary's face was a picture of innocence.

'I don't know. I don't really notice her that much.'

'Oh come on Mr Channing! You have a young servant girl working for you and you haven't really noticed her!'

'Mary!' Elizabeth Brookes spoke up once more. Thomas wasn't really sure why, but it was enough to make Mary change tack again.

'Do you often go away on business, like my father?'

'On occasion I have to go to London with my father to meet with the merchants and the bank. When we are wed, you can come with me, if you like, on my next trip.' He smiled at her.

Mary shook her head. 'I am not sure if I would like London. I think I shall stay behind with Molly and look after the house for you.'

'Have you never been to London before?'

'No,' said Mary. 'Everything I need is right here. I have my friends, my family. I have no great desire to travel to London. I have heard it is too busy with people and horses, and that it smells terribly in the summer, especially when it is hot.'

It was Thomas's turn to smile. 'It can certainly be unpleasant, especially along the river.'

Mary leant forward in her chair. 'Have you ever been betrothed to another?'

Thomas was quite taken aback. 'No. Why do you ask?'

'It's just that... well, you are quite old and I find it strange that you have not had opportunities beforehand, especially for someone of your reputation and standing.'

'Mary!' Elizabeth interjected once more. Thomas held up his hand. 'It is fine, Mrs Brookes. It is a fair enough question.' He thought about it before responding. 'I have been quite close to someone in the past, but unfortunately it was not to be.'

'Why not?' Mary was intrigued, if only because she could never imagine any woman falling for him.

'She was married previously.'

'Previously? How can that be?'

Thomas chuckled. 'Her husband died a couple of years ago. She is a widow.'

'So why can't you marry her?'

It was Mary's mother that spoke up. 'It is not right and proper for a single man to marry a woman that has been widowed. Not until a suitable period of mourning has passed. Isn't that right, Mr Channing?'

'Society does not look favourably upon it,' Thomas said, sadly.

'But you would marry her if society allowed it?' Mary asked.

Thomas felt unsure as to how to answer. 'I suppose I would. If it were deemed acceptable.'

'I think that is very sad,' Mary announced, looking at her mother. 'It would appear Mr Channing and I have much in common.' She returned her gaze to Thomas. 'Both of us are unable to marry who we want to because society demands we conform to their ideals and are respectable.' She abruptly stood up and curtsied once more to Thomas. 'Sir, I will take my leave of you now. Good day.'

Thomas scrambled to his feet and Elizabeth called out to her daughter as she headed for the door. 'Mary, come back at once. Mary!' She rushed after her, pausing momentarily as she passed Thomas. 'My apologies, Mr Channing. Thank you for coming. My servant will show you to the door.'

Thomas remained standing as he waited for the servant to appear but there was no sign of him. Eventually, after a couple of minutes, he left the drawing room and strained his ears for sounds of life. He could hear nothing. He sighed as he made his way across the hallway to the large front door. Letting himself out, he gently pulled it shut behind him and made his way out into the storm. The light was fading fast and the wind had strengthened. He pulled his coat tightly around him in an effort to keep out the chill. The dark clouds looked ominous and he glanced up at them as he made his way round the back of the grand house to the stable block to collect his horse. 'It's a sign,' he told himself as he mounted his horse, pulled it round to face the wind, dug in his heels and quickly galloped away.

Chapter Four

Early the following morning, Thomas sought out Eliza's lodgings. He had tossed and turned all night, his mind in a quandary as to what to do. Mary's words had resonated with him. *But you would marry her if society allowed it?* Yes, he would. Damn his father and damn what society determined was acceptable. So what if she was older than he was. Why did it matter if she was a widow? Her husband had died. There was nothing unusual in that. Why should they both be unhappy? Why did they have to leave it for such a long time before society deemed it acceptable for her to take another husband, one that was younger than she?

Eliza looked up as she heard his footsteps crunching up the path. She saw him approaching through the window and rushed out of her room, flying down the stairs to intercept him before her landlady heard his knock on the door. It would not do for her to receive male visitors at her lodgings and she risked being thrown out into the street should Thomas be seen. She arrived at the large oak door and managed to open it before Thomas could grab hold of the brass knocker. She raised her finger to her lips to prevent him from speaking. 'Shhhh.' She closed the door gently behind her and gestured for him to go back down the path and out of the garden. 'Why are you here?' She demanded when she reached the roadside.

'I had to see you.' Thomas glanced across at his shop. 'Come. We need to talk.'

They hurried across the street and Thomas let them both in. Closing the door behind him, he followed her through to the room at the back. She took her usual seat at the table and watched him as he urgently paced back and forth before her, deep in thought. Finally, he stopped, took a deep breath and began speaking. 'I fear I have made a dreadful mistake.'

Eliza remained silent, keen to hear what he had to say. After a brief pause during, Thomas went on. 'The girl is a brat. And a spoilt one at that. She is too young, too immature and too rude. Small wonder her father wants rid of her!'

He continued pacing, his mind racing. 'She asked me about you.'

Eliza raised an eyebrow. 'Really? And why would she do that?'

'She asked me if I have ever had feelings for anybody else, on account of my being so much older than her.'

'And what did you say?'

'I told her that there was somebody that I had grown close to. But that it was difficult.'

'I see.' Eliza put her hands together, placing them in her lap. 'And why is it difficult?'

Thomas stopped in front of the window and stared out of it, his hands clasped behind his back. 'Because you are older than I am. Because you are a widow who is meant to be in mourning, not developing a friendship with another man. And because my father would never approve of such an arrangement.'

Eliza's heart skipped a beat. 'I see. And yet, here we are.'

'I know.' He turned to face her. 'She told me that it

was unfair that society dictated we could not be with those we wanted to be with. She also implied that she, too, had feelings for another.' His face grew red as he replayed Mary's words in his head.

'Is that why you are angry? Because she has feelings for another?' Eliza looked up at him, narrowing her eyes.

Thomas responded without thinking. 'Perhaps, yes. I don't know. She obviously has no feelings for me. She thinks I am a monster. She mocked me, with my deformed foot and odd shape. She questioned my abilities as a man. She even hinted that I might be having relations with my maidservant!' He stopped himself, aware that he had gone too far.

'So you are upset that she feels you are not worthy of her.' Eliza's voice was cold.

'No. Well yes, of course. But it is more than that. It is obvious I would be taking on a child, not a wife. A young girl that has no desire to be with me or even has any respect for me. I doubt that I could ever change her. What I need is somebody that likes, understands and wants me, in spite of my looks and my ailments.' He looked down solemnly at his foot, before looking back up at Eliza. 'Somebody like you.'

Eliza's heart leapt. Just a few days earlier her hopes had been dashed. Now Thomas was clearly declaring his feelings for her. 'Are you saying you wish to marry me, Thomas Channing?'

Thomas nodded, his cheeks flushed. 'I believe I am.' He looked downcast again. 'But there is much to sort out and I may lose everything.' He fell silent again.

'Then you must work out exactly what it is you want.' She rose to leave. 'Let me know what you decide. You know where to find me.'

Thomas heard the bell tinkle as she left the shop. He sighed. 'How did I get myself into such a complicated mess?' He asked himself as he gathered up his thoughts and began putting out items for the shop. He inadvertently kicked his bad foot against a table as he lifted up a box of dried fruits and cursed. Putting the box down, he sat on a stool, took off his boot and rubbed his foot. Eliza had made up an ointment for him, one that relieved the pain when it was at its worst. He gently applied it as he wondered about her past, recalling that she had been married to a doctor and had helped tend to his patients.

He smiled to himself as he recalled their conversations. He found her to be intelligent, funny and clever. Her knowledge of medicine had astounded him, as it was rare to meet a woman who knew of such things. He also found her to be attractive and had been pleased to learn of her feelings towards him. Eliza's words had given him hope and she had certainly left the door open should he wish to pursue her further. But what would the price be should he marry her? His father would most likely ostracise him and he could possibly lose both his home and the shop should his father decide he would not tolerate their relationship.

He put his boot back on and stood up, grimacing as he forced his foot down into it and applied his weight to it. His mind was made up. He would go and see Mr Brookes and tell him that he no longer wished to marry his daughter. And then he would ride out to see his father and tell him that it was his desire to marry Eliza. So what if he was cut off from his inheritance. If his father truly loved him then he would allow him to be with her. If he didn't, then he would just have to take his chances. And then, when that was done, he would approach Eliza and ask for her hand in marriage.

Chapter Five

Richard Brookes listened in earnest as Thomas outlined his doubts over marrying his daughter. Having heard from Elizabeth about Thomas's disastrous meeting with Mary, Richard had suspected this moment would come and was already armed with a response. He remained seated as Thomas paced back and forth before him.

'She is a sweet girl and is not without attraction. Indeed, I should be the happiest man alive having been presented with the opportunity.' Thomas paused momentarily before taking a deep breath and continuing. 'But, having met with her, I fear that I am not right for her. She appears to have feelings for another and is obviously being forced into this arrangement against her will. I have no desire to make her any unhappier than she already is.' Thomas stopped pacing, turned to face Richard and put his hands behind his back. 'I therefore feel I have no alternative other than to withdraw from our arrangement.'

'I see.' Richard pursed his lips. 'And you are quite sure?' Thomas nodded. 'Yes sir, I am.'

Richard rose. 'Would you care for a drink?' Without

waiting for Thomas's response, he went to the cabinet and poured two small glasses of port. Handing one to Thomas, he gestured for him to be seated and Thomas duly obliged.

'When I first met with Mary's mother, things did not go terribly smoothly. She'd had a sheltered upbringing and my outlook on life did not sit well with her. She was only seventeen and probably felt that marriage to me was a daunting prospect, one which would unnecessarily burden her.' Richard smiled as he remembered back to the young girl he had taken for his wife more than twenty years earlier. 'But we worked it through and, in time, she grew to become the perfect wife.'

Thomas made to say something but Richard held up his hand. 'Hear me through, young man. It is only natural to have second thoughts. I had them myself at the time. But we must overcome them if we are to succeed in life and make our mark on history. I am sure your father would tell you the same. Indeed, I am sure your parents' story follows a similar path to my own.' Thomas nodded. It was true. They had entered into an arrangement as per their fathers' wishes and he had often wondered if his mother was happy.

Richard swigged his drink back and put the glass down on the table. 'My daughter will marry you, in spite of her reservations. She has no choice. You are her only suitor and I have faith in your ability to be her husband. I will back you all the way when it comes to controlling her!' He threw his head back and laughed. 'She certainly is full of fire! Her mother was much the same at her age.' His voice grew serious once more. 'So let's have no more of this. The date is set, the arrangements have been made and the invitations sent. I will see to it that Mary will be there on time and that she will become your wife. And to ensure that everything goes to plan, I will double my original offer to you for taking her hand.'

'Double?' Thomas was incredulous. The original offer had already been more than generous. The revised sum would see him very wealthy indeed. He did some quick calculations in his head and grinned. Getting to his feet, he held out his hand. 'In that case, I am sure that our agreement can be honoured.'

Richard grabbed his hand in his own and pumped it vigorously. 'That's the spirit! Now, let us refill our glasses and drink a toast to your marriage. As he refilled the two glasses, the feeling of euphoria Thomas had briefly experienced left him and the feeling of nausea in the pit of his stomach returned. Having plucked up the courage to end it, he had found himself back in the exactly same situation with no progress made. How would he break the news to Eliza? Having planned to disappoint Mr Brookes, he was now going to have to let her down once more.

Richard handed the glass to him and they chinked glasses before drinking as if to seal the deal. 'Here's to you and Mary.'

Thomas glumly raised the glass and knocked back the contents and Richard patted him firmly on the back. It was agreed. There was to be no going back. He would have to marry Mary Brookes.

Chapter Six

The meeting with Eliza had been brief and painful for him. Thomas recalled it as he stood on the church steps listening to the church bells ringing out in celebration while a feeling of dread coursed through his veins.

Eliza appeared to have taken the news well. Perhaps a little too well. If she had argued with him, maybe cursed or even struck him, he would have felt better. Instead, she had just nodded, kissed him lightly on the cheek and wished him well. That had been less than a week earlier and he hadn't spoken to her since, although he had often seen her passing by the shop on her way into town.

Thomas pulled the collar up on his coat. The cold January wind carried occasional patches of drizzle and his hair and coat felt damp to the touch. He was shaken out of his thoughts by the sound of horses' hooves. The small coach came into view, pulling up in front of the church. As it did so, the bells changed tune, announcing the bride's arrival, their joyous melody at odds with Thomas's sombre mood. He quickly turned on his heel and headed back inside the church where the small congregation awaited. He marched purposefully down the aisle and took his place before the altar, eyes fixed forward, his heart pounding as he felt everybody's eyes fixed upon his back.

Outside, Richard Brookes stepped out of the coach, a big smile on his beaming face. He took his daughter's hand as she gathered up her dress. Mary climbed out, followed by her young maid, who smoothed her dress down and checked the ribbons in her hair as the wind whipped up once more. Mary shivered as the maid removed her shawl from her shoulders. 'Come along, Mary. It is time.' Richard held her hand firmly as if to prevent her from escaping, then led her up the small stone path and in through the entrance.

Everyone turned to see them as they walked in. Mary looked beautiful in her flowing dress and murmurs of approval ran through the party of wedding guests as she slowly made her way down the aisle. She waved at some of her friends as she passed them by, drawing a stern glance from her father. 'Not now, Mary!' He hissed under his breath. The grin on her face made him wonder what trick she had up her sleeve but he quickly dismissed his thoughts when he saw Thomas stood up ahead of him. The marriage ceremony would soon be over and his wayward daughter would no longer be his responsibility.

Mary had resolved to enjoy herself. It was, after all, her wedding and even though she had no desire to marry Thomas Channing, she had decided that she was still going to enjoy the occasion. After all, the day was all about her and she was to be centre of attention – a role she fully intended to make the most of. The marriage ceremony ahead of her would soon be over and then she could return to her new home for a celebratory party. She had spent longer planning the party with her friends than she had on the wedding itself!

Following on from her chaperoned meeting with Thomas, she had been kept under the watchful gaze of her mother who had prevented her from meeting with friends and refused to let her attend any social gatherings. At first she had mutinied, which had resulted in her being locked in her room. However, as the day drew nearer, Mary's mood had lightened and while her mother knew she had not reconciled herself fully to the marriage, Elizabeth felt that she had at least resigned herself to it.

Mary glanced across the pew to her right as she walked through the church and caught sight of a young man with strawberry blonde hair. She smiled at him as she walked by, and he gave her a quick wink of the eye before turning away, placing his hands on his knees and staring at Thomas, stood at the front of the church.

She arrived at the altar alongside Thomas, who barely glanced at her as she took her place beside him. Her father took a step backwards, leaving the couple with the reverend, who opened his Bible, held it out reverentially before him, and began the ceremony.

His words were short and brief, as per Richard Brookes' instructions, and it was over in minutes. When the reverend had finished reading, he declared the couple married. Thomas leant forward to kiss his new bride. She turned her face as his lips headed towards hers and he lost his balance, nearly falling over in the process. Feeling embarrassed, he steadied himself, nervously looking around to see if anybody had noticed. Richard Brookes slapped heartily him on the back. 'Congratulations Thomas! Welcome to the family!' Richard grabbed hold of Mary's hand and placed it firmly in that of her new husband, clasping then squeezing them both tightly together. He stepped to one side and the newly weds made their way back down the aisle. Guests both sides stood and applauded enthusiastically as they walked by them, calling out their congratulations and offering words of encouragement as they passed through them.

The couple exited the church to find the threatened rain had arrived in the form of a persistent drizzle. A strong gust of wind lifted Mary's dress and she snatched her hand from Thomas in order to push it back down. Without pausing, Thomas continued on his way down the path to the wooden gate, letting himself out and going on his way, heading towards home.

Mary remained outside the church doors, greeting her friends and family, kissing her many brothers and talking excitedly with everyone. The young man with the strawberry blonde hair appeared before her. He took her hand and bent forward to kiss the back of it. 'Congratulations, Mrs Channing.'

Mary curtsied. 'Thank you kind sir.' She leant forward and whispered in his ear. 'Are you coming to the party?'

He nodded. 'Of course. I wouldn't miss it for the world.' He took a step back and bowed. 'I will see you later, Mrs Channing.' He doffed his cap. 'Good day.'

Her mother appeared at her side as he walked away. 'Who is that?' she enquired.

'Gabriel,' Mary answered, a dreamy look in her eyes.

Her mother stared after him. 'I trust you won't be seeing him anymore.'

Mary looked up at her, mischief in her eyes. 'Maybe. We'll see.'

'Mary,' her mother warned her. 'You are a respectable woman now. You have responsibilities to your husband and to your family. Please don't let me or your father down.'

Mary smiled. 'Of course not mother. Why should I do that?'

Elizabeth Brookes was unconvinced but knew there was nothing she could do about it now. She had done as her husband had requested. She had seen to it that Mary would be ready to marry Thomas Channing and she had duly delivered. Now it was up to Mary.

Chapter Seven

Although she would never have described Thomas Channing as handsome, Eliza felt he many good qualities and she found him to be a jolly soul who was knowledgeable and made her laugh. He had often remarked on how attractive he found her without ever coming across as forward. He had made her feel good about herself, which had been much appreciated after the dark times she had endured prior to arriving in Dorchester.

The sudden news that he was to marry had been a great shock to her. He had never mentioned his relationship with Mary before. The way in which he had confided everything about his daily business had given her hope that maybe, just maybe, there was a future to be had with him.

She watched him from afar as he exited the church with his new bride. Mary's long hair was flowing, her young features were strong and her hourglass figure fitted snugly into her dress. Thomas looked clumsy and oafsome in comparison; a most unlikely couple Eliza thought unkindly before chastising herself for having such malicious thoughts.

Eliza felt a pang of jealousy as they both came into view,

but it quickly turned into curiosity as Thomas continued walking out of the church grounds and into the road, leaving Mary behind at the church entrance.

She thought about going after him, but the surly look on his face and his determined stride as he marched up the road made her think otherwise. Instead, she concentrated on Mary. Who was this girl that had made such an unexpected and unwelcome entrance into her life? She certainly appeared to be popular, especially given all of the attention she was receiving from her friends and, in particular, young men. A number of them stepped forward to kiss and embrace her and Eliza was astonished at how brazen she was. She did not, of course, know that most of them were her brothers and cousins. But one boy stood out as he bowed before her, kissing the back of her hand while holding on to it for a fraction too long, before leaning into her and speaking into her ear.

An older woman had appeared alongside her. It had to be her mother for she had the same colour hair and shared many of Mary's attributes. Eliza wondered what her mother had said to her. The way Mary had looked at the boy showed that she obviously had feelings for him.

Eliza had seen enough. She decided to follow Thomas up the road to his house. She knew the after-wedding party would meet there and she wanted to see them all arrive. She approached the house and stood across the road, behind a tree. From there she could observe most of the comings and goings without fear of being noticed.

Before long, the wedding guests began arriving. The majority of them were around Mary's age and it suddenly struck Eliza that she had never seen Thomas with any friends or associates. Indeed, she had not met any when she had been in the shop and she could not recall him speaking of having any friends outside of work.

They arrived in dribs and drabs, small groups, all talking

loudly and in high spirits, quite at odds with the gloomy day. Mary arrived soon after, arm in arm with another girl of her own age. Eliza heard the cheer go up as she arrived in the front garden and she positioned herself to get a better view. Mary pushed through the throng of well-wishers congregated in the front garden to get to the front door. She pushed it open before turning and inviting everybody to come into her new home. Another cheer went up as they followed her inside and Eliza heard numerous, excited shrieks as they all entered the house.

Eliza waited a while longer before going up the lane to the rear of the house. She noted that Mary's mother was not among their number and presumed that her father wasn't there either. Indeed, as all of the revellers seemed to be of the same age as Mary, it seemed obvious to her that they were all her friends.

As the party got underway, Eliza continued to watch from the lane behind the house. At one point, Mary appeared in the garden with some female friends and Eliza shrunk back behind the hedge from where she could hear snippets of their conversation. Mary held centre stage as her friends gathered around her and Eliza strained her ears to hear what was being said.

'I can't believe you actually went through with it!' said one.

'You told me you weren't going to do it!' said another.

'What are you going to do tonight when you have to actually go to bed with him?' asked a third.

Mary was giggling. 'Oh don't worry about that. I'm not actually going to do it with him! I could never do that!'

There were more shrieks of laughter. 'So what are you going to do?' another asked when they had all calmed down again.

'Give him enough food and wine until he can eat and drink no more and falls asleep. Then I can do as I please!'

The girls giggled again and there was more excited talking before a young man appeared in the doorway and called out to them. 'Come on you lot. The musicians are here. It's time to dance!'

They ran inside, squealing as they went, and Eliza stepped out once more from behind the hedge. The light was dimming as the evening was drawing into night. The clouds had grown thicker and darker and Eliza was beginning to feel the damp seep through her clothing as the rain kept up its persistent drizzle.

As candles and lamps appeared in the windows of the house, Eliza decided to go back to her lodgings. Once there, she would change into dry clothes and return to see if she could get into the party. Few would notice her, especially as the drink was flowing and the lighting would be dim. If anybody challenged her, she would claim to be from Thomas's side of the family, perhaps a cousin, or an aunt.

Having changed, she donned another coat and quickly returned to the house. It was now dark and the sound of music was coming from within. She made her way to the rear of the house and let herself in through the back door. A small candle was burning on the kitchen table but there was nobody there. She opened the kitchen door just wide enough to allow her to peek through. Excited youngsters were running back and forth, boys chasing girls, demanding dances or kisses. She pushed through the door unnoticed and went down the hallway. The main room of the house was to her right and she could see people dancing to the musicians who were playing in a large bay window to the front. There was no sign of Thomas, but she could see Mary holding court, encircled by three young men, one of whom was the youth with the strawberry blonde hair she had seen outside the church.

She crossed the hallway and peered into the drawing room opposite. A number of people were sat around tables with candles, talking quietly while playing cards or just eating and drinking. She spotted Thomas sat in a large wing back chair in front of the fire, all by himself. A brandy glass was in one hand and an almost empty bottle was in the other. From the looks of him, he had drunk the contents of the bottle himself and he was struggling to keep his eyes open.

Eliza made her way towards him and she stood across from him without him even so much as looking up and noticing her. She picked up a glass that had been left on a side table, which already had some wine in it. She took a sip as she made her way through the party, taking up a seat in the main room where the dancing was taking place. Mary was cavorting with complete abandon, much to the annoyance of some of her female friends who had occasion to drag her away from a number of suitors, all eager to accompany her in the next dance.

Eliza remained unnoticed, quietly observing proceedings until the musicians stopped playing and the party began winding down. She was about to leave when the announcement went up for all those still standing to attend the bedding ritual, whereby the guests would escort the newly weds to their bed chamber and toast them.

Thomas found himself being dragged from his chair, causing him to come to with a start. Meanwhile, Mary's girlfriends encircled her and pushed her up the stairs, ignoring her protestations. The newly-weds were roughly manhandled into the bedroom and led to the bed.

While Eliza had no great desire to see Thomas and Mary consummate their union, curiosity overtook her and she filled her glass with more red wine before following the revellers up the stairs to the bedroom. She stood in the doorway and looked on as the guests guided the newly weds to their respective sides of the bed.

Four girls surrounded Mary and excitedly stripped her down to her undergarments. Four young men did the same to Thomas, despite his protestations and drunken attempts to fight them off. They removed his shirt as well and Eliza saw his barrel chest for the first time. His short arms were thick and covered in hair, as was his torso.

The covers on the bed were thrown back and Thomas was

pushed backwards. He fell onto the bed and lay on his back, glaring at the ceiling, as his boots and breeches were pulled off him. The girls then threw Mary on top of the bed, and there were bawdy cheers from everyone as the bed covers were pulled back on top of them. Thomas turned on to his side to look at Mary, but she promptly turned her back on him and refused to face him.

'Go on Mary, kiss him!' one of the girls cried.

Mary shook her head, defiantly. 'Never!'

'Go on Mary! It's time to become a woman!' shouted out one young man, holding a candle up to ensure he could see what was happening.

Mary remained tight-lipped, resisting the efforts of the girls to roll her over in the bed towards her new husband.

'Mary, you have to!' one of her friends hissed at her. 'It's not right. You're not married until you do it.'

Mary shook her head defiantly. 'I am going to sleep,' she declared. 'It has been a long day and I am feeling tired.' She closed her eyes and pretended to be asleep.

Thomas rolled on to his back once more and also closed his eyes. A silence fell over the room. Eliza had seen enough. She reversed out of the room and made her way downstairs.

Eliza was torn. On the one hand she felt sorry for the man she believed she had grown to love. On the other, she was delighted by this turn of events for she believed all was not lost. It was obvious that Mary would never submit to being his wife. While the marriage remained unconsummated, there was still hope. Surely it would only be a matter of time before Thomas divorced his young bride and returned his affections to her.

Chapter Eight

Thomas Channing belched and patted his stomach in a hearty manner before pushing himself back from the table. He slurped at his port, spots of the red liquid landing on his white smock, before unsteadily rising to his feet, gripping on to the edge of the table for balance. He steadied himself before stumbling to the door. He stopped in the doorway, holding on to the wooden architrave to prevent himself from falling over. 'Molly!' he yelled, lolling backwards and forwards.

A young girl appeared from the kitchen. Barely fourteen years of age, her thin face was pale from lack of sunlight and her hair was lank and unwashed.

'Where is she?' he demanded.

The young maid shook her head. 'I don't know.'

Channing grunted. 'Damn girl. She'll be the ruin of me!' He rolled forward again, taking an involuntary step. Grabbing hold of the post at the bottom of the stairs, he steadied himself once more. 'I am to retire to my room. Clear up and make good, then come and undress me.' He squinted his eyes as if struggling to focus, then swung his leg up on to the bottom step and began climbing the stairs, hauling himself up on the handrail as he did so.

Molly watched him work his way up, concerned that he may fall backwards. As he reached the top, he lurched across the landing and fell into his room. Sighing, she returned to the dining room, collected his plate and took it through to the fire chamber. The small dog looked up at her, hopefully. She shook her head at the animal. 'Nothing much for you today, I'm afraid. Just scraps.' She opened the door to the back yard and scraped the meagre offerings off the plates on to the step outside. The dog shot past her as quickly as it could, wary of being kicked. It snuffled around excitedly as she closed the door behind it. The dog would remain in the garden overnight to warn of danger should it approach in the shape of a fox or a stranger.

She washed her hands in a pail of water before drying them on her heavily stained apron. Placing the plate in the same bucket, she stared out of the window. There, at the bottom of the garden, the woman stood, close to the thin hedge that marked the boundary between the lawn and the orchard. She was dressed all in black. Molly wondered if perhaps she was a widow, still in mourning for her deceased husband. The sun was setting quickly behind her, painting the sky burnt orange, accentuating her silhouette. Perhaps sensing she was being watched, the woman abruptly turned around and glided off down the bridlepath, out of view.

'Molly!' The shout made her start, shaking her from her musings.

'Coming!' she called back, turning her back on the window, she quickly washed and dried her hands before heading into the hallway. Arriving at the foot of the stairs, she paused to scrape back her hair, remove her apron and straighten her dress. Placing the apron on the coat stand, she took a deep breath and made her way upstairs to Thomas's room. She had hoped he would fall asleep without her, but it was not to be. He was laying on the bed, his head propped up on his pillow, still fully dressed. He pointed at his boots, a drunken leer on his face. 'Come on, quick! Before she returns.'

Molly did as she was told and began yanking at his boots until they both slid off. He sat up and raised his arms, allowing her to pull his shirt over his head. He laid back on the bed, looked down at the buttons on his breeches and she began undoing them. Pulling apart the opening to his breeches, he patted at the bed beside him. Taking a deep breath, she raised her skirt and petticoat, climbed up onto the bed, laid back and closed her eyes.

He climbed on top of her, grunting, feeling under her skirts and forcing her legs apart. She let out a faint cry as she felt him enter her. Within seconds, he grunted, then rolled off her. She made to rise but his hand grabbed hold of her wrist.

'No. Stay awhile. At least until I am asleep.' He stood up, still unsteady on his feet and went to the window to turn off the lamp.

As he fell back on the bed beside her, Molly remained frozen, her eyes wide open, adjusting to the darkness that filled the room. Outside she could hear the chatter of passers-by, making their way back from the town. She lay there, waiting for the sound of his breathing to lapse into the snores she knew would come. It was a routine she had become accustomed to in recent days, one that she felt she had not control over. In the beginning, she had protested but he had always been too drunk to reason with. And now he had grown to expect it of her.

His breathing was becoming deeper and more regular as he recovered from his exertion. Finally, they gave way to snores as he fell asleep. Her own eyes were becoming heavy and she was struggling to keep awake herself. As she lay there in the dark, her own thoughts took over and she went to her happy place, where the sky was blue and the long grass was green. In her mind she was running across the meadow to play in the warm waters of the stream that had played such a big part of her childhood. As her thoughts overtook her, she relaxed, a sad smile on her face. Before she knew it, she too was fast asleep.

Chapter Nine

The Antelope was a hive of raucous activity. Mary leant across to place the newly lit candle on the windowsill and Gabriel took full advantage, nuzzling his face into her cleavage while putting a searching hand up her skirt. She pulled back, slapping at his hand, a big grin on her face. 'Oi! Stop that!'

The handsome face beamed up at her, blue eyes twinkling. 'Or what?' he demanded.

She slapped playfully at him once more and he grabbed her, pulling her into his lap. Mary could feel others looking at them, but she didn't care. 'Or maybe I will have cause to do something about it!' She reached her hand down underneath her, feeling at his growing bulge. 'Gabriel Fletcher!' she exclaimed, laughing out loud. 'Or maybe I won't,' she teased before pushing herself up from his lap and seating herself on the chair opposite him, just beyond his reach. She picked up her gin and sank it in one before wiping her mouth with the back of her hand and waving at the serving wench. 'Another!' Mary yelled before turning back to Gabriel. 'You having one?' she demanded.

He nodded in response before draining his tankard of warm

ale. 'Of course!'

'Same again,' she called after the girl who was already disappearing behind the long wooden bar. Mary leaned forward conspiratorially and lowered her voice. 'Did you arrange lodgings?'

Gabriel looked around to make sure he was out of earshot. 'I did. Do you have the money?'

Mary pulled a face. 'For all I do for you, you should be the one who pays. Why is it you never have any money?'

Gabriel looked downcast. 'You know why. Father pays me a pittance, my allowance barely covers anything. Plus I had a bad night at the George the other night.'

'Not again!' Mary sat back in her chair as the girl arrived with their drinks. She placed them in the middle of the table and picked up the coins Mary pushed towards her. When she had gone, she leant across the drink stained oak surface. 'How much this time?'

'Ten guineas.' Gabriel looked pained as Mary glared at him. 'I know, I'm sorry. I was convinced I had the beating of him. It was such a good hand as well. You know how good I am at whist. I swear he must have cheated!'

'Cheated?' Mary sat back. 'So why didn't you call him out?'

'Oh don't be so silly, Mary. My skills with the sword are terrible. Besides, would you have me killed?'

Mary softened. 'No, of course not my love. But you cannot afford to keep on losing like this. I cannot keep up with you and your demands. You appear to lose far more than you win!'

Gabriel reached beneath the table and sought out Mary's hand. Initially she resisted, but her resolve softened and she let him take hold of her. 'I'm sorry. I promise, I'll stop doing it. Just as soon as I win my money back!'

Mary pulled her hand back sharply but he just laughed, throwing his head back as he did so. It was infectious and she couldn't help but join in. As they finished laughing they fell back momentarily into their own thoughts, oblivious to the noise going on around them. Eventually, Gabriel leant forward once more. 'How is it going? The marriage, I mean. Does he treat you well?'

Mary looked glum. 'He treats me well. But he does not love me. Nor I him. He has learned to leave me well alone.'

'Does he… you know…'

'Does he what?'

Gabriel looked around once more. He spoke in a low voice. 'Does he touch you?'

Mary could sense the jealousy in his voice and she liked it. 'Yes. Of course he does,' she lied. 'I am his wife, after all.'

He fell quiet for a while, contemplating his next question. 'Is he any good? Do you enjoy it?'

'He isn't as good as you my love. He doesn't know me like you do. Nor will he.'

Gabriel appeared satisfied. 'If only you could be mine.'

'If only,' Mary agreed. 'But my father would never have countenanced such a marriage. And besides, I quite like our arrangement. It's a lot more fun!'

Content, Gabriel picked up his tankard and finished his drink. He stood up. 'Ready?'

Mary smiled and did likewise with her gin, slamming the glass back on the table. 'More than ready. I thought you'd never ask.'

Gabriel pushed through the throng of people with Mary trailing in his wake. 'Where are we going?' she called.

'A small boarding house at the end of town,' he responded. 'The woman is a widow and doesn't ask questions, nor does she gossip for she knows what is good for her.'

Mary hesitated. 'Are you sure?'

Gabriel grabbed her wrist. 'Yes, I'm sure. I have used it before.'

'What do you mean, used it before?' Mary stopped dead in

her tracks. 'You have another lover?'

'Of course not, my sweet. You are my only one. This was long before I met you.'

She felt the jealousy arising within her this time, but fought to control it. 'So you are not seeing her now.'

'No, of course not,' he responded softly before setting off and pulling her along behind him. They burst out into the wide street, the damp air filling their lungs. The sun was setting ahead of them as they hurried on their way, keen to release their urges.

'Who was she?' Mary suddenly asked, her curiosity burning deep inside her.

'I doubt you would know her,' Gabriel looked steadfastly ahead, determined to get Mary to the boarding house before she changed her mind.

'I know everyone in Dorchester!' she called, struggling to keep up with his long stride.

'Ah, but she is not from Dorchester. She was on a visit from London.'

Gabriel was lying and Mary knew it, but her desires were strong and she didn't want to spoil their evening together. It could wait. She would prise it out of him in due course. Besides, he was a man. And a single, eligible one at that. Plus he was incredibly handsome. She hated her father for the marriage he had arranged for her. But she would not let it hold her back. She would continue to live her life the way she wanted to live it. And nobody would ever take it away from her.

Chapter Ten

As the day gave way to night, Eliza hurried on her way back to her lodgings, eager to get home before the lateness of the hour invited unwanted questions from her landlady. Her face was burning red with anger. She had seen the young girl in the bedroom. His bedroom. *How could he?*

Her lodgings were not far away, deliberately chosen so as to be close to him. She could even see his shop from her window, allowing her to monitor his movements on an almost daily basis. Indeed, she now knew his routine, perhaps better than even Thomas did himself. Eliza would often watch him arrive soon after dawn to set up his shop, putting his wares out front to entice in would be purchasers. His lunch was always taken when the sun hit its zenith whereby he would dutifully bring all of his goods inside, close the front door and retire to the room where they had shared so many teas together. Then, usually within the hour, he would open up again, closing the shop just before the sun set. It gave Eliza comfort knowing that he was always close by and that she could call on him whenever she wanted.

Now her heart was in turmoil. She had seen Mary leave

the house later in the afternoon, as she did every day. She had witnessed Thomas eating his meal in the dining room, while his young maid scrubbed and cleaned in the kitchen. She had seen him rise from the table, unsteady on his feet. He had obviously called for the girl as she quickly dried her hands and ran out of the kitchen, reappearing in the dining room.

After he had pushed past her, the maid had retrieved his plate and glass from the table and return with them to the kitchen. Meanwhile, Thomas had appeared upstairs in his bedroom window where he had turned up the oil lamp, illuminating the room.

Eliza had been about to leave but something had caught her eye. The maid was no longer in the kitchen and the downstairs light had been extinguished. She wondered where she had gone. She glanced up at the bedroom window. Thomas had disappeared from view but the young girl had appeared. Eliza watched as the girl approached the bed and bent over, disappearing from view. She reappeared, standing up with Thomas's shirt in her hand. Folding it, she placed it on a chair, before disappearing from view once more.

The maid then appeared at what Eliza assumed to be the foot of the bed, and she wondered exactly what the young girl was doing. For a short while she was unable to see anybody and was about to leave when Thomas appeared shirtless at the window. He leant forward and the room was suddenly plunged into darkness.

Eliza hung around for a while longer, but no more lights appeared. She made her way up the garden path to the kitchen window and peered in. The inner door was open and she could see through to the hallway and the foot of the stairs, but there was no sign of life. She remained at the window waiting for the girl to reappear, but nobody appeared.

Feeling confused, Eliza made her way to the front of the house and peered in through the windows there. Again, there was no sign of anyone. The truth was becoming obvious to her.

Thomas had taken the young girl to his bed.

Chapter Eleven

Mary crept into the house, holding her shoes in her hands, barely noticing the apron hanging on the coat stand at the bottom of the stairs. She stood on the first step and dropped one of the shoes. 'Shush!' she chastised herself, feeling quite tipsy. As she turned around to pick it up, she caught sight of the garment and grabbed at it. 'Sly old fox!' she said to herself, a wicked smile spreading across her face.

She put both shoes down and picked up the apron. Quietly making her way upstairs, she approached the bedroom door. Pushing it open, she peered into the darkness of the room and waited for her eyes to adjust. She could hear Thomas gently snoring and could see his misshaped foot sticking out from under the bedsheets. She took a step inside and crept silently to the bottom of the bed. The young servant girl was laid next to him, his arm across her stomach. She had woken up at the sound of her mistress entering the room, her eyes wide with fear as she saw Mary looking down on her.

Mary lifted a finger to her lips. 'Say nothing Molly,' she whispered. 'Don't move. Stay exactly where you are.'

She'd had her suspicions that her new husband was taking advantage of the girl. Not that she could blame him. Mary herself had been driving him mad with desire just by refusing to sleep in the same bed as him. Now she had the proof she needed to continue to spurn his advances towards her.

'Thomas!' she shouted. 'Thomas! Wake up! Now!'

Her husband awoke with a start, taking his arm off the young girl next to him in bed as he flung himself round and sat bolt upright. 'What the devil?' he exclaimed, trying to gather his senses.

'What, exactly, is the meaning of this?' Mary pointed at the girl alongside him who was now curled up in a ball at the top of the bed, hugging her knees into her chest, trying to make herself as small as possible.

Thomas, wide-eyed and now fully awake, stared down at the servant girl next to him as if he had never seen her before. 'Molly?' he spluttered. 'Why on earth are you here?'

Mary laughed out loud, mocking him and his attempts to deflect blame. 'You really are a weak man Thomas Channing. Sleeping with the servant girl? My God! Have you no shame?' She laughed once more as Thomas jumped out of bed, putting distance between himself and Molly. He fell over as he landed on his bad foot, grimacing in pain. Mary laughed again, tears rolling down her cheeks as she continued to mock him.

'Stick with your serving wench!' She bundled the apron into a ball and threw it at Molly. 'For you will never have me! You are a weak, pathetic excuse for a man. I never wanted you. I will never love you. And I will never bear you a child.' Still laughing, she turned on her heel and marched out of the bedroom to her own chamber across the landing. 'And, should you try and force yourself upon me, I shall make sure the whole town knows about the carnal desires you have for the servant!'

Thomas, still on all fours on the floor, watched her fly out of the door, his mouth wide open in shock. Only now did he consider the hour and wonder where Mary had been while he had been asleep in bed. But, as the door slammed shut to her room, his heart felt heavy and his stomach churned. Molly looked at him in fear.

'I'm sorry,' he whispered. 'I'm so, so sorry.' He waved at her to leave and she quickly jumped off the bed and scampered out of the room, clutching at her apron as she went. As he heard her scurrying down the stairs back to her room, he shook his head with shame and buried his face into his pillow.

Chapter Twelve

'Couldn't you just kill him for me?'

At first, Gabriel looked shocked, but a grin quickly spread across his face. 'Mary Brookes, what are you suggesting? You'd have me hang for you?'

Mary snuggled into him, the hay prickly against her skin, pushing through her chemise. The sweat from their lovemaking had cooled, causing her to shiver. She pulled herself closer to him. 'No, of course not. We'd have to be clever. Perhaps you could arrange an accident at the store, or maybe a fall when he is out riding.' Her Dorset accent, so despised by her father, was at its strongest when she was with Gabriel.

Gabriel picked at his teeth with a piece of straw. 'Don't be so daft. Besides, why change anything. You get to see me whenever you want. You've got plenty of money. And you don't even have to lay with him, especially now you've caught him playing with that servant girl of yours.'

Mary shuddered at the thought. 'The poor girl. He must have forced himself on her. She's so small she couldn't fight him off. If he tries that with me…'

Gabriel squeezed her shoulder. 'If he tries that with you, he'd have me to answer to.'

'So you would kill him for me.' Mary looked up at him, her eyes big and hopeful.

'There you go again, talking of killings and all that. You must stop that talk right now.'

Mary fell quiet. Gabriel extricated himself from her hold and pulled up his breeches. Arching his back, he did up the buttons, sat up and then pulled his braces over his shoulders. 'I've got to go.'

'Please don't.'

He leant over and kissed her gently on the forehead. 'I've got to.'

'I can't stand it any longer,' she blurted out. 'You've got to help me!'

Gabriel stood up. 'How? How can I help you? You are a married woman. He has rights. He owns you. He can do anything he wants with you and there's nothing you can do about it. You are just a chattel.' His voice softened. 'Like I said, we can still see each other, just as long as we're discreet. No more meeting at the Antelope. No more walking anywhere together. I can arrange to come here whenever you want, or at the mill or at Mrs Caudle's lodgings if you want a proper bed to lay on. Just as long as you're paying,' he added, a twinkle in his eye.

He climbed down the ladder and made his way to the door. He peered out cautiously before pushing the door open slightly. 'I'll see you soon. I promise. I'll get a message to you.' He squeezed through the gap and sprinted across the lane, disappearing into the trees opposite.

Mary lay back on the hay bale, thinking. If only Thomas was gone. She could have the house, the shop, the money. And Gabriel. After a suitable period of mourning, of course. She giggled to herself. She had to appear respectable, even if she wasn't.

Chapter Thirteen

Eliza watched from her vantage point as Thomas left the house. His foot must be playing up even more so today as his limp was pronounced, his face screwing up in pain with each step. She so wanted to help him, to go to him with her medicines and give him some more wintergreen to ease the pain. She missed their talks over cups of ginger tea, putting the world to rights, discussing foreign spices and the mysterious countries they came from. China, India, The Silk Route; they all seemed so far away and exotic.

Why did he have to go and marry Mary Brookes? she thought to herself as he limped down the road. The girl was the talk of the town, with gossip-mongers and fishwives quick to tell stories of her errant and promiscuous ways. Marriage to Thomas may have given her respectability, but it hadn't caused her to change her behaviour. If anything, she was even worse. She had cuckolded Thomas and now she was running wild.

She reflected on her own past and wondered if she was so different. She had been married at sixteen, to a man twice her age. A doctor by profession, he had married her after his first wife had died in childbirth. The passing of her own father had seen her left homeless, evicted by the landowner for whom her father worked as a labourer. It was a marriage of convenience for both of them. The doctor got a wife, cook and housekeeper while she got a roof over her head.

In spite of his profession, he was not a kindly man. He would drink heavily and fall into fits of rage. Eliza was frequently the recipient of his violent outbursts as his fists did their worst. In the beginning, he would apologise, tending to her cuts and bruises, promising never to do it again. But, in time, his resentment towards her grew, blaming himself for being unable to save his beloved first wife while taking it out on Eliza. Eventually, he stopped making excuses for his behaviour altogether.

The beatings stopped when she fell pregnant at eighteen. He tended to her, cared for her, revealing a softer side that she had seldom seen. But then, one dark stormy night, he was thrown by his horse and arrived home, battered and bruised and angrier than she had ever seen him before. He took to the brandy immediately and it wasn't too much longer before he began insulting her, pointing at her belly, calling her fat and useless. She refused to rise to the bait, which only made him worse. Finally, he snapped. She couldn't remember what had happened after that. When she awoke, in a pool of blood and the baby was gone. In the years that followed, she was never able to conceive again.

She resolved to leave the marriage as soon as she could, but it was impossible without means and money. However, as his medical practice grew, she began helping him, working alongside him, mixing his medicines and potions. She studied plants and herbs and he taught her about their properties, how they could be used in the treatment of all sorts of ailments.

Eliza secretly harboured her own dream of being a doctor but knew this was impossible. Only men could be doctors. Only men could decide who would be doctors. The few women who had tried to open that door had been ridiculed and, on occasion, prosecuted.

But the knowledge she gained helped her to finally escape her loveless and violent marriage. It had also given her the opportunity to help those less fortunate than herself, those who could not always afford to pay for medical assistance. Finally free of him, she set off on her own journey, visiting small towns and villages, giving aid to those who needed it.

Which is how she came to arrive in Dorchester.

When Thomas disappeared from view, she stepped out from behind the hedge. As she did so, the servant girl appeared in the yard with scraps for the chickens. Eliza needed to speak with her, to find out exactly what had happened the previous evening. She approached her, making her way up the neatly tended garden path. 'Good morning.'

Molly was startled. She looked around, wondering who the strange woman was talking to. Eliza arrived before her. 'Calm yourself, child. Tell me, what is your name?'

'Molly.'

'And is your master here?' Eliza already knew the answer but needed a reason to talk to the girl.

Molly shook her head. 'No madam. I'm afraid you have just missed him. But you will find him at the shop in High East Street.'

'And the mistress of the house?'

Molly shook her head again. She had no idea if the mistress was in or not. After the events of the previous evening Mary's bedroom door had remained closed and while she suspected she may have gone out early in the morning, she was not sure. 'I'm afraid I don't know madam. She may be in her chambers, but I haven't seen her and she has not appeared yet for breakfast.'

Once again, Eliza had known the answer. She had seen Mary slip out just after dawn, making her way hurriedly down the road, a skip in her step. 'So, Molly. Tell me, are you well?'

Molly was surprised. Nobody ever asked her how she was, not even the master who she felt was, in the main, a kindly man, in spite of recent events.

'Yes, thank you madam. At least, I am as well as can be expected.'

Eliza studied her face. She could not be more than fourteen years of age. Her dark hair was lank around her face and she looked like she could do with a good wash. The hem of her dress was caked in the mud of the yard and the front of her apron bore testament to her cleaning and cooking duties. 'I heard a commotion last night for I live close by and it awoke me. Is everything all right with the master and his wife?'

'Yes,' Molly answered, nervously, for she knew she was lying and she hoped the lady would not be able to tell. 'I believe so,' she added for good measure.

'It's just that I heard some shouting. I don't like to pry but if there is anything I can do, I have experience in these things and may be able to offer assistance. I have my medical bag to hand if you require anything.'

Once again, Molly gave a nervous shake of the head. 'The master and the mistress had a disagreement over something. I'm not sure what it was about.'

'But you were there, weren't you.' Eliza softened her tone of voice. 'You know exactly what happened, don't you.' She moved closer to the girl. 'It's fine, you can tell me. I won't pass it on to anybody. It will be our secret.'

Reassured, Molly wrung her hands together, keen to offload to someone about what had happened the previous night. 'Very well, I will tell you. Mistress Mary went out last night and Master Thomas ate alone as usual. He was feeling annoyed so he got drunk, which happens most nights now.' She hesitated, unsure if she should continue. Eliza took her by the hand and squeezed it gently.

'Go on.'

'Well, I helped the master to his bed and he insisted I lay with him awhile until he fell asleep. But nothing happened, I swear!'

'Of course not, child.' Eliza gave her a reassuring smile. 'Then what happened?'

'Well then the mistress returned and saw me laying on the bed next to the master and she went mad at him.'

Eliza smiled. 'And you are positive the master didn't touch you?'

Molly hesitated. 'No. Well, not really. It was all over very quickly. He was too drunk this time.'

'So he forced himself on you?' Eliza was taken aback. 'And you say he has done this before?'

Molly was now close to tears. She nodded. 'Yes. At first, he just wanted me to lay next to him as his wife would not. So I did, but then he wanted more. I didn't know what to do. He is the master. I have to do what he tells me for I have nowhere to go. If I am thrown out into the street, I don't know what would happen. And normally he is so kind. It is only in the evening when the mistress isn't here that he drinks heavily and changes.'

Eliza was appalled. Her suspicions were correct. Thomas was a brute. Her own memories came flooding to the fore. 'You poor girl. Would you like me to examine you? I can make sure you are all right and not with child.' Before Molly could object she grabbed her by the arm and dragged her back into the house. 'Get up on the table and raise up your skirts.'

Molly did as she was told. She climbed up on to the kitchen table and hoisted up her skirt. A quick examination confirmed Elizabeth's worst fears. Thomas had violated her and the young girl was no longer a woman of virtue. Eliza pulled down the skirt and probed at her stomach. 'Does this hurt?'

'No.' Molly was bemused. She had never been examined before.

Eliza tapped at her stomach a few more times before standing back. 'Fortunately, you don't appear to be with child. But you must be careful. If the master does it to you again you must tell me. And if you miss your bleeding, you must also tell me.' She knew that even if Molly was with child, it would be a few weeks before anybody could tell and the marriage between Thomas and Mary had only taken place three weeks earlier. 'How long have you worked here?'

'Less than a year madam.' Molly climbed down off the table and smoothed down her skirt.

'And this has only happened since the master married the mistress?'

Molly nodded. 'Yes madam. Before then I don't think he even noticed me. I preferred it then.'

'And the master of the house doesn't sleep with the mistress?'

'No.' Molly shook her head once more. 'Apart from on their wedding night, she has never visited his chambers, not once.'

Eliza knew that the marriage was not consummated on the wedding night. And now she knew that they had never had relations. But his treatment of the young servant girl was unforgivable. Her feelings towards him had changed. The burning in her heart had turned to rage. Thomas had spurned her in favour of Mary and while Eliza understood it was a marriage of convenience, she could never forgive him for taking advantage of such a young girl. He was no better than her former husband had been.

She leant forward and grabbed the girl by both arms, holding her firmly and looking into her wide, innocent eyes. 'What he did to you, Molly, is unforgivable. He has no rights to you, do you understand?'

Molly nodded, her mouth open.

Eliza continued. 'If he does anything to you again, you must speak with me. I can protect you, but only if you let me know what is happening and when it happens. Do I make myself clear?'

She nodded once more. 'Yes madam.'

'And you must tell nobody about what we have spoken of today. To do so could result in grave danger for you – and me. Now, I must take my leave of you. But I will return regularly to check on you. If you need anything, you must ask me. If you feel unwell, you must tell me. And if the master touches you, you must come to me. You will find my lodgings at the end of High East Street, on the corner opposite Mister Channing's shop. Just ask at the door and the lady of the house will bring me. Goodbye Molly. And please take good care of yourself.'

She let herself out of the back door and walked purposefully down the path. Molly stood in the doorway and watched her leave, unsure of what to think or feel, but glad that she was able to confide in her. Perhaps the lady could make the master stop. Perhaps she might even take her away to a better life. Who knew? All Molly could do was hope.

Chapter Fourteen

Thomas was surprised when Mary suddenly appeared in the shop. He was in the back room enjoying a coffee made from fresh beans that had arrived that very morning. The black brew was bitter to the taste, but not unpleasant, and he was sure that the fashionable households of Dorchester would desire it once word got out that he had some for sale.

The bell tinkled as Mary pushed inside and wound her way through the large sacks of produce that were positioned around the shop.

'Oh, it's you.' Thomas sounded disappointed although inside his heart was pounding. In spite of the way she treated him, he still had feelings for her and was hopeful that she would come to her senses one day. However long it took, he was prepared to wait, just as long as the gossip-mongers stopped wagging their wicked tongues.

Mary made her way to the counter, pausing to pick up some chocolate. She broke a piece off and put it in her mouth, screwing her face up at the taste. 'I'm not sure if I like it or not. What is it?'

'It's to make a drink called chocolate. It's very popular

in France and Spain although there it is reserved for royalty. In London there are chocolate houses where it is melted in hot water and you can drink it, although it is still very expensive. It is very fashionable there. I am hoping it will take off here although unfortunately it's not selling very well at the moment.'

'I only asked what it was. I didn't want a lecture.' She sneered at him. It was too easy, but she still enjoyed putting him down at every opportunity.

Thomas resisted the urge to tell her to get out. Instead, he forced a smile. 'So what brings you in here?'

Mary continued winding her way through the shop goods, running her hands over everything and occasionally sniffing at the various spices and fruits that were in small wooden crates. 'I was just curious. I wanted to see what my husband does for a living.' She emphasized the word "husband", putting as much disdain into her voice as possible. She went on. 'So you are just a shopkeeper really. Nothing special. Not a merchant, like my father.'

He bit his tongue again. 'Yes. I'm *just* a shopkeeper. But, as you can tell, it finances your lifestyle. Talking of which, where were you last night?'

'Only out with friends.'

'But you came home late.' As soon as he said it he wished he hadn't.

'It's a good job I did! How else would I have known you were taking advantage of that poor girl as soon as my back was turned! I should throw you out for bringing disgrace upon us. Imagine if it ever got out? There would be hell to pay! My father would have you horsewhipped!'

'Don't turn this on me, Mary!' Thomas snapped back. 'I know about your cavortings and dalliances. Do you take me for a fool?'

'You are a fool!' her retort was like a slap in the face. 'But I don't care. You can have her. At least she is saving me from you and your advances. As for what I get up to, it is none of your business!'

'Of course it is my business!' Thomas made his way around the counter to confront her. 'It's my reputation at stake, as well as yours. Do you think I don't hear the women gossiping about me in my own shop? Do you care that the menfolk don't invite me to their gatherings anymore? It's embarrassing. You –' he pointed at her '– are embarrassing.'

She smiled sweetly as she stood in front of him, challenging him to do something, her hands on her hips. He took a backward step, involuntarily retreating. Grinning, Mary went around the counter to the shop's till. 'I guess this is where you keep all of our money.'

'Keep away from there Mary. That's got nothing to do with you.'

Mary ignored him, pulling open the wooden drawer. 'It looks like you've had a good day.'

'It hasn't been too bad. At least not until you arrived.'

Mary ignored the barbed comment. She pulled out a few coins and waved them at him. 'I need this for housekeeping. And a new dress. Plus I have some additional expenses I have incurred.' She pushed the drawer back in.

'Put it back Mary.' Thomas tried to sound stern, but it was to no avail. 'Mary, please, put it back.'

Mary ignored him, walking past him to the door of the shop. She paused as she opened the door. 'Goodbye, husband. I may see you later. But if I am late, don't wait up. And as for that poor servant girl of yours, you have my blessing. She is welcome to you.'

The bell tinkled as Mary slammed the door behind her. Thomas watched her saunter back up the High Street towards town. He sighed, feeling dejected, and sat down heavily on a wooden chair behind the counter. He put his head in his hands and shook it as he pondered his fate. Damn her and her ways!

He would have his revenge on her one day. Perhaps he would throw her out and take Molly for a wife instead. At least she did not spurn his advances. Indeed, she behaved more like a wife than Mary. She cooked, she sewed, she cleaned; in fact, she tended to his every need. She never mocked him. She even bathed his bad foot when he asked. She dressed and undressed him. And she laid with him. He smiled as he remembered their fumblings and wondered exactly what had happened the previous night. Had he had relations with her? The truth was, he couldn't remember. Mary was driving him to drink and his memory was hazy. He could remember going to bed. And he could remember Molly taking off his boots. But the next thing he could remember was being woken by Mary shouting at him, with Molly laid next to him in bed. But she was on top of the covers while he was beneath them. And she was still fully dressed. Had he? He shook his head again. He simply could not remember.

Sighing once more, he stood up and opened the till. He removed what was left of the larger coins and took them through into the back room. A large, iron safe stood in one corner. He removed the key from his waistcoat pocket, opened the safe and deposited the coins in small stacks, alongside some papers. He kept a shilling back, putting it in his pocket. He would give it to Molly tonight. Perhaps he would tell her to buy a new dress or just to treat herself. She would be pleased. And maybe, just maybe, she would treat him too.

Chapter Fifteen

The gentleman laid the timepiece on a piece of blue velvet. 'It's a John Bushman, made in London, presented in a silver case. The chain is also in silver.' He wasn't sure if he was wasting his time with the presumptuous young lady before him, but as he hadn't had a customer all day he had decided to indulge her. Besides, she was young and pretty and it wasn't as if he had anything better to do.

Mary picked it up and balanced it on the palm of her hand. 'It feels quite heavy.'

'Indeed it does madam. It has gilt verge movement and a silver champlevé dial. The case has been designed and made by John Willoughby, also of London. We can engrave it if you wish. Is it for someone special?'

'Oh yes.' Mary blushed. 'Someone very special. But I won't have it engraved as I wish to take it now.' She placed it back on the velvet. 'How much is it?' She flashed him her sweetest smile.

The gentleman slid the velvet back towards him. He didn't want the lady to suddenly make a grab for it and made good her escape when she learned the price. Experience had taught him well and his knees were no longer up to the job of chasing priggers up the street, especially those more than half his age. He picked up the pocket watch and dangled it from its chain. It spun around it catching the sunlight, dazzling Mary as it shone in her eyes. 'Ten guineas.'

'I'll give you eight.'

He was taken aback. He hadn't expected her to barter, let alone have the money to pay for it. As if sensing he doubted her ability to pay for the piece, she took eight coins from her clutch bag and presented them in the palm of her hand.

'I couldn't possibly let it go for less than nine.' He stared hungrily at the coins, knowing it could be weeks before he made another sale like this.

'Nine it is then.' She put the coins down on the counter, withdrew another from her bag and placed it on top of them. 'Please can you wrap it for me.'

'Of course, madam. I will do it straight away.' He swept up the money from the counter before she could change her mind and took a square of silk from behind him. Returning the watch to its case, he wrapped the silk around it and secured the package with a piece of ribbon. He handed it to her. 'Thank you, madam. I hope your friend appreciates it.'

Mary slipped the gift into her dress and patted it. 'Oh I'm sure he will. Thank you and good day sir.' She exited the shop and headed towards Mrs Caudle's lodging house. The modest house was close to the town's boundary on a small road that led nowhere except to fields, farms and labourers' cottages. She knocked on the small wooden door and heard footsteps echoing down the hallway. The door opened and a short, stocky woman with grey hair tied up in a bun appeared before her. 'You must be Miss Brookes' she stated.

'Yes,' Mary replied. 'Is Mr Fletcher here yet?'

'He is indeed.' Her voice was cold and unfriendly. Mary

went to push past her, but she stood her ground. 'Aren't you forgetting something?'

Mary gave her a quizzical look, then remembered. She delved once more into her small bag and pulled out a penny. She handed it to the woman who then stood aside. 'Up the stairs, second door on the left. You've got an hour then you must be gone. I have somebody else after you have finished and will need to ready the room.'

Mary climbed the stairs, two at a time, eager to see Gabriel and present him with his gift. She burst in through the door and he was sitting on the bed, his boots and tunic already off. He looked so handsome she felt she would burst with desire.

'Have you got the money?' he demanded as soon as she closed the door behind her.

She set the small package on the dressing table and opened her bag once more. 'I have. Four guineas. Is that enough?'

He pulled a face. 'I suppose it will have to do. It will at least get Jacob off my back. For now. Can I promise him more next week?'

Mary handed him the coins and threw herself on the bed beside him. 'I'll see what I can do.'

Gabriel pointed to the small package. 'What's that?'

Mary giggled. 'Oh, nothing much. I bought you a present. A small keepsake to remind you of me.'

Gabriel's face lit up. 'A present? For me? What is it?'

Mary got off the bed, went to the table and picked it up. As she approached the bed, he made a grab for it. She giggled again as she quickly removed it out of his reach. 'You'll see. But first, take off your shirt.'

Gabriel quickly pulled the shirt over his head. The days working at the mill had left his body toned and firm from lifting sacks of grain. Discarding the shirt on the floor, he held out his hand. She obliged and began undoing the buttons on his breeches as he pulled at the ribbon and removed the silk. Holding up the watch, he whistled softly. 'Did you really buy this for me?'

Having pulled down his breeches, she stood up and kissed him hard on the lips. 'I did! Do you like it?'

'I love it! It's incredible. How can I ever repay you?'

Mary lay back on the bed, putting her hands above her head. 'I'm sure you can work it out. But be quick. We only have an hour and then I have to go and buy myself a new dress.'

Gabriel took one last look at the pocket watch before putting it gently down on the dressing table and diving full length on top of her. He kissed her all over her face before their tongues entwined. 'I love you Mary Brookes!' he exclaimed before burying his face into her neck, kissing and nibbling her.

'I love you too, Gabriel Fletcher!' She gasped as she felt him force himself inside her. Closing her eyes, she gave in to the feelings that were coursing through her body before she felt him shudder, then collapse on top of her. She suddenly opened her eyes, fear running through her. 'Did you withdraw?'

Gabriel's face was still buried in the pillow and he was breathing heavily. 'What?' His response was muffled.

She pushed him off to one side and sat up. Raising her skirts she looked down at herself. 'Did you pull out?' She already knew the answer as the stain beneath her began spreading. 'Gabriel! No! What have you done?'

Gabriel rolled onto his back, still panting. 'It will be fine. I'm sure there's nothing to worry about.' He didn't sound convinced. Mary rushed to the chamber pot and quickly filled it with water. She splashed the cold liquid onto herself while squatting over the pot, trying to get his seed out of her.

'I don't believe it!' She cried. 'How could you?'

Gabriel balanced himself on his elbows. He was grinning at the sight of her splashing herself. 'Not very dignified Mary.' He tried to make light of the situation.

Mary was still frantically cleaning herself, splashing water everywhere. 'If you have given me a child Gabriel Fletcher, I don't know what I'll do. It will be the ruin of me.'

'I think that ship has already sailed Mary. It will be way past Portland Bill and nearing France by now.' He stood up and pulled on his breeches, before putting his shirt back over his head. Tucking his shirt in, he then put on his waistcoat. He picked up the timepiece, attached it to the material and delicately placed it in the waistcoat pocket. He practiced removing it a few times, flicking the silver lid up and down, perfecting the technique. The sight of him admiring the watch she had bought for him made her soften. She stood up and dried herself off.

'You're sure you like it?'

'I love it. And I love you.' He grabbed her and pulled her body to his, holding her tight and kissing her once more. 'It will be all right. Don't worry. Everything will be fine. And, if you are with child, I will help you get rid of Channing so we can all be together forever.'

'Truly?' she asked, wide eyed.

'Truly,' he confirmed.

She nestled her head into his chest. 'Thank you Gabriel. You don't know how much that means to me to hear you say that.'

Chapter Sixteen

The trip out to Maiden Newton took a little over an hour. The eight mile trip was taken in a small carriage pulled by a brown pony. As they swept up the drive, Mary gasped in amazement at the size of the sandstone building before her. For once, she was in awe of something that related to Thomas Channing.

'Is this really where your parents live?'

'Yes. Do you like it?'

'I do. It is incredible. Is this where you grew up?'

'It is.' Thomas pulled the pony up short and jumped down from his seat. He helped Mary down as the large doors opened on the house and his parents appeared.

'Thomas! My dear boy! It's so wonderful to see you.' His mother rushed down the grey steps and grabbed her son's face, smothering him in kisses before pushing him back, gripping him by the arms. 'Let me take a good look at you. My word, you are so handsome!' She kissed him once more, before relinquishing her hold on him, her face beaming. His father held out his hand.

'At last, Thomas, you have come to see us.' He shook his son's hand warmly before turning to face Mary. 'And you must be my son's new wife.'

She held out her gloved hand and curtsied. 'Sir. It is a pleasure to finally get to meet you.'

Mr Channing bowed and held the back of her hand to his lips. 'The pleasure is all mine.'

Mrs Channing stepped forward and took Mary's hand and she curtsied again. 'Come on inside. We have some afternoon tea for you to enjoy.'

Thomas retrieved Mary's bag from the carriage and followed them up the stairs to the front door. Mary was led straight through into the landscaped gardens at the rear of the house where she was introduced to other members of the family, including Thomas's uncle. Mary couldn't help but notice the family resemblance, with all of the men having stocky builds and short, muscular arms. With formal introductions over, they enjoyed tea and bread with thickly cut slices of cured ham. When they were finished, Mrs Channing made her excuses and stood to leave. 'Come on Mary, let's leave the gentleman to discuss business while we go and have a chat whereby I can get to know you better.'

They entered the drawing room and sat opposite each other in small chairs looking out over the gardens from where they could observe the men. Mrs Channing spoke first. 'So, Mary, I must confess I know very little about you, although I do know of your family. Your marriage to Thomas did come as quite a shock to us though. We knew nothing of it until afterwards! I was quite upset at first, but now you are here I can see why Thomas has fallen for you. Please, tell me all about yourself, how you met Thomas, and all about the wedding day.'

Mary gulped. What should she say? That her father had married her off to the first man willing to take her on? One who had been paid handsomely for staying around long enough to see it through? And that she loathed the sight of Thomas and wished he had never been born? She smiled sweetly and took a deep breath. 'Well, where to begin?'

Mrs Channing sat back, expectantly, her piercing blue eyes looking straight into Mary's eyes.

'My father wanted the best for me and felt that Thomas would make the perfect husband' Mary began. 'I had not met him until an accord had been struck. As to the wedding, it was all rather rushed as my father wanted the matter concluded as quickly as possible.'

'Oh. I see.' Mrs Channing sounded disappointed. 'Are you with child?' It was a perfectly normal question given the circumstances surrounding their union but Mary felt a tremor go up her spine as she recalled her time spent with Gabriel the previous day.

'No! Nothing like that. We did not have knowledge of each other until our wedding night.'

Mrs Channing looked relieved. 'Well that's some comfort,' she joked. 'Although hopefully, that will soon follow. So, tell me more about the wedding.'

'There isn't much to tell really. It was held at St Peter's Church in Dorchester and was attended by family and friends. I don't know why my father or Thomas did not send out invitations to you and for that I am truly sorry. But in truth, it was a cold day, the ceremony was over in minutes, then we returned to Thomas's house for a party. It was all rather jolly.'

'And how are you finding married life?'

Mary gulped again. 'It is strange, living in a new house with my husband. It is certainly taking some getting used to.'

Mrs Channing nodded in agreement. 'I can only imagine. I remember when I was first married to Richard, although there was some courtship so at least I was able to get to know him before I moved into our home. Still, no matter. You are here now and will be staying for some time so I can get to know you.'

'Pardon?' Mary thought she must have misheard Mrs Channing.

'You will be staying with us for some time. Thomas has

business with his father to attend to and the shop will be taking up a lot of his time so he has asked if you may stay here awhile so we can keep an eye on you and prevent you from falling into boredom. He is quite worried about you.'

So that's why we are here, thought Mary. *To keep me away from Gabriel and my life in Dorchester.* She pouted angrily. *I won't have it!*

Mrs Channing stood up and rang the bell. A young manservant arrived promptly and Mary stood to leave. 'Take Mrs Channing up to her room please.' Mary stood to leave. 'We shall see you at dinner tonight Mary. I very much look forward to talking with you later. It will be served at eight o'clock. Please don't be late. Thomas's father likes everyone to be punctual with their timekeeping.'

Mary followed the man out of the room and up the wide staircase that dominated the hallway. She marvelled at the splendour of the place and glanced briefly at the portraits that lined the walls as she climbed the stairs. Finally, she arrived at her room. The young man held the door open for her to enter. As she went in he said 'You're Mary Brookes, aren't you?'

She looked at him. 'What if I am?'

He grinned. 'I've heard all about you. I'm surprised to see you here in this house.'

'Well you had better get used to it and control your insolence! You do realize that I could have you whipped!' she snapped.

His grin transformed quickly into a sneer. 'You could. But I doubt it.' He tapped the side of his nose. 'I think you will stay very quiet if you know what's good for you. But, if you need anything, just let me know. I'll be sure to sort you out.'

He laughed as he exited the room. Mary looked around. Her case was on the bed. How could Thomas do this to her? How dare he? Feeling in a state of utter despair, she threw herself on the bed alongside the case and began sobbing uncontrollably.

Chapter Seventeen

Mary had been staying with Mrs Channing for little over a week and it was beginning to take its toll. Being separated from her beloved Gabriel was one thing. Being on her best behaviour in what was a very confined and stuffy atmosphere was another. She was feeling like a tethered horse, unable to run free and burn off her excessive energy. She longed for Gabriel's touch. She also longed to frequent Dorchester's numerous taverns and meet up with her friends for a drink, to catch up with gossip and to just have some fun!

Mrs Channing was polite, but was constantly asking questions of her. She wanted to know about her background, her family, her friends, what she got up to when Thomas was at work, how was she coping with being a wife and running a house. She even wanted to know when they would be having their first child! At least Thomas wasn't around to mither her. And, with him away, she didn't have to make excuses for not sharing the same bed as him for that would surely have attracted unwanted attention from his doting parents.

Her only respite from the monotony of living at the house

came when she visited Thomas's Uncle Peter. In his forties, he was more handsome than his brother and certainly more fun. As the younger brother he'd had a more carefree upbringing, away from the family business. He had never married and resided in a more modest house in the village. He took on the role of chaperone, taking her to the local inn on occasion where she could enjoy a gin or two, flirt with the menfolk and soak up the friendly atmosphere. Indeed, Mary enjoyed his company so much she even suggested that perhaps she could stay with him.

Much to her surprise, both Mrs Channing and Peter agreed to the arrangement. Peter duly arrived on horseback with another horse for Mary and the two went riding together while her things were transported to his home.

Initially, she enjoyed her time there. He was less fastidious about time keeping and Mary began to get the sense of freedom that she had lost while staying with Mrs Channing. But it was to be short-lived. Uncle Peter quickly tired of her untidiness, complaining about her leaving things around the house, and her constant, frivolous chatter. The novelty of having a young lady in the house soon wore off and Mary was returned to Mrs Channing's household within the week!

Finally, after what felt to Mary like months but was, in reality, just a couple of weeks, Thomas returned with his father and said they would be leaving for Dorchester. The trip back passed in silence, with neither speaking to each other. Thomas attempted to engage in conversation with her, but she pointedly ignored him, preferring to look dead ahead with a glazed expression on her face.

As soon as Mary got home, she retired to her room, locking the door behind her. When night fell, she heard him climbing the stairs. Within a short time, she could hear loud snoring coming from his room. She got up, went to her dresser and scribbled a quick note, leaving it unsigned. As soon as she believed it was safe to do so, she quietly exited her room, crept down the stairs and opened the front door. She ran down the path, turned left into the lane and made for a large oak tree by a broken wooden gate. She scaled the gate and sought out the flat stone partly hidden by the hedgerow, and lifted it up. There was nothing beneath it, which didn't overly surprise her although she did feel a sense of disappointment. Depositing the note, Mary carefully replaced the stone, taking care to ensure it looked as if it hadn't been disturbed.

Mary quickly returned home before her absence was noticed and climbed into bed. She thought excitedly about Gabriel. Hopefully, tomorrow he would find the note and, when she returned to the stone, he would have left a response. With any luck, she would be in his arms at Mrs Caudle's lodgings within just a few hours.

Chapter Eighteen

Molly saw Eliza standing at the end of the garden, watching the house from her usual vantage point. She opened the back door and filled the pot with water from the well. Returning to the kitchen, Molly waved at Eliza, beckoning her to come in. Molly then hung the pot over the fire to boil the water, before busying herself with removing the scales from the large pike that Mr Channing had presented her with the day before. She knew that much of the day would be spent preparing the fish for dinner and it was a job she hated, especially the removal of the fish's scales.

Eliza appeared at the door. 'Good morning Molly,' she called out as she came into the kitchen, depositing a selection of vegetables on the table. 'How are you today?'

'I'm fine thank you, mistress Eliza. What have you brought for me today?'

Eliza ran through the ingredients, pointing them out although Molly already knew what they were. 'We have green beans and carrots.' She delved into her bag and bought out two flat cakes. 'And I have made an extra special treat for the master of the house and the mistress – should she decide to eat with him tonight!'

Molly stopped what she was doing with the fish and looked over. 'What are they?' she enquired.

'Corn cakes. I'm sure the master will love them. Just heat them up in a pan before you serve dinner and put them on the plate alongside the fish. It's my own special recipe. I'll have to give it to you and show you how to make it when I have more time to spare. It really is very simple. But don't have any for yourself. They are strictly for the master of the house and his wife.'

Molly looked crestfallen. 'Oh. Why?'

'They will be too rich for you and will cause problems with your stomach. Speaking of which, how is it today?'

Molly placed both hands on her belly, looking down at it. 'It is much better today, thank you. That balm you put on me yesterday certainly helped. What was it?'

'It's an ointment made with wormwood. I'm glad it has helped. If you require any more, just let me know.' Eliza pulled up a chair and sat down. 'I see the mistress is back.'

Molly nodded. 'Yes. The master brought her home yesterday.'

'And how is she?'

Molly picked up a small knife to begin on the laborious process of removing scales from the fish, moving the small knife from head to tail. 'I don't rightly know. She went straight to her room last night, coming out only after the master had gone to bed and was snoring away.'

Eliza was intrigued. 'Really? Where did she go?'

Molly giggled. 'Went off to meet her lover I reckon. She ran out of the house in the dead of the night, soon after the master was asleep.'

'Did you see her?'

'Only briefly, for I was downstairs having just finished

cleaning up after the master's dinner.'

'Did she see you?'

The young girl shook her head. 'No. She flew down the stairs and straight out of the door.'

Eliza was deep in thought. 'So you weren't with the master last night. After dinner, that is.'

Molly shook her head again. 'No. Now that the mistress is back hopefully he will have no need of me.'

While Mary was away, Thomas had frequently taken Molly to his bed whenever he had stayed at the house. Now that Mary was back, he would have to be more careful as he would not want to give his young wife cause to ridicule him again.

Molly continued scraping at the pike, removing the thin scales. 'There. I am done.' She cut the tail and the head off the large fish, picked the body up with both hands and placed it to one side. She then cleared the table, scrubbing it with a brush. Once she had removed all remnants of the scales, she returned the fish to the table and proceeded to split the belly.

'You must let me know straight away when you have your course,' Eliza said. 'I am hopeful your stomach ailments are a sign that it is on its way. I fear that, should you fall with child, the master will banish you from the house.'

The concerned look that suddenly appeared on Molly's face showed that this was something she had not considered. 'Won't the master want to keep the baby for himself?'

Eliza shook her head, a sad expression on her face. 'No, for it would bring shame upon him.'

'Couldn't he just kill the baby?' Molly stuck her hand inside the open belly of the fish and pulled out its innards.

'Of course not, Molly.' Eliza smiled sadly. 'He would not even let you stay in the house while you are with child. As soon as your belly starts swelling, you will be forced to leave.'

Molly turned the fish upside down. She peered inside it, looking for the layer of film that covered the spine. Having located it, she deftly removed it in one swift movement, just as her mother had taught her. 'But how can I stop it? Master Thomas is most insistent. I am unable to refuse him. Should I tell the mistress?'

Eliza shook her head. 'I don't think telling Mistress Mary what is going on will help you. It will only make her angry at you and she may even throw you out herself. You should tell the master that you are afraid of falling with child and that you would prefer it if he withdraws should he insist on taking you.'

Molly began trimming at the fins of the fish with her sharp knife, throwing them to one side with the entrails. 'But he is usually so gone with the drink he is unable to control it.'

'Then I have some lily root and rue you can try. Just put it inside yourself afterwards. But, if you get the chance beforehand and you know that he wants you to go upstairs with him, cut a lemon in half and insert it inside you.'

Molly looked incredulous. 'Will that work?'

Eliza laughed. 'It may do. It seems to have qualities that will prevent his seed from finding its way into your belly. And besides, it's better than nothing!'

'Have you ever used it?'

'No, for I have never needed to.' Eliza shook her head, sadly.

'But you have had a husband.' Molly took the unwanted parts of the fish and threw them into the yard. The chickens began clucking excitedly as they ran towards it, only to be beaten by the dog who hungrily devoured the entrails as the hens complained loudly at him.

Eliza was lost in her thoughts for a moment. 'Yes, I had a husband. For a while. It all seems so long ago now.'

Molly lifted a pail of water onto the table and began washing the fish, removing the last of the debris and blood. 'So what happened to him?'

'He passed, unfortunately.'

'Was he much older than you?'

Eliza shook her head. 'Yes, he was quite a lot older than me.'

'Could you not have a child?'

'Yes, I could.' Eliza looked dreamily off into the distance. 'Indeed, I was with child once. A boy.'

'You had a boy?'

'I did. But alas it was not to be. He did not survive childbirth.'

The room fell silent as Molly finished cleaning the pike. Eliza was in a world of her own as she recalled that fateful day. She could not – she would not – let the same fate befall poor young Molly. 'It was God's will,' Eliza suddenly announced. She stood up. 'I must leave, for I have things to do.' She pointed at the two corn cakes. 'Don't forget to serve those with dinner tonight. If the master likes them, let me know and I will show you how to prepare them for him. And don't have them for yourself. They will upset your digestion and you will not thank me for it!'

Molly smiled, removing her hands from the fish and wiping them on her apron. 'Thank you, Mistress Eliza. I am much obliged to you. And thank you for all of your help and advice. I don't know how I coped before I met you.'

Eliza paused briefly as she exited the door. Looking over her shoulder, she said 'You are most welcome, child. I will return again tomorrow with another treat for your master. He will think you are the best cook he has ever had!'

Molly closed the door behind her, using her foot to keep the dog from entering. She knew he would try and eat the rest of the pike, for he had a taste for it now. She smiled to herself. She was so lucky to have such a lady for a friend. Eliza was kind, sweet, considerate and so worried about her welfare. She didn't know where she would be without her. She looked up at the shelf to where the fruit was kept and spied a couple of lemons. Normally, she would have put them both inside the fish while it was cooking. Instead, she resolved to put just the one in, and keep the other for herself. Just in case.

Chapter Nineteen

Thomas got up just as dawn was breaking and put on his Sunday best. A fine embroidered waistcoat with black velvet jacket, white breeches and highly polished boots. He winced as he squeezed his foot into the tight fitting boot and tested it before gingerly getting up from his chair and putting his full weight on it.

Mary could hear the floorboards creaking as he made his way down the stairs. As if sensing she was awake, he stopped halfway and called out to her. 'Mary. Are you coming to church?' Hearing no reply, he continued on his way. Only once she had heard him close the front gate behind him did she open her eyes.

While Sundays were a day of worship for Thomas, they were a day of partying for Mary. His efforts to make her go with him, if only for the sake of respectability, had fallen on deaf ears as she far preferred to stay in bed for as long as possible before rising, mid-morning, and getting ready to receive her guests.

Her Sunday gatherings had become legendary amongst her circle of friends in Dorchester. They had begun at her parent's home when, as a thirteen year old, all her friends would arrive soon after her parents had left the house. Fine wine, cooked hams, fruits and sweetmeats would all be on offer as young Mary had the household servants running around ensuring her guests were happy, pandering to their every whim.

It was a tradition that Mary had been keen to uphold and while Thomas had been aware of what was happening in his absence, he had long since given up trying to stop her, in spite of the expense and excesses that she went to.

Today was to be especially significant for Mary, as it was to be the first time that she would be able to see Gabriel – and it would be the first time that he had come to the house since the day of her wedding. It was a bold and provocative move, but having been kept locked away at Thomas's parent's house for so long, she just didn't care.

Gabriel had taken two days to respond to the note she had left him. In it, he explained that he was helping his father at the mill and was unable to meet with her until Sunday at the earliest. Feeling frustrated at not being able to see him, she told him to come to her party at the house for she cared not what other people would say or do.

She called Molly up to her chamber as she ran her hands through the numerous new dresses she had treated herself to since returning to Dorchester. Having chosen a red dress, which she felt reflected her intentions that day, Molly helped her into it then patiently stood by while Mary worked her way through a large selection of ribbons to put in her hair. She decided upon the yellow ones and Molly dutifully arranged the ribbons in Mary's hair and on her dress. When she was done, Mary sent Molly back to the kitchen to begin preparing the food in time for the arrival of the guests.

About two dozen had received invitations, which was a reduced number from her days living under her father's roof. Friends had come and gone, some married, some leaving for London and Exeter to follow professions. Many had stopped coming altogether, in part because of the excesses of Mary's behaviour. Her reputation was becoming increasingly sullied and to be associated with her was to risk bringing shame. While the young men of the district looked forward to experiencing far more than society thought decent, the young ladies were becoming acutely aware of the potential damage, perceived or otherwise, that could be done to their reputations by associating themselves with Mary Channing.

As the guests began to arrive, Mary danced and cavorted, gin in hand, playing the errant teenager instead of the lady of the house. As she danced, she would frequently raise her skirts to reveal her shapely calves, much to the delight of the many male guests who outnumbered the girls by a ratio of three to one. When her beloved Gabriel arrived she screamed in delight, running towards him and nearly bowling him over as she leapt into his arms.

For many, this was a step too far. Some of her guests immediately made their excuses and left, vowing never to return. But Mary did not care. This was to be her day and she was going to make the most of it. As the drink flowed, she danced with Gabriel, ignoring the etiquette that was required of each dance and touching him at every opportunity.

As the drink began to take its toll, packs of playing cards were produced and the guests fell into different groups playing whist and brag, even though gambling was forbidden on Sundays, the day of worship.

Mary took the opportunity to whisk Gabriel away, up into her chamber, where she leapt upon him. Downstairs, the couple's absence was noted, resulting in yet more guests choosing to leave in disgust, with yet more mutterings about Mary's unseemly behaviour under her husband's roof.

Eventually, Mary and Gabriel returned, with Mary holding his hand, even though he was clearly uncomfortable. He made a show of pulling out his pocket watch. 'My word, is that the time?

I really must go.'

Mary pulled a face, pouting. 'No, Gabriel, you cannot. Not until I say so.'

Gabriel returned the watch to the pocket on his waistcoat. 'I am sorry Mary, but I have chores to attend to. It was difficult enough to come here as it is. If I do not return shortly, my father will have cause to beat me. If I stay much longer, your husband will return and most likely do the same.'

'He would be no match for you!' Mary exclaimed. 'There is no way he could best you in a fight.'

'Maybe that is so, but I must still leave. I'm sorry.' He made his way to the front door and a number of other guests stood to leave as well. As the door opened, a gentleman stood before them, filling the doorway. 'Sir?' Gabriel enquired.

'I should ask the same of you!' the man responded in a booming voice, forcing his way through the throng of young men stood before him. He stopped in the hall. 'Mary!' he bellowed, his voice echoing around the vestibule. 'Mary! Where the devil are you?'

Mary appeared at the door to the drawing room. Upon seeing the man, she immediately retreated, then hurried away. He strode purposefully after her. 'Mary!' he shouted again, his deep voice causing everyone to look up. As he marched through the drawing room he lunged at the revellers, brushing cards and coins from the table. 'Gambling? On a day of worship? This is disgraceful behaviour and I won't have it! Get out of this house now! Leave immediately!'

The young men did as they were told, scrambling towards the door before he could hit them with his riding crop, which he was now swishing in their general direction.

He paused momentarily, breathing heavily, his voice red from exertion. 'Mary!' he bellowed once more. Mary crouched down behind a table but he spied her. He made his way towards her. 'Stand up! Now! What...' He gestured around the room, noting the cards on the table with a few pennies left behind, along with discarded glasses of wine and plates of food. '… is the meaning of this?'

The sight of her father in law in full flow made Mary feel like a small child again. She stood up, head down, hands clasped before her. 'I'm sorry sir.'

'Sorry? Sorry! Sorry doesn't even begin to cover it! This is atrocious behaviour.' Richard Channing's voice went up another level. 'This is completely unacceptable. You are the lady of the house, the wife of my son, and my daughter in law. You have a standard and a reputation to uphold. I don't know why Thomas has been unable to stop you. If you were my wife I would have beaten you black and blue by now!' He flexed his riding crop threateningly and Mary flinched, wondering if he might actually be moved to do it.

'You have made my son a laughing stock!' he continued. 'You have ruined both his name and his finances. Instead of behaving like a lady of means, you act like a spoilt brat, spending money on frivolous things and cavorting with members of the opposite sex when your status demands decorum. I will have it no more! Do you hear me?' He brandished his riding crop again. 'No. More. Enough, is enough!'

He turned on his heel, striding out of the house, leaving the front door wide open behind him. Mary was shaking. It had been many years since somebody had chastised her and she was not used to it. She wondered what Thomas would do upon his return. Would be beat her as his father had suggested? If he did, she would at least have cause to leave him. But where would she go? Her father would undoubtedly turn her away, ashamed of the position she had put herself in, telling her to return to her husband at once. Perhaps she could turn to Gabriel? Again, Mary knew this was fanciful thinking. Gabriel would turn her away as soon as look at her. She was fast coming to the conclusion that as long as she had access to Thomas's money, Gabriel was a more than willing accomplice to her deviant ways. But as soon as the money was gone… she shuddered as she thought about it.

She snapped herself out of her thoughts. Thomas would no doubt return soon, probably with his father. She should make good the house. 'Molly!' she called. The young girl appeared almost immediately and Mary realized that she had must have witnessed her dressing down. No matter. She would deal with her later. First, she needed to set Molly to work. 'Tidy this all up before the master returns home. When he comes, tell him I have taken to my bed for I am not feeling well.' She smirked. 'And Molly.'

'Yes mistress.'

'Do whatever it takes to placate him. Whatever he needs, you are to give it to him. Do I make myself clear?' As Molly nodded, Mary recovered her poise and stood up straight. Nobody was going to tell her what to do. Least of all, Thomas. And certainly not his father! She would show them. Nobody would ever tame her and make her change her ways!

Chapter Twenty

Richard Channing found his son at the Kings Arms, just below Cornhill. He was sitting in front of the large inglenook fireplace, a tankard of ale in his hand, looking decidedly unhappy. Richard got himself a brandy, ordered another ale for his son, and went over to him. Thomas barely stirred as he sat down opposite him.

'She'll be the death of you, you know.' Richard paused momentarily to take in the aroma of the brandy before taking a large gulp. As the landlord put down the tankard of ale next to Thomas, he gestured for another brandy. 'I'll have the same again please landlord.'

Saying nothing, Thomas drained the last of his tankard and picked up the fresh one.

Richard gulped down the rest of his brandy, swallowed loudly and breathed out. He cupped the empty glass in both hands. 'It has to stop. Before it's too late. They'll have you blindfolded, riding backwards on a horse through town as a cuckold if you don't. Do I make myself clear, Thomas?'

Thomas nodded sullenly as the landlord returned with a

second brandy for his father.

'I'm going to have to cut your lines of credit before it's too late. I will inform the bank in the morning. You can order supplies for the shop through me. Mary will no longer have access to your – my – money. The way she is going, you will end up ruined and relying on poor relief. The shame and stigma will never go away and I simply will not let that happen.'

Thomas looked up. Richard thought he saw a wetness in his eyes but chose to ignore it. His son really needed to be a man.

Eventually, Thomas spoke. 'I know. She has become too much for me. I have no control over her. I threaten her, she laughs at me. She takes what she wants, then takes some more. She helps herself to the money at the store. She spends it all on hats, clothes and shoes. She acts like a child, pouting when she is unable to get her way.' Thomas held his stomach and turned to his father. 'The whole affair is even upsetting my digestion. I keep getting cramps and having to take to the pot at the most inconvenient of moments. What am I to do?'

Richard grunted at him. 'Damned if I know. I never had this problem with your mother or your sisters. I thought the family she came from was fine, upstanding. Small wonder they wanted rid of her! But you must get her under control. You need to put an end to the endless gossip that is going on about you and Mary. It's gone too far and you must put a stop on it.' He softened his voice. Speaking in a hushed tone, he said 'What are you going to do about this braggard that she has been seen with?'

Thomas shrugged his shoulders. 'Perhaps I should challenge him?'

Richard shook his head. 'No. To do that would be to acknowledge you know what is going on behind your back. I know the owner of the mill where the boy's father is employed. If I suggest he have a word with him with regards to his future employment, it might give him cause to send the boy away, somewhere out of the area.'

Thomas sat upright. 'Really? Could you do that?'

'I don't know. But at least I can try. We can perhaps put in an order for grain to stock at the shop in order to curry favour.'

They fell silent as the landlord returned with Richard's second brandy. As soon as he was out of earshot, Thomas spoke. 'But what am I to do for money? I cannot simply drop out of society.'

'As I said, you can order your supplies through me and use my account. Pass your household bills on to me and I will settle them. If it helps, perhaps you should move back home so we can look after you and keep an eye once more on Mary. I'm sure your mother would love to get her hands on her!' Richard suddenly laughed at the thought of his wife taking her young daughter in law in hand.

'But what about the shop?' Thomas suddenly looked miserable again. The thought of returning to the family home where his relationship with Mary would be under scrutiny, as would her behaviour, was not a favourable one to him.

'Close it awhile.' Richard leant over to his son. 'It's not as if it is successful at the moment anyway. The drop in trade has been noticeable since gossip of your wife's antics has hit the streets. Everyone is leaving the shop well alone and they will no doubt continue to do so while she is allowed to carry on in such a wanton manner.'

Thomas slumped back in his chair. His options were limited and he gloomily accepted what must happen. 'When would you have us arrive at the house?'

'Tomorrow. It is for the best. I'm sorry my boy, but there is no other course that I can see that is available to you.' Richard Channing stood up, put his hand on his son's shoulder and squeezed it gently. He knocked back his brandy in one and slammed the glass back down on the table. 'There! It is done. I will expect you for lunch. I shall tell your mother to make the arrangements.' With that he marched out of the inn, leaving Thomas to consider his fate.

Chapter Twenty-One

'I won't go – and you can't make me!' Mary steadfastly refused to leave the house and go back to the Channing's house with Thomas.

'You have no choice. Pack up your things and get yourself ready.' Thomas regarded her sternly.

Mary laughed at him. 'You can go. I am staying here. I hate it there, away from my friends. Your mother locks me up as if I am a toy.'

'Please Mary. I need to get my affairs in order.' Thomas pleaded with her. 'Thanks to you, my finances are a mess. We need to cut our cloth accordingly. By staying there, if only for a short while, it will enable me to get everything back in order.'

'You can do what you like.' Mary pouted, an obstinate look on her face. 'It isn't my fault you cannot earn enough money to keep me.'

Smarting from her comment, Thomas shook his riding crop at her but she just laughed at him, mocking him even more. 'If you use that on me then that will be the end of us. I will leave for my father's house immediately and you will never see me again.'

'Don't tempt me!' Thomas growled. 'Look, it is only for a short while. Just a few days, that is all. Just long enough for me to go to London with my father. As soon as I have refinanced with the bank and the merchants, things will return to normal. In the meantime, you must stay at my parent's house.'

Mary screwed up her face and crossed her arms in front of her. 'You do what you like. I will not leave this house.' She pushed past him and ran up the stairs. Thomas heard the door to her room slam shut and shook his head sadly. He knew it was pointless. He would have to leave for his parent's home without her.

As soon as he had gone, Mary wrote a note and left it under the tree for Gabriel. With Thomas away for a few days, she hoped he would be able to come and see her at the house without fear of being caught out by Thomas or his father.

Mary returned home and walked through the house. She quite liked it. While it was nowhere near as big as grand house she had grown up in, it was a good size. She went into Thomas's bedroom and casually opened his drawers, picking through his belongings. There was nothing of any real value and the pot where he kept his money was empty. She wondered how serious his financial predicament was. It was true; she had been spending a lot of money on clothes and trinkets for herself. But it was because she was bored. Why didn't Thomas understand that? She had also been paying off a lot of Gabriel's debts, plus financing their meetings at the lodging house whenever they met. Mary had long since given up on Gabriel ever having the money to treat her. All of his promises had turned to dust. She wondered if she was beginning to tire of him. Apart from their lovemaking, he didn't have anything else to offer. They couldn't even meet up in the local taverns and inns anymore to enjoy an evening out together.

Finding nothing of value in Thomas's room, she returned to her own chamber. She opened up her purse but, apart from a few coppers, there was scarcely enough in there to keep her while Thomas was away. Her thoughts of throwing a big party in his absence evaporated.

Feeling disappointed, Mary made her way down to the kitchen, where Molly was preparing the meal for that night. She picked up a morsel of salted meat and popped it in her mouth, chewing at it slowly. 'What is for dinner tonight?' she asked.

'I have some cold meat and turnips.'

Mary screwed her face up. 'I don't think I would like that.'

Molly shrugged her shoulders. 'I'm sorry mistress, but it is all we have in the house. The master did not give me any money for food this week.'

Mary was shocked. What if Thomas had told her the truth? Were they really poor? Had he really run out of money? 'What am I to eat?' she demanded of Molly.

Molly shrugged once more, holding her hands up. 'I'm sorry mistress. We have eggs and some bread left over, but apart from tonight's meal, that is all.'

Mary wandered slowly out of the kitchen, feeling bored. She considered walking into town but with no money to spend it seemed pointless. Even though it had been less than an hour since she had left the note for Gabriel, she decided to return to the spot to see if he had responded. She walked slowly down the road and then hurried up the lane to the gate, once she was sure nobody had seen her. She climbed the gate and dropped down the other side. She leaned back over the gate and looked both ways up and down the lane before dropping to her knees and lifting the stone. Her note was still there.

She sat down under the tree and pondered her predicament. If Thomas really had run out of money, then she would have to return to her own home. She wondered what her reception would be. Would her father send her on her way to the Channing's house? She suspected he would even escort her there himself. Much as she hated to admit it, she was stuck with Thomas and there was nothing she could do about it.

As the sun began setting, Mary slowly made her way home. Molly greeted her with dinner as soon as she arrived back, but she just picked at it, not feeling at all hungry. She stood up to get some wine but the decanter was empty. 'Molly!' she called.

Molly appeared at the door within seconds. 'Yes, mistress?'

'Bring me some wine.' Mary held up the empty decanter.

Molly shook her head. 'We have none, mistress.'

Mary groaned and dismissed her with a wave of her hand. She held her head in her hands. No money, no wine and no Gabriel. This was not how it was meant to be. Suddenly feeling very lonely, she decided she might just as well go to bed. Perhaps she should have gone with Thomas to his parent's house after all.

Chapter Twenty-Two

'Where is everybody?' Eliza had arrived with a small bag of food and had let herself into the kitchen through the back door.

Molly shook her head. 'The master left a couple of days ago. The mistress has been around but went out earlier today. I am the only one here.'

Eliza placed the bag on the kitchen table and began unpacking it. 'Where has the master gone?'

'The mistress said he has gone to London. She was meant to stay with his parents but she refused to go.' Molly grinned. They had an awful argument about it, too.'

'Really?' Eliza grinned as well. 'I saw the closed sign on the shop yesterday and wondered where he had gone.'

'According to what I heard the other day, he hasn't got any money left. The mistress has spent it all!'

'Oh dear. What did the mistress say about that?'

'She didn't believe him. But she has been complaining about the fact there is very little food in the house and we have run out of wine.' Molly picked up some of the items Eliza had placed on the table. 'I can't pay you for these. The master hasn't given me any money.'

'That's fine, Molly. I came to give you some more cookery lessons. When is the master back?'

'He told me he would return on Thursday.'

'That's tomorrow.'

'Is it?' Molly seldom knew what day of the week it was, as all of her days were identical, comprising of cooking, cleaning and running around after the master and the mistress of the house.

'Yes, it is. Well perhaps he can give you some money when he gets back and you will be able to repay me. In the meantime, I have come to teach you how to make mutton stew and the corn cakes the master likes so much.' She ran through the ingredients and then took out a small, black pouch. 'This,' she said, holding it up, 'is my secret ingredient.' She opened it and Molly peered inside.

'What is it?'

Eliza tapped the side of her nose. 'It's a special spice. You can only use it in small amounts but it adds taste to every dish you prepare. Just sprinkle a small amount into the dish as you prepare it then mix it in well. The master will love it!'

Molly grabbed the large pot from the stove and they chopped up the root vegetables Eliza had brought with her. After placing them in the pot, they added water and placed it on the stove to heat up. Eliza then unwrapped the mutton and got Molly to chop it into small pieces, before putting them in a pan and browning them over the fire. Once the meat had sealed, they added it to the pot of vegetables. Eliza then opened up her pouch. 'Molly, take a pinch.'

Molly did as she was told.

Eliza nodded at the pot. 'Now just sprinkle it in and stir it in slowly until it dissolves.'

Molly rubbed her finger and thumb together over the pot letting the powder fall into the stew.

'Now add some cornstarch, along with the juices from the

mutton that you have collected in the pan.' Eliza watched as Molly poured the greasy liquid into the pot and then added two spoonfuls of cornstarch. She nodded her encouragement. 'Now stir it all in together and leave it to thicken up. Slowly cook it for at least four hours, until the mutton has softened. Leave it to cool overnight, then add another sprinkle of powder and heat it through before you serve it for dinner tomorrow. Understand?'

Molly nodded. 'What is it called?'

'What? The powder?'

Molly nodded. 'Yes.'

Eliza thought for a second. 'It hasn't really got a name. Let's call it Molly's Magic Mixture.'

'I like it.' Molly smiled, pleased to hear her Eliza use her name.

'Good. Now clean off the pan and I will show you how to make the corn cakes.'

While Molly sluiced out the pan, Eliza got all of her ingredients together for the cakes. Molly finished washing out the pan and put it to one side.

Eliza stood back from the table. 'You have some ground maize and a little bit of flour. Now you need to add two eggs, some salt, some black pepper and a little bit of water. Now, have you got a large bowl to mix it all in?'

Molly grabbed a bowl, and poured the ingredients in before breaking two eggs carefully over it.

'Good!' Eliza encouraged her and handed her the pouch again. 'Now add the Molly's Magic Mixture. Sprinkle it in, like I showed you.' Molly took a pinch and sprinkled it over the mixture. 'Good girl. Now, add a bit of water and begin kneading it through until it has all joined together.'

Molly kneaded the mixture until it had all bound together and stood back, sweating at the effort.

'Now roll it flat.' Eliza picked up a mug. 'Use this to cut it into circles.'

As soon as Molly had finished, Eliza picked up the pan. 'Don't do it now, but when the master is ready for his dinner just quickly heat them through on this, turning them over halfway through cooking so they are brown on both sides. You must serve them hot.'

Molly smiled. 'Thank you mistress. I don't know what I would do without you.' She hugged Eliza warmly and held her tight.

Eliza pushed her away. 'Don't be so silly, child.' She handed her the small black velvet pouch. 'Now remember. This is the secret ingredient. Whatever you do, make sure you add this to every meal and mix it in well. Can you do that for me?'

Molly nodded her head vigorously. 'Yes, mistress.'

'Good. When you run low, let me know and I will get you some more.' She glanced out of the window. 'Time is pressing on. I really must go as I have some house calls to make.'

Molly hugged her once more, then waved goodbye from the doorway as Eliza made her way down the garden path and disappeared from view.

Chapter Twenty-Three

Thomas returned the following evening to find a bountiful meal before him. Amazed by Molly's sudden improvement as a cook, he tried to get Mary to join him for dinner but to no avail. Mary announced she was feeling unwell and refused once more to vacate her room.

After two days on the road, Thomas was ravenous. He tucked in to the hearty meal, delighting in the taste and quickly clearing the plate. 'Molly!' he bellowed.

Molly arrived almost immediately, drying her hands on her apron. 'This stew is wonderful!'

'Thank you, sir.' She beamed.

'Is there enough for a second portion?' He held out his empty plate.

'Certainly, sir.' She grabbed it off him and turned to leave.

'And if you have any more of those corn cakes, I'll have some more of those as well.'

Molly was beaming as she set the second portion of stew down before him, before skipping back to the kitchen to heat up some more corncakes.

Thomas hungrily set about the second portion. He picked up the second batch of corncakes as Molly delivered them to the table. 'These are incredible. Where did you learn to make them.' He dipped one into the mutton stew and shoved it into his mouth, his eyes rolling in pleasure.

Molly couldn't help but smile, happiness flooding through her. 'I have been having cookery lessons.'

'Really?' Thomas grabbed another one, broke it in half and continued mopping at his plate. 'From whom?'

She shrugged. 'Just a friend.'

'Well she is very good. You must continue to learn off her.' He went silent for a second. As Molly made to leave, he suddenly spoke. 'I am sorry if I have taken advantage of you in recent weeks, but my marriage is not working and I have needs that my wife will not see to.' It was a poor excuse for an apology, but it was the best he could do.

Molly stood still, listening but not speaking for she knew not what to say. Finally, she plucked up the courage to speak. 'I am concerned what will happen to me if I fall with child.'

The thought hadn't even occurred to Thomas. The only thing on his mind was the damage Mary was doing to his reputation. He hadn't even considered what damage he could do to his own should he give a child to Molly. He nodded to her. 'You are right, of course. It would bring shame on the house. And you. Of course, I am sorry. I shall endeavour to behave in a manner more befitting of the master of the house in future.'

But even as he said it, a ball of anger was growing in his belly. Why was it he always found himself apologizing to his wife? And now he found himself apologising to his maid as well. He was the master of this house. It was high time he started acting like it. He narrowed his eyes as Molly turned to leave, the anger turning to lust. 'Before I dismiss you, I would like you to pour me some more wine.' He held up his glass, a mean look in his eyes.

The decanter was close by his side. Warily, Molly went over to him and picked it up. She poured it slowly, taking care not to spill any on the white linen cloth. Putting the decanter down, she replaced the lid. As she did so, Thomas grabbed her round her waist, pulling her down on his lap. His hands reached up under her skirt as she tried in vain to push him away. His lips were suddenly on hers and she gave in, fearing that he would turn violent should she resist. She closed her eyes and concentrated on the place in her head where everything was peaceful and nothing could hurt her. As he lifted her on the table and forced himself between her thighs, she thanked her lucky stars that she had remembered to insert half a lemon inside herself earlier that day.

Chapter Twenty-Four

That weekend, Mary was stirred out of her misery by the arrival of one of Thomas's old school friends. Nial was charming, witty and handsome, and Mary was bewitched by the new house guest. Determined to play the perfect hostess, Mary ran around ensuring food and drink was readily available and she joined the two men at every opportunity. Thomas was bemused by her sudden turnaround in health, but was just happy to see her up and about and acting as he felt a wife should.

They all sat around the table as Molly brought in their dinner. Under Eliza's guidance, she had made a pork and apple stew, which was served from a large casserole dish, accompanied by lots of corncakes. As the wine and port flowed, Mary flirted outrageously with Nial. Thomas became increasingly withdrawn as the evening progressed, feeling excluded from the conversation and ignored by his wife. He took to the brandy before eventually excusing himself, claiming that he had to be up early the following day.

He attempted to kiss his wife goodnight as be passed her by but she recoiled, pushing him away. Feeling humiliated once more, this time in front of his old school friend, he stomped off upstairs, slammed the door and fell into bed.

Seemingly unaware of his friend's mood, Nial moved closer to Mary until they were sat side by side, their legs touching beneath the table. Mary raised the wine to her mouth, feeling slightly heady and enjoying the attention. 'My, my sir. Is that a stirring I can feel beneath the table?'

At twenty-six years of age, Nial was well versed in sexual encounters and he could sense that the opportunity was in the air. If he had any feelings of loyalty towards his friend Thomas, they had been firmly pushed to the back of his mind. 'I fear it may well be madam, for it is certainly getting very hot in here.'

Mary giggled and snuggled even closer to him. Her right hand dropped to his knee beneath the table and she began rubbing it gently. Nial responded by draping his left arm around the back of her chair where his hand could touch her bare shoulder and he ran the tips of his fingers up and down the nape of her neck. Their faces got closer together and Mary could feel his breathe on her cheek. She took a swig of port, swallowed and turned her head to face him. Their noses touched and they both burst out laughing. Then, as their eyes met, they held their gazes as they both moved in to kiss. It was long and sensual. Beneath the table, Mary's hand had crept up his thigh and was now nestling in his groin. His interest in her was obvious and she squeezed him gently, causing him to gasp. He gripped her neck and pulled her closer into him, feeling her body on his, putting one hand on her bosom.

They quickly jumped apart as Molly entered the room to clear the plates. 'Will that be all mistress?' she asked as she stacked them on top of each other, taking care not to look at either of them.

'Yes. That will be all. Thank you Molly. You can go to your room once you have finished cleaning the kitchen. Goodnight.' As soon as the door closed, they kissed once more.

'I suppose I should go to my lodgings,' Nial said, breathlessly, his lips almost touching hers.

'I suppose you should' agreed Mary, her hand still resting on his crotch.

'They will be expecting me,' he whispered once more. 'If I don't go soon, the door will be locked and I will be unable to get in.'

'That will be a shame' said Mary, quietly. 'For then you will be all alone in the dark and the cold. I fear there will also be rain tonight.'

'I believe you are right,' he agreed. 'And I hate getting wet.'

'That would be most disagreeable' said Mary. 'Then perhaps you should stay.'

'Do you have a room?' he enquired, quietly.

She nodded. 'I do. But it is not prepared for guests. If I had known you were going to stay I would have got Molly to make up a bed for you. Perhaps I should ask her to prepare it for you.'

'There is no need to go to all that trouble. All I need is a bed to lay on, a blanket for warmth and a pillow for my head.'

'I'm not sure I can find one at this late hour. Perhaps you would consider sharing mine.'

'If the master of the house has no objections, then that would certainly be preferable,' he said, after kissing her again. He brushed a strand of hair back over her ear and she felt herself go weak at his touch.

'I think the master of the house is long past making a decision. So the mistress of the house will have to decide on his behalf,' she said, squeezing his crotch once more. They enjoyed a long, final kiss before getting up from the table as one. Mary turned, grabbing him by the hand. Putting her finger to her lips, she led him across the hall to the stairs and up to her room. Once inside, they quickly undressed each other and threw back the covers.

Their lovemaking was frantic and Mary struggled not to call out as he entered her. As soon as it was over, the spell was broken. They both lay on their backs, an invisible barrier between them. 'I'd better go,' he finally said.

Mary rolled over, facing away from him, feeling ashamed. 'Yes, you should.'

He dressed quickly, picking up his boots and made his way to the door. 'Will I ever see you again?' he enquired.

She shook her head. 'No. I don't think that would be wise.'

He closed the door quietly behind him and crept down the stairs. Molly watched him leave from behind the kitchen door, then skipped across the hall to lock the door behind him. Upstairs, through the top window on the landing, Thomas also watched him go. It would be the last time he would ever see his old school friend.

Chapter Twenty-Five

Mary was in a state of panic. Her course had not yet happened and she was normally as regular as clockwork. Her stomach ached again and she wondered if that was a symptom of being with child. She had been fretting since the episode with Gabriel and now she'd also had relations with Nial. She chastised herself for being so careless. She had to work out a plan of action, one that would not raise the suspicions of her husband.

The fact she had never consummated the marriage meant even Thomas couldn't be taken for a fool. To fall into bed with him now would certainly arouse suspicion, especially if she then suddenly announced that she was expecting. As an option, it was the most obvious one, but Mary found the idea abhorrent. The mere thought of his touch left her feeling cold.

The only other alternative was to induce a termination. But how was she to go about it?

Mary contemplated asking her mother but quickly dismissed the idea. Her mother would demand to know why she didn't want to keep the baby. After all, it would give her the respectability her parents craved while sealing their family's union with the Channing name.

She decided to ask Molly instead. Perhaps she would know. She headed down to the kitchen where Molly was preparing yet more corn cakes. Mary detested them, believing they affected her digestion and gave her stomach cramps. She had long stopped eating them, but Thomas couldn't get enough of them.

'Molly?'

Molly stopped what she was doing and turned around, wondering why the mistress had come down to see her. 'Yes mistress Mary?'

Mary had initially chosen her words carefully as she didn't want to raise suspicion, but then it struck her. She didn't need to tread carefully. All she had to do was turn the tables on the servant girl. 'I know my husband has been forcing himself upon you.'

Molly gasped. 'No he hasn't mistress, I swear!'

Mary smiled. 'It's fine. I don't care. I cannot abide the thought of sleeping with him myself and I know he has needs that must be tended to. I am only grateful that you are able to help him with those needs.'

Molly's mouth opened and closed like a fish stranded on a river bank.

'But mistress…'

Mary reassured her once more. 'Honestly, it's nothing. But I do need to ask you something.'

Molly pushed back against the table, leaning against it for support, gripping its edges tightly. 'Yes mistress?'

'Now I'm not saying it would happen. But it could. And if it did, it would bring shame on the master which I cannot allow.'

'What's that, mistress?'

'What would you do should you fall with child?'

Molly looked shocked. 'But mistress!'

'Oh, I know it is hardly likely and I'm sure the master is most careful. But what would you do should it happen?'

Molly's mouth opened and closed in quick succession again as she contemplated her answer. 'I don't rightly know mistress. I hadn't really thought about it,' she lied. 'But I think I know somebody who would know.'

'Really?' Mary's curiosity was piqued. How would Molly possibly know somebody who had that sort of knowledge. Unless, of course, it was her mother. Mothers usually knew that sort of thing, especially those living in the farming community. Unwanted babies were expensive to raise and it wasn't unusual to dispose of them, either before or after birth.

'Yes. It's a lady I know. She has knowledge of medicine.'

Mary narrowed her eyes. 'How would a woman have knowledge of medicine?'

'She was married to a doctor. She used to work alongside him.'

'Oh, I see. Could you ask her for me and let me know what she says. Just in case,' she added.

'Yes, of course. The next time I see her I will ask.'

'Do you know when that might be?' Mary was anxious for an answer.

Molly shook her head. 'No. But I know where she lives. I can call on her if you like.'

Mary nodded. 'Yes. Please do that. Can you go now?'

'Now, mistress?'

'Yes. I am keen to learn what to do in this matter, should it happen. But be quick. You have chores to finish before the master gets back.'

Molly began removing her apron, wiping her hands as she did so. 'Of course, mistress. I'll go straight away. Her lodgings are not far so I shouldn't take more than a few minutes.'

'Good' Mary nodded once more. 'And Molly?'

'Yes mistress?'

'Don't tell a soul. And especially don't mention it to the master of the house.'

'Of course, mistress.' Molly hurried away down the garden path and Mary felt a sense of relief. Hopefully Molly would obtain the information she required and she would be able to extricate herself from this awful predicament.

Molly returned soon after, her face covered in sweat from running up the hill. Mary heard her come in and quickly made her way back down to the kitchen to greet her. 'Well?' she demanded as Molly sought to get her breath back. 'Did you meet with her?'

Molly bent over double, her hands on her knees, trying to recover. She stood up once more. 'I managed to see the lady. She recommends ratsbane.'

'Ratsbane? Isn't that a poison?'

'Yes, mistress. But, according to the lady, it can be taken in small doses for medicinal purposes. If you mix a pinch of the powder with water, then drink it quickly, it should bring on the desired effect.'

Mary thought about it. 'What's in it? Won't it kill me?'

'Kill you? Is it for you?' Molly's eyes opened wide.

Mary realized she had just made a mistake. 'Yes.' There was no point hiding it. 'But you mustn't tell anyone. It must be our secret. My course is late and it is possible I may be with child, but I am not ready for one yet. So, will this poison – this ratsbane – kill me?'

Molly shrugged her shoulders. 'I don't know. But according to my friend, a small dose will be enough to kill the child and may cause you to be unwell for a few days, but that is to be expected. The only alternative is to see someone who will rid you of the baby, but that is dangerous and may cause you harm.'

Mary knew that to deliberately kill your unborn child was to incur the wrath of the authorities. If she was to do it, it needed to be done discretely. Ratsbane it was then.

'Do you know where I can get this ratsbane?'

'There is the apothecary shop in the high street. Mister Wolmington's. You can get it there.'

Mary rushed to her room and grabbed her bag. She could send Molly but there was no guarantee the girl would come back with the right stuff. The girl also had to finish her chores before Thomas returned, or he would question what she had been up to. Checking she had some money, she put on her hat and made her way to the apothecary shop. She loitered outside briefly, plucking up the courage to go in, before entering.

'Hello Mary. Fancy seeing you in here.' The shop assistant was one of the young women who had attended many of the balls and dances Mary used to hold before she had married Thomas.

'Hello. Erm…?'

'Amy. Amy Clavel.'

Flustered, Mary struggled to maintain her composure. 'Amy. Of course! What are you doing here?'

'I am apprenticed to work here. My father is a friend of Mr Wolmington. What are you doing here?'

'I need to buy some ratsbane. We have problems with rodents and must lay some traps.'

Amy went to a shelf and pulled a tin down. 'How much do you need?'

Mary had no idea. 'How much do you think I'll need?'

Amy shrugged her shoulders. 'How many rats do you have?'

'A fair few I'd wager.'

'I'll give you a farthing's worth. That should do it.' Amy opened the tin. 'Oh, it's empty. Hold on a minute. I'll go and have a look in the back.'

As Amy disappeared into the back, Mary was beginning to have second thoughts about the whole venture. But before she could leave, the door to the shop opened and in walked another three customers who formed a queue behind her. Feeling trapped, Mary had no option other than to wait for Amy to return.

She eventually reappeared empty handed. 'We haven't got any ratsbane, but I have asked Mr Wolmington and he says to give you powdered mercury. It will do the same job, and probably far quicker too. Do you still want a farthing's worth?'

Mary didn't know. 'I guess so.'

Amy measured out a good measure of the powder and poured it onto a sheet of paper. She then carefully folded the paper into a small envelope, creasing it as she went so it would hold firm without spilling its contents. Mary handed over her farthing and Amy passed the small package to her. Shoving it into her bosom, Mary quickly retreated from the shop. Arriving home, she immediately sought out Molly.

'They didn't have any ratsbane, so they have given me mercury instead. Should I use it?'

Molly didn't know. 'Would you like me to go and ask my lady friend?' she offered.

'Yes. Please. Go now for I need to know if it will work.'

Molly headed out into the April sunshine and ran all the way to the lodgings where Eliza was living. Eliza received her in the parlour.

'Hello Molly. What can I do for you now?'

It's the mistress. The powder she asked about? It was for her. She believes she may be with child!'

Eliza was shocked. 'She wishes to dispose of the baby she is to have with her husband?'

'I doubt very much the master is the father of the child.' Molly grinned. 'Anyway, the mistress couldn't get any ratsbane so they gave her mercury instead. She wants me to ask you if that will work?'

Eliza smiled. The trap was set and it would be an even quicker outcome than the one she had been slowly working towards with Molly. Indeed, if all went well, she could kill two birds with one stone and nobody would be any the wiser. 'Tell her it will work, but that she must take a large pinch. Mix it with boiled milk and rice and give it to her for breakfast. She will feel some pain, but it will pass. If it doesn't work first time, do it the following morning and continue to do so until the deed is done.'

Chapter Twenty-Six

Mary awoke early the following morning. She was keen to put her plan in action so rose early and made her way down to the kitchen. Molly had not yet risen so Mary decided to make breakfast for herself.

The embers of the fire were still glowing and she stoked them up before adding more wood. Blowing on it, the fire took quickly and the flames reached up to the chimney. As they died down again, she took the pot and poured in some milk, returning it to the fire.

As the milk began bubbling, she poured in a cup of rice and began stirring with a large wooden spoon. As it came to the boil once more, she took the small paper envelope from her bosom, opened it up, then sprinkled in a good measure of the powder to the pot, stirring all the while. She wondered if it would be enough, so took out the envelope and added the rest of the powder, just to be on the safe side. As the mixture began to thicken, Thomas came into the kitchen.

'Good morning Mary. What gets you up at this hour.'

'Good morning Thomas.' Keen to allay any suspicions he

may have had, she determined to remain civil. 'I felt hungry so decided to have some breakfast. Molly isn't here yet, so I have made it myself. Would you like some?'

Thomas was pleasantly surprised. Not only was Mary being polite to him, she was now offering to make him breakfast. Wonders would never cease! He sat down in a chair and pulled himself closer to the kitchen table. 'Why not? I may as well make the most of this unexpected fortune.'

Mary spooned a large portion from the pot straight onto a plate and placed it in front of him. Thomas picked up a spoon, gathered up some of the rice and raised it to his mouth, blowing gently on it to cool it down. Satisfied it was the right temperature, he took a mouthful and chewed the contents, struggling to swallow it. Eventually, after several attempts, he managed to gulp it down. 'What in the devil's name is this gruel you have served up?' he spluttered.

Mary was taken aback. 'Rice and milk. Why? Don't you like it?' She sounded hurt and Thomas immediately regretted his outburst.

'I'm sorry. It is just that it's a bit gristy. What have you put in it?'

Mary looked concerned. 'Just rice and milk. Perhaps Molly didn't clean the pot properly. Would you like me to make you another?'

Thomas could see she was trying hard and felt guilty. 'No, it's fine. I shall persevere.' He spooned another portion into his mouth and, without chewing, managed to quickly swallow it down. He looked up to see Mary studying him, a worried look on her face. It encouraged him to try again. However, after just a few spoonfuls, he gave up. Pushing it away from him, he made his excuses. 'I'm sorry. To be honest, I'm not really that hungry. I'll have something later.'

Mary picked up her own spoon and tried some from his plate. She wrinkled her nose and spat it straight back out again.

'Ugh. I'm sorry. This is indeed gristy.' She took the contents, tipped them back into the pot, then removed the pot from the fire. 'I'll give it to the chickens when it has cooled down.'

Thomas, feeling decidedly unwell, ran upstairs to his room clutching his stomach as he went. Upon arrival, he grabbed hold of a chamber pot and promptly threw up. Hearing him retch, Mary quickly disposed of the pot's contents in the garden. She then proceeded to thoroughly wash the plate and the pot so as to get rid of the concoction. Perhaps this wasn't such a good idea after all!

Molly appeared at the back door holding some vegetables. She looked surprise to see the mistress in the kitchen and thought she might be in trouble. 'Is everything all right mistress?' Upstairs, they could both hear Thomas retching.

Mary laughed. 'No, not really. He insisted on eating the breakfast I made for myself. I'm obviously nowhere near as good a cook as you are Molly!'

Molly smiled with delight. It was unusual for the mistress to engage in conversation with her, let alone praise her.

'I'll tell you what, Molly. Can you go and see your friend and ask if she can help poor master Thomas with his ailment. He appears to be most unwell and I feel totally responsible.'

'Of course, mistress. Would you like me to go now? I fear she may not yet be up.'

Mary heard Thomas make use of the chamber pot once more. 'No, not now. But maybe she could come later on this morning and have a look at him. Meanwhile, I shall go into town and see if I can get some ratsbane. I am not sure I will be able to take the mercury I purchased yesterday. I fear it will bring on the most violent of reactions.'

Chapter Twenty-Seven

Molly arrived with Eliza later that morning. Carrying her medicine bag with her, Eliza looked every part the doctor. Molly went through the house looking for Mary but was unable to locate her. She did, however, find Thomas curled up in bed holding his sides and groaning softly to himself. She emptied his pot, which seemed to comprise of vomit and blood. After emptying it, she cleaned it out and returned it to the side of his bed. He appeared to be in a state of fever and hardly stirred as she went about her business.

She returned to the kitchen where Eliza was waiting for her. 'There is no sign of the mistress and the master has taken to his bed.'

'I see. So what exactly happened?' asked Eliza.

'I don't rightly know. I believe mistress Mary made some breakfast and then master Thomas came in and decided to have some. He then became violently ill and started being sick. Now he is up there making strained noises. He looks most unwell and doesn't appear to know what is happening around him.'

Eliza smiled to herself. She wondered exactly how much

mercury Mary had put in the dish. Enough to kill a small horse from the sounds of it! 'I think master Thomas has had enough of solids for one day. Bring me his wine and I shall mix up a potion for him, one which should help settle his stomach.

Molly shot off to the dining room before reappearing with a decanter full of red wine.

'There's a good girl. Now remove the lid and give it to me.' Molly did as she was told and Eliza took a small bottle from her bag. She removed the cork from the neck and poured some white powder into the decanter. She replaced the cork on the bottle and carefully placed it back in her bag. 'Give me the lid for the decanter!' she demanded and Molly handed it over. 'Thank you.'

She replaced the crystal lid back and gently swirled the bottle around, ensuring the powder dissolved into the wine. She handed the decanter back to Molly. 'Put that back where it came from. Tell the mistress to give him a glass of that with dinner. If he can't eat dinner, tell her to insist that he drinks the wine anyway as it will settle his stomach and also aid his sleep.'

Molly nodded her head. 'Are you going to go up and see him?'

'No,' said Eliza. 'Unfortunately I don't have time, for I have other calls to make. Just pass on my instructions to the mistress and everything will be fine.'

She picked up her bag and turned to leave. 'By the way, Molly. I may have some good news for you.'

Molly's face brightened up. 'Yes mistress?'

'I have been speaking with a dear friend of mine who has recently arrived here from York. She has need of a cook to work at her manor house. I have recommended you for her household. Would you be interested?'

Molly was wide-eyed. 'York?'

'Yes. It's a beautiful city, just a few days from here by coach. All your expenses will be paid and you will be working alongside other household servants. Do tell me you would like to go, for I am sure you will be an asset to her.'

Molly nodded vigorously. 'I would love to go. But when?'

'Tomorrow morning. The coach leaves at dawn.'

'Tomorrow?' Molly was incredulous. 'But what about the master? What if he does not give me permission to leave?'

'Oh don't worry about him. I shall call on him tomorrow morning after you have left to check on his condition and inform him of your decision. By then, it will be too late as you will be on your way. How does that sound?'

'You would do that for me?'

Eliza smiled warmly at her. 'Yes, of course I would. After all, aren't we friends?'

Molly couldn't believe her luck. To land a position in a big house had always been her aim. To have such a job presented to her like this was beyond her wildest dreams. She threw herself at Eliza, hugging her in delight, before regaining control of her senses and stepping back. 'I'm sorry. But I couldn't help myself. Thank you.'

Eliza laughed. 'That's fine. Don't worry about it. Now go and pack your things. You will leave first thing in the morning.'

Chapter Twenty-Eight

Thomas was feeling very ill indeed. Even though there was nothing left inside him to vomit up, he was still retching. His throat was sore, his body ached and his headache was hammering away loudly inside his skull.

He was surprised when Mary appeared in the room. At first he thought her to be an apparition. *'Am I dead?'* he asked himself. He had been drifting in and out of consciousness for the best part of five hours now, with no sign of improvement. She sat alongside him and even took his hand in hers, squeezing it gently. 'I must be dreaming,' he said out loud as he adjusted his position, rolling on to his back. He drifted back into a fitful sleep but was soon awoken by another fit of dry heaving.

Mary had sent Molly off to find Eliza once more, but she returned after a fruitless search. Feeling worried about the worsening condition of her husband, Mary then sent Molly to go and get the physician.

She returned with the doctor within the hour. Concerned at the deathly pale colour of Thomas Channing's face, the doctor proceeded to carry out a quick examination. 'What has he eaten?'

he asked Mary as he prodded at Thomas's stomach and tested his joints.

Mary answered. 'He had some boiled rice and milk this morning.' She felt it prudent to leave out any mention of the mercury.

'Mmmm. The doctor carried on feeling around Thomas's body, looking for clues. He felt his forehead, which was hot and clammy to the touch. 'He appears to have a fever. Did anybody else eat the same meal?'

Mary shook her head. 'No. Thomas complained that it was inedible so I threw it away. Soon afterwards he was violently ill and took to his bed.'

'I see.' The doctor stroked his beard before bending down to pick up his physician's case. He put it on the bed. Opening it, he took out a tube and placed it alongside Thomas. He then requested some water and Molly was dispatched to the kitchen to get some. When she returned with a full bowl, he added some oil to it and set it to one side. He inserted the other end of the tube into Thomas's throat and forced it down, much to the discomfort of those watching. Fortunately for Thomas, he had lost consciousness again and was unaware of the intrusion. The doctor then took out a feeding funnel and inserted the tip into the tube. Holding the funnel above Thomas's head, he carefully poured the solution into it and the mixture flowed down into Thomas's stomach. As his stomach swelled, Thomas suddenly came to, leant over and began vomiting the vile liquid back up again.

The doctor pulled the tube back out of Thomas's throat and asked for some clean water.

Once again, Molly was sent down to the kitchen to collect it. As they awaited her return the doctor delivered his verdict. 'I would suggest that your husband has been poisoned.'

'Poisoned?' Mary asked innocently. 'But how?'

'Perhaps the milk you gave him had turned bad. Anyway,

I have administered a speedy application of proper remedies. He needs to rest. Don't give him any more food; just water. He will need to flush out his digestive system in order to recover. Hopefully you will see some improvement within a few hours.'

He washed his equipment in the water Molly had provided before taking his leave. 'I shall call by tomorrow to check on him. In the meantime, stay by his side and ensure he is kept comfortable.'

Molly showed the doctor out as Mary pulled a chair up beside the bed. She was surprised at her own concern. Just a few weeks earlier she wanted him dead, yet now she felt responsible for his condition. She wondered if it was the mercury. All the more reason not to take it, she thought. She would go back to the apothecary as soon as she was able to get some ratsbane. Hopefully, it would have a far gentler effect on her.

When Thomas came to a couple of hours later he felt a bit better, but had a raging thirst. Mary offered him water and he sipped at it before demanding wine. 'It will take the edge off this damned awful feeling I have and hopefully numb the pain,' he muttered.

Mary duly obliged, returning with the decanter of red from the dining room and a glass. She filled it and Thomas gulped it down like a man possessed. 'My sense of taste must be playing me up for this wine also tastes vile. No matter. Give me another one.' He handed the glass back to her and she immediately poured him a second glass. This time, he took his time drinking it.

'Would you care for another one?' Mary asked as he eventually finished his glass.

Thomas shook his head. 'No. The taste is not to my liking, unfortunately. But hopefully it will help me sleep.'

'Rest now,' Mary agreed, mopping his brow with a cold sponge.

'But I am now feeling hungry,' he declared, his mood improving suddenly.

'The doctor said you weren't to eat anything until you have flushed out your system.'

'Well how long is that going to take?' Thomas demanded.

Mary didn't know. 'I think we should await the return of the doctor in the morning and see what he says.'

'Just get me some dry bread and cheese, Mary. If I don't have anything, I fear I shall die.'

Mary made her way down to the kitchen to get something for him. While down there, she suddenly heard Thomas vomiting again, crying out in agony as he did so. She rushed back upstairs to find him hanging off the bed, his face in the chamber pot.

She helped him back into the bed, propping him up with some pillows. He looked gaunt and pale with blood, wine and spittle all around his mouth and in his stubble. 'I fear I am dying Mary. Please, get me my papers, a quill and some ink.'

'Don't be so silly, Thomas. Of course you are not dying.' Mary tried to reassure him.

Thomas shook his head wildly from side to side. 'Please woman, just this once, do as you are told. Get me my papers and my quill.'

Mary went to his study and returned with a sheet of parchment, a quill and a small bottle of ink. Thomas pulled up his knees to use them as a surface and began scribbling furiously on the parchment.

'What are you doing?' Mary enquired.

Without looking up, Thomas answered 'My will.'

Mary grinned. 'Don't be so silly Thomas. You are not dying.'

Thomas paused his scribbling momentarily, glaring at her. 'I think I am dying. I have never felt this ill before. Woman, I fear you may have poisoned me.' He dipped his quill and continued with his writings.

'Now you are really being silly.' Mary hoped he was joking. 'Why would I poison you?'

'Because you wish me dead.' Thomas said, matter of factly, as he signed the paper and put it to one side. 'Send word to my father that I wish to see him. Impress upon him it is a matter of urgency. Now leave me for I must sleep. Goodbye Mary, for I fear I shall sleep well and long.'

'Do you still want the bread and cheese? I can get it for you if you like.'

'No, Mary. I wish to be left in peace. Now go.'

Mary organised a messenger to send word to Richard Channing at his home in Maiden Newton. The evening light was beginning to fade and she doubted she would see Thomas's father until the following morning. She returned to his room and took up residence by his side once more. He was in a fitful sleep, a fever on his brow. On occasion he would call out in his sleep.

By now, she was beginning to worry. What if he didn't survive? What would she do? She picked up the parchment by his side and quickly read through it. Unsurprisingly, he had bequeathed his entire estate to his father. This in itself was not unusual, for she was sure that his father would not see her on the streets, not with her taking her son's name. But, as she continued reading, she came to a sentence with filled her with dread. "*I give my wife one shilling for I have every good reason to give her no more.*"

She put the parchment back down on the bed beside Thomas. What did he mean by "*I have every good reason to give her no more*"? She considered tearing it up and burning it, but knew she would be in trouble should Thomas recover and ask to see it. She pondered it some more and began recalling the events of that day. It had all started when she had made him breakfast, something she had never done for him before. He had fallen sick soon after.

She took the pouch of mercury from her bosom and opened it. She sniffed carefully at the tiny amount that was left, but it didn't smell particularly dangerous. She did consider tasting it, but decided against it. Perhaps if the powder was off, it would do her harm as well. She would return to the Mr Wolmington's shop to ask exactly what the powder was and how it should be administered. She had put rather a lot in, when perhaps a smaller dose was all that was required.

She placed her hands on her belly, her thoughts racing. Was it worth all that pain to get rid of the child? And what if Thomas did die? If she was to be left nothing in the will then perhaps the unborn child would be her saving grace. Richard Channing would no more see his grandchild cast out into the street than his daughter in law.

She watched Thomas as he slept, still lost in her thoughts. They returned once more to what he had said. *"Woman, I believe you have poisoned me!"* How could he think her capable of such a thing? The thought was preposterous. And yet… the more she thought about it, the clearer the picture became. She had made him breakfast. She had put a powder in his meal. He had eaten it and fallen ill, while she had avoided eating it – albeit on account of him complaining about had badly it tasted – and not fallen ill. When Thomas's father arrived, Thomas would tell him the same tale, of how she had made him breakfast and he had been sick. He would surely draw the same conclusion.

She suddenly remembered Molly's friend. She was the one who had recommended the powder! All she had to do was get her to tell Richard Channing that it was she that had prescribed the powder for Mary and that it had never been intended for Thomas. She smiled briefly before another thought crossed her mind. They would demand to know what the powder had been purchased for! Once Thomas and his father discovered that it had been to kill her unborn child, she would again be in the same predicament.

She sat back, a glum look on her face, and held on to Thomas's hand. He was not a bad man. And it was becoming obvious that Gabriel no longer had need of her. Perhaps it was time to grow up, stop protesting about her arranged marriage and start being a dutiful wife. Besides, if she shared his bed, her immediate problem of being with child would be solved for Thomas would surely believe he was the father. Thomas may be weak, but he clearly had feelings for her and perhaps, in time, she could grow to love him. She squeezed his hand, gently. 'I promise my dear Thomas that, when you wake up, you shall see a change in me. We shall be as one, Mr and Mrs Channing. I feel we could be quite a formidable team. All you need to do is get well. And soon. Please be well when you wake up in the morning for I shall be waiting.'

Chapter Twenty-Nine

Molly opened the back door and let herself out. Her belongings were tethered together in a sheet and wrapped in twine. She did not have much. Indeed, she was leaving the Channing household with exactly what she had arrived with a year earlier.

It was still dark, although the first showings of the sun were beginning to appear on the horizon, making silhouettes of the trees on the crest of the hills that overlooked the town. A chill wind cut through her, the last remnants of winter providing a last hurrah before giving way to the subtle warmth of spring. She pulled her cape closer around her neck as she hurried up the hill.

Eliza was waiting for her outside the front gate. She too had a bag containing her belongings. Molly smiled. 'Are you coming with me?' The thought pleased her as the journey would be long and she had no idea where she was heading.

'I am. My friend suggested I go and stay with her for a while and I believe my time here has drawn to an end. There is nothing left her for me now, especially with you leaving.' She linked arms with Molly as they headed down the hill to the George where they were to join the coach to London, before heading on up to York. As they made their way along the cobbled streets, Molly briefed Eliza of the events that had taken place the evening before, of how Mary had given the master some wine and he had been vomiting ever since. Molly had found the whole affair amusing. Mistress Mary had never made her husband a meal before, and the first time she had he had been violently ill! Eliza laughed out loud at her recounting of events. 'And how is the master now?'

Molly went quiet. 'I am not sure. He has hardly eaten anything and he was still very unwell overnight. The mistress has not left his side.' She suddenly brightened up. 'But I am sure he will be feeling better this morning. Just as long as she doesn't make him any more breakfast!' They both laughed out loud again, before scampering to the side of the road as a lone horseman shot by at full gallop, the steed's eyes wide open and its flank covered in sweat. The rider did not spare his whip as he urged the horse to go even faster. They turned and watched as he reined the horse in outside the Channing's house, dismounted and rushing through the gate to the house.

'That must be master Channing's father,' Molly mused. The mistress sent for him last night. I do hope the master is better.'

Eliza pulled her linked arm closer to her as she span her round to continue on their journey. 'I am sure the master will be fine. It is you we have to worry about now. That, and your new life in York.'

Molly felt a mixture of fear and anticipation. What was going to happen to her? She had never been out of Dorchester before and now she was heading to London and beyond! A thought suddenly crossed her mind. 'Weren't you supposed to tell the master that I was leaving today?'

'Yes, I was,' Eliza nodded. 'But I will be unable to as I have decided to come with you.'

'But they will worry and wonder where I have gone.'

'They will be fine,' Eliza reassured her. 'Just as long as they get a new maid and the mistress doesn't take up cooking! I will write them from London to inform them of your great adventure.'

The George came into view and the stagecoach was already being prepared in the courtyard, with four horses being hitched to its front. Molly now felt a huge wave of excitement running through her. The fear of the unknown was banished. And with her friend Eliza beside her, she felt she could conquer the world.

The Burning of Mary Channing

Chapter Thirty

Richard Channing tethered his horse to the front railings and charged up the path. He banged long and hard on the front door, waking Mary from her slumber. She sat bolt upright as she gathered her thoughts and remembered where she was. She looked at Thomas. Was he still alive? She leant close to his face to see if he was breathing. He stirred, startling her and causing her to jump back. 'He's alive!' she exclaimed.

The banging continued. Wondering why Molly hadn't answered the door, she went to the top of the stairs and called down. 'Molly! Are you there? Molly!' She wondered if Molly was out in the back garden feeding the chickens and collecting the eggs. She thought that she might make Thomas eggs for breakfast. He would like that. She smiled at the thought of nursemaiding Thomas back to health.

She made her way downstairs calling out as she did so. 'I am coming!' As soon as she released the bolts on the door, it was flung wide by Mr Channing, who was panting heavily. 'Where is he?' he boomed as he entered the house, forcing his way past her.

'In his room,' Mary called out as she ran up the stairs after him. 'He is sleeping.'

Richard reached his son's room, threw open the door and ran to his bedside. He picked up his hand. 'My dear boy. What has befallen you?' He took in the physical appearance of his son, a grave look of concern on his face. 'My God, you look awful. What has happened.'

'It was something he ate.' Mary arrived at his back.

'What was it? Tell me!' Richard released his son's hand and felt his forehead. It was cold to the touch. Thomas stirred slightly, but did not awaken.

'Just some boiled milk and rice. I made it for his breakfast, yesterday.' Mary was keen to show her father in law that she was trying hard to be a good wife and had changed her wayward ways.

'And did you have some?'

Mary shook her head. 'No. Thomas complained that it was inedible so I disposed of it. It was not long after that he took to his bed.'

Richard Channing grunted. 'Have you called a physician?'

'Yes. He came yesterday afternoon. He cleared his digestion with a pump. Thomas has been sleeping ever since.'

Richard put his face near to his son's so he could hear him breathing. It was shallow and irregular. He looked gaunt and pale and his body was lifeless. He picked up the will laying at Thomas's side and quickly read through it. 'My son fears he is close to death. What have you done to him?' He roared at Mary, forcing her to take a backward step.

'I have done nothing, sir, and I will not have you accuse me of such things nor speak to me in such a manner!' She stiffened her back and pouted. This was her house and she would not tolerate Richard Channing speaking to her like that. But if she thought it would make her father-in-law apologise, she was wrong. He grabbed her roughly by the elbow, forcing her backwards out of the room before dragging her down the stairs, forcing her to take them two at a time in order to keep up with his stride.

'I will speak to you in any damn manner I want, madam, and you should be wise to treat me in accordance with the fact you are living in my son's house. A house, by the way, which will revert back to me should he die, so you had better hope and pray that he makes a full recovery!' They arrived at the front door. He grabbed the door knob with one hand, pulled the door open and launched Mary off the top step. She landed on her hands and knees, a look of surprise on her face as she span around to face her aggressor. He stood in the doorway, anger written all over his face. 'Be gone madam and never darken my son's door again!'

Mary was in shock. She stood up, brushed herself down and looked around to see if anyone had witnessed her shaming. She fancied there was a face in the upstairs window of the house next door, but couldn't be sure. She crept around to the back of the house and made her way into the kitchen. Where on earth was Molly? There was no sign of the girl. Mary was feeling annoyed, both at her treatment at the hands of Richard Channing but also at the disappearance of her maid. She peered into Molly's cramped quarters under the stairs. The state of the covers suggested that the bed had been slept in, but there was no sign of her. She returned to the kitchen. She was about to call out into the garden but remembered she wasn't meant to be in the house. Instead, she made her way into the yard to where the chickens were housed. Again, there was no sign of Molly. The small wicker basket for collecting the eggs was hanging on a rusty nail. Mary picked it up, entered the coop and collected the eggs as the chickens gathered at her ankles, clucking impatiently for their morning feed. As soon as she had gathered the eggs, she grabbed some handfuls of grain from a sack and scattered it around the yard.

She then wondered where the dog was. Normally he would by at her heels, whining at her for scraps of food. She decided to go and look for it, heading for the spot where it liked to lay at night, inside a small outbuilding used to store firewood. She entered, calling out for him as she did so. There was no response. She went to the end of the stack of logs and turned the corner. The dog was laid there. Dead. All around his mouth was remnants of vomit and, in amongst it, there was undigested rice.

There was no longer any doubt about it. She had poisoned her husband and the dog, resulting in its death. All she could hope for now was that Thomas didn't suffer the same fate.

Chapter Thirty-One

R ichard Channing gently tried to stir Thomas from his sleep. Eventually, Thomas opened his eyes but they were vacant, unseeing. A rash had spread up his neck and, upon lifting his night shirt, Richard noted it was all over his torso.

'I need to go to the toilet,' Thomas suddenly mumbled. He tried to sit upright but struggled to maintain his balance. Richard picked the chamber pot up and offered it to him. Thomas began rapidly scratching at his rash while he struggled to crawl over to the side of the bed. Eventually, with the help of his father, he managed to relieve himself before falling back on the bed, his legs dangling over the side. Richard noticed how Thomas's toes were strangely coloured and the skin was peeling, as if they had somehow been burnt. He helped Thomas back under the covers, picking up his legs and swinging them round for him before pulling the blankets back over him.

Thomas was groaning all the while, his hands were trembling and he appeared to be fading fast. 'Please Thomas, stay with me,' his father pleaded. 'You have so much to live for. You must survive this.' He was disturbed by a gentle knock on the door behind him. A gentleman in a black suit holding a medical case stood before him.

'I'm sorry to intrude sir. There was no answer when I knocked, so I let myself in. How is he?' The doctor handed Richard his card as he made his way to the bed. He examined him quickly, opening Thomas's eyes and taking his pulse.

'Not good,' Richard responded, reading but not really taking in the details on the card he held in his hand.

The doctor leant over Thomas, placing his right ear on his chest. He listened for a while before standing up. He took his wrist and felt for a pulse. It was weak. He shook his head, sadly. 'I was hoping that, following on from my efforts yesterday, he would be showing signs of improvement. Alas, I fear he is not long for this world. Is he your son?'

Richard nodded. 'Yes. How did this happen?'

The doctor shook his head. 'It will require further investigation, but I would presume he has been poisoned.'

'Poisoned?' Richard was aghast. 'But how? All he has eaten is rice and milk.' He picked up the empty wine glass on the bedside cabinet and noticed the staining at the bottom. He sniffed at it. 'And perhaps some wine, looking at this.'

'So I gather,' the doctor responded. 'I spoke with the lady of the house yesterday. But she has not been taken ill.'

'No. Apparently she refrained from eating after Thomas complained it was inedible. What sort of poison are we talking about?'

'As I said, it will require further investigation. But my hunch would be either mercury or arsenic, although his bodily functions seem to suggest that arsenic is not the culprit here.' He picked up his hand and studied his fingernails. 'Mmmm. Strange.'

'What is?'

'Well his fingernails would suggest arsenic, but the growth would suggest this has been happening over a period of time.

Either way, it is not prudent to summarise now. We can find out afterwards.'

'After what, exactly?' Richard furrowed his brow and bit his lower lip. He already knew the answer.

'After death.'

Richard was silent for a moment. 'How long as he got left?'

'It is difficult to say exactly. The poison is in him and it is only a matter of time. It could be hours, it could be days. But it is highly unlikely that he will be able to purge it from his system. I'm sorry.'

The doctor gathered up his bag, put his gloves on and offered his hand. Richard shook it, gravely. 'Let me know when it is done and I will make the necessary arrangements. I'm sorry Mr Channing, but there is nothing that can now be done. May God take mercy on his soul and deliver him safely without any further suffering. Good day sir.' He closed the door quietly behind him, not noticing the door opposite being quickly pushed shut. Mary was hidden behind it and she had heard everything.

In a state of panic, she silently gathered up some of her belongings and bundled them up together in a small cloth sack. She contemplated running back to her parent's place but was unsure as to what her reception would be. Perhaps Gabriel would provide a solution? It was possible. She would head for the mill where he worked. But first, she needed to pay a visit to the apothecary. She needed to try and cover her tracks.

Chapter Thirty-Two

Mary walked boldly into town, her brazen attitude belying her feelings of despair. She made her way to Mr Wolmington's apothecary in order to speak with him regarding her purchase the previous Monday. He gazed at her, his mouth wide open in disbelief, as she entered the shop. She stood back until the shop had cleared of all customers, before approaching the counter.

'May I speak with you Mr Wolmington.'

'On what matter, Mrs Channing.' Wolmington had already heard that her husband had been poisoned and that she was being been accused of administering it.

'I came here last Monday and purchased some powder from you.'

Wolmington raised an eyebrow. 'That you did.'

'I asked for some ratsbane. Unfortunately you did not have any.'

'That is correct. We took delivery on Wednesday. Apparently you have a rodent problem.'

Mary grimaced. How could she reveal the real reason why she wanted the ratsbane without explaining that she was with child by another man. 'That's right. We have rats in the yard. Our dog was unable to cope with them and they were stealing eggs from the chicken coop. You then recommended I buy some mercury.'

The apothecary nodded. 'Yes. It will have the same effect, but is far stronger.'

'I have a favour to ask of you.' Mary gave him his best smile, one that she knew worked well on men for she had used it many times in recent months to good effect. She clasped her hands across her chest and pushed up her bosom for good measure.

Mr Wolmington was unmoved. 'Go on.' He said.

'I fear that a mistake has been made. One that is not of my own making. You see, my maid mixed up some rice and milk with the powder you gave me in order to put out for the rodents.' Her words tumbled out quickly. 'Unfortunately, she put the plate to one side and my husband came down thinking it to be breakfast. He ate some of it before I could tell him not to. And… well, I guess you know the rest.'

Mr Wolmington picked up his clay pipe. He carefully filled it with tobacco, damped it down with his thumb, picked up a taper and went over to the stove. Opening the door, he put the taper in to the embers and twirled it until it caught light. He offered the flame to the end of his pipe and sucked at it until the tobacco had caught. He took a few deep puffs as the smoke filled the shop, causing Mary to wrinkle her nose and cough slightly. He exhaled, sending more smoke in Mary's direction. Finally, he spoke. 'So what is the favour you would like to ask?'

Mary took a deep breath. 'Well obviously there has been a mistake, one for which I cannot possibly take the blame. I purchased the powder from you in all innocence. It was never intended for my husband. He obviously ate it in error.'

'You still have not asked a favour of me.'

'I fear that the magistrate will not look kindly on me if it becomes known that I purchased the powder from you. Perhaps, if you could find it within your heart, you could…'

Mr Wolmington took another couple of sucks on his pipe. The smell was quite pungent and Mary was feeling a little light headed. 'Could what?' he asked after what seemed to Mary to be an eternity.

The man was being infuriatingly obtuse. Feeling she had no other option other than to come straight out with it, she took the plunge. 'Could tell those that might have cause to ask, that you have not seen me and that I did not buy the powder from you.'

'Aha. I see.' He puffed again at his pipe. 'And why would I do that?'

'Because it was never my intention to poison my husband!' Mary was becoming increasingly exasperated at Mr Wolmington's slowness in the matter.

Wolmington nodded once more. 'But you did.'

'Did what?'

'Buy the powder from me and poison your husband with it.'

'Yes, I know I did. But I didn't mean to. It was his mistake, not mine.'

'So what have you to fear? Just explain it to the magistrate the way you just did to me and I am sure it will be as clear to him as it is to me.'

Inside Mary was crumbling. It was obvious that Mr Wolmington would not cover for her. 'I fear that I will hang. Nobody will believe me. Why would they? I know what they are all saying about me. I fear that my husband's demise will precede that of my own. And I am innocent! I did not do it. I swear!'

The old man crossed his arms and smoked his pipe some more while pondering Mary's predicament. 'You know that I cannot lie for you, for it is a sin to lie. It is for God to decide if you are innocent or not. I am afraid I cannot, and will not, help you.'

Mary was defeated. Bidding Mr Wolmington good day, she burst out of the shop feeling close to tears. Another thought came to her. She had to find Molly's friend. It was she that had recommended she purchase the ratsbane for her "problem." And it was she that said she could substitute the ratsbane for the mercury. If she could get her to tell Thomas's father that it was all an innocent mistake, then surely everything would be all right. She would have to bear the consequences of the reasons behind the purchase after, but she could not think that far ahead. Instead, she must deal with the matter in hand. She racked her brain to remember what Molly had said about where she lived. Damn that Molly! Where was she? How could she disappear like this in her hour of need?

She remembered Molly saying it was close to Thomas's shop, on the corner. She vaguely recalled a lodging house being located there and set off at a pace. Within a couple of minutes, she was stood outside a large, red-brick house. The garden was in need of some attention and the inside looked dark and foreboding. She went up the path and knocked on the door. Within a short while she heard footsteps approaching and the door creaked open. A small woman of middle age stood before her.

'Do you require lodgings?'

'No. Well, yes. Well, maybe. Although at the moment I am looking for one of your guests. A lady.'

The woman put her head to one side, still holding the door. 'We have a few ladies here at the moment. Do you have her name?' Her tone was brusque.

Mary shook her head. 'No. All I know is that she had a knowledge of medicine and my servant said she lived her.'

The lady shook her head. 'A knowledge of medicine you say? I don't have anyone like that staying here.' She went to close the door.

'Please! You must help me. I am sure she said she lived here.'

The woman's face appeared to the side as the gap in the door narrowed. 'I'm afraid there is nobody here by that description. Now I really must go.' She shut the door firmly leaving Mary feeling perplexed. She was sure this was the house. Where else could it be? She walked up and down the street looking at the houses but none of them appeared to be offering rooms.

With the light fading fast, she knew she must find somewhere safe to lay her head. She would not make the mill before dark and besides, she felt it unlikely that Gabriel would offer her shelter anyway. She contemplated returning to the lodgings house where she believed Molly's friend had been staying, but decided against it. She had a friend who lived closed by, one with whom she had shared many adventures and regularly confided in. Keeping close to the bushes that lined the road, she made her way through the back streets until she arrived. A candle burned in the window and she crept up to it to peer inside. Her friend was sat by the fire, rocking back and forth in a chair, darning a dress.

Mary tapped on the thin glass of the window. 'Katherine!' she said, urgently. 'Can I come in?'

Katherine looked up, a look of surprise on her face. 'Mary?' she mouthed. Mary nodded. The girl came to the window, opening it. 'What are you doing here?'

Mary gestured to the door. 'Let me in!'

Closing the window, Katherine went to the front door. Mary pushed her way past her as soon as the door was open. 'Quickly, close it, before someone sees!'

Katherine did as she was told, sliding a bolt across for good measure. She turned to see Mary making her way in to the front room and chased after her. 'You are the talk of the town. Did you really poison poor Thomas?'

Mary slumped into a chair. 'No! Of course not! Well, not

really. It's all been a terrible mistake.'

'So what are you doing here?'

'Thomas's father has thrown me out! I have nowhere to go. Can I stay here? Just for a short while until this whole retched affair has been sorted.'

Her friend looked at Mary nervously, shaking her head. 'I don't know. I don't think it would be wise for you to stay here. Jack, my husband, will not like it.'

Mary leant forward and grabbed hold of both of her hands. 'Please. I have nowhere else. It won't be for long, I promise. Just until Thomas has recovered and tells everyone the truth.'

Her friend relented. 'Jack is away in Honiton on business for a few days. I am not expecting him back until Saturday at the earliest. You can use the attic room. But you must be gone before he returns.'

'Thank you!' Mary gushed, relief running through her. 'If it is all right with you, I shall go there now for I am exhausted. It has been a very long day. I can only hope and pray that Thomas is well again soon.'

Chapter Thirty-Three

Thomas Channing passed away on the evening of Saturday twenty-first of April, 1705. He had been suffering for five days. The effects of the poison had spread throughout his entire body before finally arriving in his lungs. No amount of further purging by the doctor could help and so it was, with the hour approaching nine o'clock in the evening, he coughed his last breath, and died, a pained look on his stricken face.

The recriminations began almost immediately. As his mother wept by his side, his father requested his son's body be opened so that an autopsy could be performed to determine the exact cause of death.

The following afternoon, the surgeon stood over Thomas's body, the doctor at his side. 'Are you ready?' he enquired.

'As ready as I'll ever be.' He pulled back the sheet that was covering the body and the surgeon picked up a knife. He split the belly and they both turned away as the smell hit them. As soon as he had recovered his composure, the surgeon resumed cutting and slicing, peeling back the skin, flesh and muscle, to reveal Thomas Channing's innards.

Thomas's stomach and organs revealed the true extent of his suffering. His lungs were discoloured. His stomach and part of the liver were black. Black spots were scattered throughout his intestines. 'I think we are in agreeance with your original findings,' the surgeon said solemnly as he stepped back from the table, wiping his hands. 'It most definitely looks like mercury to me.'

The doctor leant over Thomas's body and peered inside one last time. 'It must have been an agonizing death. Poor man.' He stood upright and picked up one of Thomas's hands, studying the fingernails. 'It's strange. The fingernails definitely look like he has been given arsenic over a period of time. But the rash on his body, the peeling of the skin on his toes, as well as the nature of his death certainly would suggest that mercury was the culprit here.'

The surgeon shrugged. 'Maybe whoever carried out this deadly deed got tired of waiting for the arsenic to take effect. Or perhaps they got their powders mixed up. Either way, they got what they wanted.'

The doctor nodded, deep in thought. 'Perhaps. But that's not for us to determine. Anyway, there's nothing more to see here. You might as well stitch him back up again and prepare the body for his family to collect.

The surgeon worked methodically as he made Thomas's body presentable again. After cleaning his tools in a bucket of water, he removed his bloodstained apron and wiped his hands one last time.

Meanwhile, the doctor sat down and completed the autopsy report, confirming that it was his belief Thomas had been poisoned to death, with the most likely compound being mercury. When he was done, he signed it and handed it to the surgeon, who quickly cast his eyes over it before putting it down on the desk and picking up the quill. He too signed it with a flourish. The report would be delivered to the magistrate within the hour for he was keen to have sight of it.

'It's a damned ugly business. And a damned ugly death.' The doctor put his long coat back on.

'I understand it was at the hands of his young wife?' The surgeon had heard the gossip in his local tavern.

'So it would appear.' The doctor picked up his hat and gloves. 'It's a shame, really. She is a pretty young thing. I met her at the house. I believe she was too much for the unfortunate Mr Channing to handle. She's been leading him a right merry dance from what I hear.'

'So why would she do it?' The surgeon dried his hands on an old cloth and reached for his own jacket.

'Who knows?' the doctor shrugged his shoulders. 'According to the gossip that is going on around here, she is not a girl of virtue. Perhaps Mr Channing tried to put his mark on her and bring her to heel. If he did, then he has paid for it with his life.'

Hooking buttons on his jacket, the surgeon headed for the door. He donned his hat and picked up his riding crop. Looking at his pocket watch he said 'The inn down the road is open. Would you care to join me for a drink?'

The doctor responded immediately. 'Why not? That is an excellent idea, sir. This affair has rather put me off my dinner. I think a strong brandy should line my stomach rather well in readiness for my wife's cooking. The magistrate's house is on the way. I can drop off this report and let him break the news to the poor boy's father.'

Chapter Thirty-Four

Richard Channing prowled around the magistrate's office, his face set firm. He glanced at his pocket-watch just as the door opened. A diminutive man with whispy white hair and pince-nez attached to the bridge of his nose entered, carrying the autopsy report with him. He went around his desk and sat down heavily in his chair. The April sunshine was streaming through the large window, illuminating the dust as it swirled around in the air.

'Well?' Channing was impatient to learn the results.

The magistrate ignored him and said nothing, continuing with his reading. Channing clicked his tongue in anguish, but remained silent. He knew he would know soon enough. Finally, the magistrate sat back, removed the pince-nez from his nose and placed them delicately on the large oak desk. He pushed the report across the desk towards Channing. 'The doctor's report is pretty much as expected. He was most definitely poisoned. It is the doctor's belief that the poison used was most likely mercury, although there are signs of arsenic in the body as well. The doctor has suggested that the arsenic was making slow progress, so mercury may have been added to speed up the process. The discovery of the dog in the garden as good as confirmed it. It's likely she disposed of the remains of the meal without thinking about how it would affect the animal.'

Channing picked up the report and grunted. 'Yes. She's not exactly the cleverest of girls in my opinion. So what happens now?'

'Well first, we must find her. I have officers out looking for her but without success. But I'm sure she won't get far. Where can she go? Her parents have disowned her and her friends claim not to have seen her anywhere. Her face is well known around these parts, so it is unlikely she will remain at large for long.'

'Are you sure her parents aren't protecting her?' Channing sank back into the chair facing the magistrate, suddenly feeling exhausted. The events of the past few days were starting to catch up with him.

'It is possible, but unlikely. Her father claims he hasn't seen her since her wedding day and says he would most likely shoot her on sight should she darken his door. From what I know of the man, I wouldn't be in the slightest bit surprised if he did. But the officers have carried out a thorough search of Brookes' property, from top to bottom, and there is no sign of her.'

Channing grunted again. 'What about her supposed man friend? Have you tracked him down yet?'

'We have our suspicions as to his identity and have spoken to the boy. He denies it, of course. But he is not in a position to harbour her as he still lives with his parents and they are not at all well disposed towards her.'

'Can I know who he is?'

The magistrate smiled weakly. 'I don't think that is wise Mr Channing. I do not want another murder on my hands. Besides, while the boy is not entirely blameless, surely it is the girl who has led him on. You remember what you were like as a young man? I myself was quite the dandy! There are girls that will and girls that won't and who are we to judge? I am sure you will remember well the days when your groin ruled your head.'

'I wish to involve myself with the investigation.' Channing stood to leave, choosing to ignore the bawdy comment regarding what he got up to in his youth. 'I shall ask around as people may be more inclined to speak with to me with regards to the whereabouts of the Brookes girl than to your officers.' He slapped his riding crop against this boots as if to emphasise the point he was making.

The magistrate put his hands together and leant forward on his desk. 'Of course, Mr Channing. Your assistance in this matter would be most appreciated. But do please be careful. There is a law to uphold and it is my duty as the Queen's representative to see that is exactly what happens without any outside interference.'

Channing left the office, his mood foul. His son had been murdered and the magistrate was expecting him to stand to one side and do nothing! He jumped on his horse as the stable boy handed him the reins. He had no intention of letting the magistrate conduct affairs and bring Mary Brookes to court. He would do everything necessary to ensure justice was served and his son's death was avenged. Kicking his heels fiercely into the horse's sides, he rode off at speed, heading back into town.

Chapter Thirty-Five

'Katherine? What was all that commotion about?' Mary appeared at the top of the stairs just as her friend arrived at the bottom. 'It was two officers of the law,' Katherine explained, looking harassed. 'They asked after you.'

'What did you tell them?' Worry was spread across Mary's face.

'I told them you were not here. But you cannot stay here any longer. It is getting dangerous and my husband will have plenty to say to me if he finds out, all of it unpleasant.'

'But where can I go?' Mary pleaded.

'That is no longer of any concern to me, Mary. I'm sorry but you must leave.'

'Katherine, please.' Mary made her way down the stairs and grabbed hold of Katherine's arm as she turned away. 'I have nowhere to go. Please help me. I will soon be gone, just as soon as I can make arrangements.'

'But how will you make arrangements, Mary? You can't make them while you are hiding up in the attic! You must come to your senses and give yourself up.'

'I cannot! I know how it looks and I promise you, I didn't do it. I need to find the woman that was friends with my servant, Molly. Can you just go to the house and see if Molly is there? Please, I am begging you.'

Katherine softened, momentarily. 'Well I do have to go into town for some provisions. I can go past your house and have a look for you, I suppose.'

Mary hugged her. 'Thank you. You are a good friend. I mean it. Don't go to the front of the house for Thomas's father might still be there. Instead, go around the side, down the lane. It comes out at the back of the house. Go up the path to the back door and just push it open, for it is seldom locked. If Molly is to be found anywhere, it will be there.'

'What shall I tell her?'

'Tell her that I need her. Bring her to me. Then we can find her friend and I will get her to explain everything.'

'What do you mean by explain everything?'

Mary looked down at her stomach and placed both of her hands upon it. Katherine gasped. 'You are with child!'

'I am. It is an accident. I never meant for it to happen.'

Realisation dawned on Katherine. 'It's Gabriel's!'

Mary nodded sadly. There was no point saying that she wasn't actually sure who the father was, as it might also be Nial, Thomas's friend. It would only paint her in a worse light than she already was.

'Does he know?'

'Who? Gabriel?' Mary shook her head. 'No. And he mustn't. It was my intention to end it.'

What? With Gabriel?' Katherine held her hands to her face in shock.

'No, silly! The life of the baby. I had to in order to save suspicion. Thomas would have known it wasn't his.'

Katherine had been there on the wedding night. She had seen how she had turned her back on Thomas. She had implored her at the time to become his wife and commit to him but Mary had ignored her. 'You should have had relations with Thomas that night of your wedding.'

'I know,' Mary said glumly. 'I was so stupid. But I never wanted to marry him. I loved Gabriel. I told my father it would never work, but he told me he knew what was best for me. Now look at the mess I am in!'

'But to rid yourself of the baby? That would see you hung!'

'I know. I am damned if I do, damned if I don't,' Mary said, ruefully. 'Which is why you must find Molly for me.'

'But what good can possibly come of it? If you confess to trying to kill the child within your belly, then you will be prosecuted for infanticide. If you don't, you will be hung for poisoning your husband. Oh Mary. What have you done?'

The full horror of how events would look to those that would judge her began to dawn on Mary. She felt a panic rising within her. 'Just go and get Molly. Then I will see what can be done to present my actions in a better light.'

Grabbing her shawl, Katherine left the house and made her way to Mary's house. On the way she was gripped with fear. It didn't matter how Mary presented it, she would surely face the gallows. Hiding Mary away from the magistrate and his men could well see her face the same fate. On the way, she passed several small groups, talking in hushed tones. She recognised some of the faces and could tell they were keen to involve her with their news, but she hurried on by, a fixed smile on her face, offering greetings and making excuses as she went on her way without stopping to learn more.

Finally, at some relief to herself, she arrived at the Channing home. She had never before noticed the small lane to the side of the house, never having had cause to use it. She hurried down it, keeping close to the high stone wall that bordered the property. At the end, where the wall finished, a gap appeared leading into the garden. She could see the chickens pecking at the soil as she made her way up the path to the back door.

Without knocking, she silently opened the door and went in. She could sense that the house was empty and there was a chill in the air as the fire had long since gone out. She shuddered as she crept across the flagstone floor to the inner door. She put her ear to it and listened intently, trying to hear voices or any sign of life the other side. When she was sure there wasn't anybody there, she gently prised the door open, peering through. The hall was empty. The only noise was the ticking of the grandfather clock, which took up residence at the bottom of the stairs.

Pushing through, she looked left and spotted the small door under the stairs, cut into the wooden panelling. This must be Molly's room. She gently knocked on it before pulling open the door. The room was dark and it took a while for her eyes to adjust. With no window, there was no natural light to be had, so Katherine opened the door wide to see inside. The single iron bed was against the main wall, with a crumpled blanket and a pillow on it. The pillow had an indent, where someone's head had laid. A dresser was slotted in under the stairs. Katherine noted that there was nothing on top of the dresser, not even a hairbrush. Katherine stepped into the room and opened the top drawer on the dresser. It was empty. She pulled out the other two drawers to find that they, too, were also empty.

It was obvious to her that Molly had left.

She withdrew from the room, then froze. She could hear muffled voices. She fancied they were outside, to the front of the house. She went back through the kitchen, being careful to quietly pull the door to behind her. She didn't want to leave any evidence of her visit. She opened the back door, turning as she did so to make sure nobody was following her and gently closed it as she exited the house.

'Hello madam.'

Katherine screamed as she jumped, completely caught by surprise. The officer was stood behind her, on the bottom step. 'My word, you caught me unawares!' She regained her composure as she got her breathing back under control.

'My apologies, madam. I didn't wish to startle you. But I was wondering what you might be doing here.'

Katherine gathered herself. She recognized him as one of the men who had visited her house earlier that day. 'I was looking for Mary' she answered, garnering as much authority as she could in her voice.

'And did you manage to find her?' The officer smirked slightly as he said it.

'Well no, obviously not.'

'But why are you coming out of the back door?'

Katherine made to push past him but he stood firm and she had to relent. 'Because nobody would answer the front door,' she answered, huffily.

'But I was stood at the front door, madam.'

Her ruse was rumbled. There was nothing for it other than to pull rank on him. 'Do you know who my husband is?'

'No madam. Should I?'

'Yes you should. He is a good friend of Mr Channing, as well as Mr Brookes, and he would not have you speak this way to me. Now stand aside before I report you.'

Unsure as to what to do and slightly fearful of any consequences, the officer stepped backwards off the step. He waved her past him, doffing his cap as she went. 'Please accept my apologies. I had no wish to offend. Have a good day.'

The officer followed behind her at a leisurely pace, as she made her way back down the lane. As she turned right to go back down the hill, he turned left and went into the front garden. His colleague was there, stood at the front door. 'What's was that all about?' he asked.

'I am not sure. It was a young lady. She was coming out of the back of the house.'

'It wasn't Mary was it?'

The officer laughed. 'No. I know exactly what she looks like. I've seen her down the Antelope on more than one occasion with her friends. But I did recognize her.'

'Where from?'

'I'm not sure. Let me think awhile.' He paced the garden for a few moments, racking his brain. Finally, it came to him. 'This morning. It was the house we went to this morning. I believe her to be one of Mary's friends.'

'So why would she come here?'

'She said she was looking for Mary. But I don't believe her. I reckon she was looking for something else. Whatever it was, she didn't find it for she left empty handed. It is very strange though. I think we should let the magistrate know.'

Chapter Thirty-Six

'Where is she?' Richard Channing demanded.

Katherine shrunk back inside the hallway as he forced his way in. 'She is upstairs. In the attic room at the top of the house.'

The two officers came in behind him and charged up the stairs. The magistrate followed them in and stood alongside Richard Channing. Katherine felt like a young child who had been caught stealing, such was her embarrassment.

A commotion ensued upstairs as the two officers forced their way into the attic room, before all fell quiet. After a brief while, both men returned, empty handed. 'No sign of her,' one of them said, holding his hands up by way of an apology.

Richard turned to Katherine. 'I shall ask you again. Where is she?'

Katherine looked up the stairs, a puzzled look on her face. 'I promise you sir, I have no idea. She was here earlier. She asked me go looking for Molly, her servant.'

'These men came here yesterday looking for Mary. Why did you not assist them?' Richard demanded.

I don't know,' she stammered. 'She made me promise.'

'But she murdered my son!' Richard shouted right in her face, causing her to flinch.

'Murdered? Mary told me he had been poisoned and that he was unwell, but that it wasn't her doing. I'm sorry. I mean it. I had no idea he was dead! But she said that she is innocent and that she didn't do it!'

'Well I have an autopsy, a doctor and an apothecary who will tell you different. Plus several witnesses who have come forward saying she wished my son dead!'

Katherine withered, collapsing into a chair. 'Please don't tell my husband, for he will beat me,' she pleaded.

'And you, madam, will deserve it!' Richard shouted at her once more. 'Indeed, I have a good mind to beat you myself!' He turned on his heel and marched angrily out of the house. The magistrate leant forward. 'We may bring charges against you for harbouring a murderer. We shall have to wait and see. Please send your husband to see me at his earliest convenience.'

Katherine was weeping. 'Please sir! I was only doing what I thought best. I didn't know Mr Channing was dead. She didn't tell me. Only that she had accidentally poisoned him.'

'Accidentally, eh?' The magistrate looked unimpressed. 'I doubt that very much. She will be going to hell just as soon as she has stood trial and been declared guilty.'

'But sir, you can't!' Katherine looked up at him, her eyes red with tears.

'And why would that be, madam? What could possibly save her from the gallows or the stake for murdering her husband of just thirteen weeks?'

'Because, sir, she has told me that she is with child.'

Chapter Thirty-Seven

Mary had made good her escape just as soon as Katherine had left the house. With her situation becoming increasingly desperate, she knew that her story would not be believed. Even if it was, as soon as the news broke that she was attempting to kill her own child she would be arrested, regardless of Thomas's condition.

She set off on foot heading east, away from Dorchester. As the amount of traffic on the road increased, she turned off it, instead crossing fields and pushing through hedgerows to keep out of sight. Intermittently running and walking, she finally came across Thornton Wood and headed into its dense interior. Finding an area covered with soft moss, Mary decided to sit down against a large oak tree and gather her thoughts while she recovered.

Within a short while, she relaxed her guard and was lulled to sleep by all the birdsong that was going on all around her as the creatures busied themselves feeding their young. The cracking of a twig brought her to with a start. Two young boys were stood before her. 'Who are you?' the older of the two urchins enquired.

Mary got to her feet, using the tree behind her for support as she stiffly inched her way up its trunk. 'I could ask the same of you,' she responded.

'I'm Jack,' the boy said. 'And this is Tom. He's my brother.'

'Oh,' said Mary. 'Pleased to meet you. Can you tell me the way to the nearest town or village?'

Jack pointed back over her shoulder. 'Puddletown is that way.'

'Thank you. How far is it?'

'The boy shrugged. 'Not long, if you walk quickly. So what's your name?'

Mary felt no need to lie. They would probably forget her as soon as they left anyway. 'My name is Mary.' She brushed herself down, removing remnants of moss and dried leaves from her dress. She picked up the shawl that she had used as a blanket while she slept. 'I'd best be on my way then. Thank you.'

The boys watched her go. 'She seemed nice,' said Jack to his younger sibling. 'But we'd best get some kindling for the fire or mother won't be happy. He pointed to a clearing in the trees. 'Come on. Race you!'

They sped off, Jack in the lead, his younger brother trailing in his wake. Mary heard them go as she headed back out of the woods. She found what looked like a small track, the grass flattened from regular use. Before long she was stood on the edge of the wood from where she could see smoke and rooftops. The track turned into a bridleway and she made good progress until, just a short while later, she arrived at the town's boundary. Mary knew the small town quite well, as a few of her friends lived there and she had visited the place often. 'I think it's time to pay someone a visit. Who shall it be?' She ran through the small list of friends in her mind, eventually deciding upon a young man called Peter. She had spoken at some length to him at a party she had held the previous summer and he had let it be known that anytime she was passing, Mary should come and see him. 'There's no time like the present,' she thought out loud as she set off at a pace towards the north of the town.

Within a short time, Mary arrived at a cottage. With a low thatched roof and thick oak beams running through its walls, it was smaller than Mary had expected. She marched up the path and banged on the heavy front door three times. It was opened by an elderly woman, wearing a tattered dress. 'Yes?'

'Is Peter in?' Mary said sweetly, giving her a warm smile.

The woman looked suspiciously at her. 'And who might you be?'

'Mary. I'm an old friend.'

The woman didn't look convinced. 'Mmmm. I'll just see.' She closed the door on Mary and bellowed to Peter. Mary could hear a conversation going on the other side of the door. Eventually it opened and a strongly built youth appeared, a shock of red hair shaped around his freckled face. He was holding a small axe in one hand and beads of sweat were on his brow. 'Mary!' he exclaimed. 'What on earth are you doing here?'

'I was in the area and I thought I might just pop round and see you. Can I come in.'

Peter looked unsure. 'Probably best not. My mother doesn't like strangers.' He stepped outside, closed the door behind him and placed the axe against the wall.

Mary's disappointment was obvious. 'Oh.'

'I'm sorry. You should have sent word.'

'I know. But the truth is I'm in a bit of a bind and could really do with somewhere to stay for the night.'

'Why? What's happened?' Peter began brushing pieces of wood and bark from his breeches, still looking at her.

Mary obviously couldn't tell him what had happened in Dorchester and news of what had befallen her husband obviously hadn't made it as far as Puddletown yet. She thought quickly. 'I came over on one of my father's wagons for I fancied a day away from Dorchester. Unfortunately the wheel has broken and cannot be repaired until Monday. So I am stuck here. Do you know of any rooms in the town I can take?'

Peter shook his head. 'No, I'm sorry. But I tell you what. I have my own lodgings just over there.' He pointed at a small outbuilding. 'You can have it until Monday. That way you can stay a couple of nights and we can catch up tomorrow.'

The look on Mary's face made it obvious what she was thinking. Peter laughed. 'Don't worry! You can have my bed and I will stay in the house with mother. Your reputation will be intact. Although, should you reconsider, you know where you will find me!'

Mary punched him playfully in the arm. 'Peter!'

He took her to his lodgings. It was just one small room, with a stove at one end and a small bed at the other. 'It used to be for storing wood,' he explained as Mary peered inside. 'But I turned it into a little home for myself last summer. I could no longer stand my father's snoring!'

Mary laughed. 'Peter, it's perfect. I shall be very comfortable here.'

Peter looked pleased. 'I am glad you like it. We have some stew in the pot indoors. I will bring some to you, so you will not go hungry. I will also fetch you some water. Please make yourself at home while I finish chopping the wood. I won't be long.'

Peter left Mary to settle down. The small, one room cottage was quaint and Mary mused that it was like being in a doll's house. She sat on the bed and tested it for comfort. Overcome with fatigue, she lay down on top of the blanket, curled herself up into a ball and closed her eyes. Within seconds, she was fast asleep.

Chapter Thirty-Eight

'Tell the officer what you told me.' The young mother held Jack by his shoulders.

The man squatted before him, giving Jack a friendly wink as he did so. 'Your mother tells me you met a nice lady in the woods today.'

Jack nodded. Getting no further response, the officer prompted him again. 'What did she look like?'

Jack looked up at his mother. 'Go on,' she encouraged him. You are not in any trouble.

'She was wearing a green dress and her hair was quite dark, like mother's. She was very pretty.' The words fell out of the youngster's mouth in a hurry.

The officer looked up at his colleague before returning his gaze to Jack. 'And what was her name?'

'Mary,' the boy screwed up his face before he answered. 'Can I go now? He looked back up at his mother, who in turn looked at the officer.

'No, not yet,' he said. 'What was she doing?'

'She was laid against a tree. She was sleeping.'

'Have you ever seen her before?'

Jack shook his head. 'No.'

'So what happened next?'

'Me and Tom went off to get firewood for mother and she went for a walk.'

'I see.' The officer stood up. 'And do you know where she went walking to?'

'Yes. She said she was coming here.'

'What? Here? To your home?' The officer looked puzzled.

'No!' the boy pulled a face. 'Not here! She asked where the nearest place was and we said it was Puddletown and she set off walking towards it.'

The two men looked at each other. 'Thank you Jack, you have been most helpful.'

They both let themselves out of the front door. 'What has she done?' the mother called out as they began walking away.

'She killed her husband' they said in unison, before mounting their horses and heading at speed back to Dorchester.

Chapter Thirty-Nine

A persistent knocking at the door finally stirred Mary from her sleep. At first, she wondered where she was. As the events of the previous day came back to her, she quickly stood up and looked fearfully out of the window. She was relieved to see Peter stood there with a tankard of water and some bread. Mary quickly opened the door, squinting in the bright sunshine as it flooded in, filling the room with light. 'I was in a lovely sleep. You have just woken me up.' She rubbed at her eyes as she tried to focus.

Peter pushed past her and went to the small table in the middle of the room. 'So I see. I'm sorry. But I've brought you some food.' Placing the items upon it, he turned to the stove, opened the door and began poking at it, stirring the embers. As the heat was released, he gently blew on them, adding kindling. Finally, after a lot of coaxing, the small pieces of wood caught light and he added a couple of logs on top before closing the door. Having completed his task, Peter pulled out a chair and sat opposite Mary, who was chewing at the bread.

'It's a bit stale,' she grumbled as she chewed.

'I know,' Peter said. 'It's last night's. Mother will be making more later on. Just put it in the water first, for that will help.'

Mary dunked the crust in the tankard before taking another bite. As she ate, Peter drew a big breath. 'Why have you really come here, Mary?'

'What do you mean?' Mary gave her him her best smile, but Peter was unmoved.

'The hue and cries were around early this morning. They are looking for you.'

Mary swallowed hard, nearly choking. As she recovered, she asked 'You haven't told them I am here, have you?'

'No, not yet.' Peter sat back in his chair, folding his arms. 'But if mother gets to hear, then I will have no say in the matter. She isn't happy about me allowing you to stay as it is.'

They both fell quiet. It was Peter who eventually broke the silence. 'They say you have poisoned your husband. Is it true?'

Tears welled up in Mary's eyes. She nodded. 'Yes,' she blubbed. 'But I didn't mean to.'

'How could you not mean to?'

Mary recounted the story of how she was worried that she was with child so had consulted with a friend of her servant. The woman had recommended ratsbane, but when she couldn't get any, she had purchased mercury. She had put it in her food with no intention of ever giving it to Thomas. He had eaten some before falling ill. And now he was poisoned and everyone was blaming her. Meanwhile, the servant and her friend were nowhere to be found. Tears streamed down her face as she stressed her innocence.

Peter listened intently before leaning forward and placing his elbows on the table, his hands clasped together. 'So what are you to do? It's only a matter of time before they catch up with you.'

'I know,' Mary sobbed. 'I just need some time for Thomas

to recover so he can tell them it isn't my fault, or for my servant to reappear.' She suddenly had a thought. 'You don't think she could have done it, do you?'

Peter looked at her sternly. 'You have just told me that you yourself made the meal and put in the powder. I don't see how your servant could have done it.'

'But with her disappearance, perhaps they will think it is her, not me who has poisoned him!'

'Perhaps,' said Peter. 'Though I doubt it. After all, it is you they are seeking, not her.'

They fell silent once more. Mary drained the cup of water and stood up. 'I suppose I should leave.'

'Yes, you must. But I have had a thought. If it is time you need until your husband is fully recovered, I may be able to help you travel to somewhere else. Have you anywhere you can go and stay where news will not reach them of your woes?'

Mary thought about it. 'I have family to the north of here. Perhaps I could go there. They would surely welcome me.'

'Whereabouts?'

'They live in a village called Charlton Horethorne, near Sherborne. I went to my brother's wedding there. Could you really help get me there?'

Peter stood up. 'Yes, I will make ready my horse. But we must be quick. The gossip is spreading faster than a wild fire and we must make haste. Give me a few moments and I will return.'

Fifteen minutes later, he returned on his horse. 'Here, jump up.' He leant down and grabbed her arm as she stuck her foot in the stirrup and swung herself up behind him. Putting her arms around his waist, she nuzzled into his back as he stirred the horse into a trot. Before too much longer, they were on the main road heading north to Sherborne.

Chapter Forty

Peter arrived home to find a cordon of men awaiting him in the yard. He had been seen leaving Puddletown on a horse at speed with a woman matching Mary's description hanging on to him for dear life.

The faces were unfriendly. Richard Channing leant forward on his steed. 'Where have you been, boy?'

Peter dismounted and began removing the saddle from his horse. 'I have been visiting friends.'

'Friends you say?' Channing smirked and looked around at his colleagues. 'And who might these friends be?' he enquired.

'You wouldn't know them,' Peter answered, lifting off the saddle. He turned to carry it into the wooden barn behind him, leading the horse as he went. Tethering the horse in front of a water trough, he came back out into the warm sunshine and headed off to his small cottage.

Richard Channing dismounted and headed him off. 'You took Mary Brookes with you, didn't you?'

Peter shook his head and went to speak but Channing stopped him. 'Don't lie, boy. We know she left with you. Were you aware that there is a reward for her capture?'

'A reward?' Peter raised his eyebrows.

'Yes, a reward. And are you also aware that harbouring a murderer carries a grave sentence.'

'A murderer?' The full extent of what Mary had done suddenly struck him, as did his own predicament. 'Mary told me she had accidentally poisoned him. She said he was recovering and that she just needed time to clear her name. She was hopeful that her husband would make a full recovery and absolve her from all blame!' Peter looked around, nervously. 'I'm sorry. I had no idea.'

'Well it's time to make up for your mistake.' Channing poked at his chest with his riding crop. 'You can either return with us to Dorchester and be charged with being an accomplice. Or you can take these two officers –' he turned and pointed at the officers with his crop '– to where Mary is holed up so they can bring her back to face justice.'

It didn't take long for Peter to make his mind up. It was a stark choice and he held no real feelings of loyalty for Mary. He nodded his assent. 'I will go with you and bring her back, just as soon as my horse is rested.'

Channing looked up at the sun. It was already mid-afternoon and he knew that the journey would take at least half a day. 'You will leave at dawn tomorrow with the officers. I shall await you in Dorchester.' He mounted his horse. It whinnied as he turned it around. 'God speed, boy. I look forward to making your acquaintance again soon, along with that of Mary Brookes.'

Chapter Forty-One

'Your husband has made a full recovery. You must come back now.' Peter lied, knowing that the truth would make it almost impossible to get Mary to return willingly. He gave her a warm smile, as if he was happy for her.

'Really? He has recovered! Oh that is wonderful news!' Mary hugged him in joy. She released him, a sudden look of concern crossing her face. 'But will Thomas tell them the truth about what happened?'

'He already has. He has stated that you are not to blame and that the food he ate must have been off. He wishes to speak with you and he is worried about you. Please, quickly say farewell to your cousins and come with me. The sooner we leave, the sooner you can return to clear your name.'

Mary went to say her goodbyes to her hosts, who were bemused by both the sudden arrival and then departure of their unexpected visitor. Having said her farewells, she went into the courtyard where the two officers were awaiting her. Saying nothing, they turned their horses and began the long journey back to Dorchester. Once again, Peter held down his arm for Mary to swing up behind him on to his horse. As soon as she was settled, he set off after them.

It was dusk before they arrived back at Dorchester. A small crowd had gathered outside her house and she had to endure a range of insults, jeers and accusations as she stiffly dismounted and was led up the path into the house. She pointedly ignored them, holding her head high as she skipped up the steps to the front door.

The house felt cold and unwelcoming as she was directed to the study. Inside, she found Richard Channing and the magistrate awaiting her. She wondered where Thomas was, but concluded that he must still be recovering upstairs in bed. Richard Channing's face was stern, but Mary dismissed his look, assuming he was still angry with her for inadvertently poisoning Thomas. Surely Thomas would not allow his father to throw her out onto the street? It would bring too much shame upon the family name!

The magistrate moved toward her, a sad look on his face. 'At last, we meet. You have led us quite a song and dance, I must say.'

Mary smiled, sweetly. 'I am sorry sir, but I feared the worst. Thankfully, I hear my husband has recovered so I am able to return to clear my name.'

'Recovered? Recovered!' Richard Channing's face had turned a dark pink colour as he spat the word out. 'Have you not heard?'

'Heard what?' Mary looked surprised.

'Thomas is dead!' Channing spat the words out, glaring menacingly at her.

Mary staggered backwards and nearly fainted. The two officers at her side caught her by the elbows before she could collapse to the floor. She steadied herself. 'It is not possible!' she exclaimed, with tears in her eyes. 'Peter told me that he had made a full recovery and had said I was not to blame!' As Mary spoke, she realized the full extent of Peter's betrayal. He had told her what she had needed to hear in order to get her to willingly return to Dorchester.

Channing pointed at her, accusingly. 'You killed my son and I shall see to it that you will pay with your life.'

Mary gasped, putting her hands to her mouth. Channing continued. 'The Justice of the Peace will meet with you tomorrow so you can answer for your sins. Until then, you are to remain here under house arrest until such time as your pretrial has been arranged.'

'But I have done nothing!' she appealed. 'Where is Molly, my servant? She will explain everything!'

The magistrate spoke softly. 'Your servant has disappeared, probably too scared to remain in the house. I am afraid your actions speak for themselves. You poisoned your husband then fled the scene of your crime. There can be no doubt in anyone's mind that you – and you alone – are responsible.' He waved his hand at her, half turning as he did so. 'Get her out of my sight!' he shouted to the two officers. They dragged her away, up the stairs to her room, where they left her sobbing into her pillow.

'Can you believe that?' Channing poured himself a brandy and sat down behind the desk in a large, leather chair.

The magistrate shook his head. Upstairs he could hear Mary crying. 'No. It is as if butter wouldn't melt in her mouth. She has a cold heart and a manipulative manner. I am convinced as to her guilt. I cannot imagine anybody else differing in their opinion.'

Downing his brandy in one, Channing poured another without offering the magistrate one. Swirling it in his glass, he stared out of the window at the small crowd who were still hanging around, hoping for news of the proceedings going on inside. The two officers returned and he pointed out of the window. 'Disperse the crowd. Tell them there will be no further news until tomorrow morning at the town hall when we shall hand Mary over to the court.'

As they left the study, Peter stepped warily into the room.

'What is it?' Channing said tersely, glaring at him.

'You said there would be a reward, sir?' Peter spoke meekly.

Channing cleared his throat, hesitating before reaching into the pocket of his jacket and removing a small pouch. He shook it so Peter could hear the sound of its contents jangling before throwing it to him. 'Here. Have it. Your thirty pieces of silver. Now be gone before I change my mind and have you whipped, for that is what you truly deserve!'

Peter caught the pouch, weighed it briefly in his hand, before reversing out of the door. He thought briefly about saying something but decided against it. Best get out before Mr Channing could change his mind and turn on him.

The two men watched him leave and the magistrate reached for his pocket watch. 'The hour is getting late. I must go. I have much to prepare before tomorrow.'

Channing sighed heavily. 'I shall meet with you at the court in the morning.'

The magistrate turned. As he left the study, Richard Channing turned to look out of the window to see the officers pleading with the crowd to go home. The magistrate made his way down the path, through the gate and on through the crowd without stopping. Tomorrow, Mary will face her accusers, he thought, glancing up at the ceiling. Upstairs, in her room, he could hear Mary still sobbing her heart out. For the first time since he had received news of his son falling sick, Richard Channing smiled.

Chapter Forty-Two

Mary was greeted by a few jeers from the packed gallery as she was manhandled into the courtroom. The Justice was busy writing with his quill, his face stern and his cheeks ruddy. Mary stood before him in silence, her head lowered.

Finally, after what felt like an eternity, the Justice stopped, blotted his scribblings and passed it to the attendant who stood alongside him. For the first time since Mary had entered the room, he looked up at her. Mary felt herself shrink under his gaze. 'So what do we have here?' he called out, knowing full well who the girl was that was stood before him.

'Mary Channing, my Lord.' The magistrate stepped forward to present himself.

'And who is the complainant?' Again, the justice of the peace knew the answer, but the gravity of the charges before him demanded that procedures must be followed to the letter.

Richard Channing stepped forward. 'I am, my Lord. Richard Channing, father of the deceased.'

'Thank you.' He picked up some papers and scanned them briefly before looking once more at Mary. 'I have read the charges laid against the defendant by Mr Richard Channing, father of the deceased. Mary Channing, nee Brookes, of East High Street, Dorchester, you are charged with petty treason following the murder of your husband, Thomas Channing, formerly of East High Street, Dorchester. How do you plead?'

Mary looked nervously around. 'Not guilty,' she said, meekly.

'Speak up girl. I can't hear you! How do you plead?' The justice looked to the back of the room, gauging the reaction of the crowd. He was pleased to see many of them nodding in approval at his reproachment of the accused.

'Not guilty.' Mary's voice was louder but still contained a slight tremor.

The justice dipped his quill in some ink and made some notes on the paper before him. He nodded to his assistant. 'The defendant has entered a plea of not guilty. Record it for the court.' The assistant nodded and also dipped his quill into his ink well before writing on his own sheaf of papers.

The Justice addressed the magistrate. 'Where is the defendant being remanded?'

'She is to remain under house arrest at her house in East High Street,' the magistrate confirmed. 'She will be attended to at all times by my officers. We are of the opinion that the defendant will be safer there.'

'Does this meet with your approval, Mr Channing?' The Justice held the quill, just above the paper in readiness for his response.

Mr Channing gave him a slight nod. 'Yes. I shall personally take charge of her internment and guarantee her delivery to the court.'

The Justice made some additional notes, blotted the ink and once more handed it to his assistant who scrambled across his desk to grab it. 'We shall return here tomorrow morning at ten o'clock for the pre-trial hearing.' He addressed Mary.

'Tomorrow, you will have a chance tomorrow to explain yourself and mount your defence – should you have one.' He rose and the room joined him as one. As he departed the room a chorus of voices broke out in the gallery, hurling insults and making threats at Mary. She was bustled away by the two officers, past Richard Channing who sneered at her. 'I will see you tomorrow, Miss Brookes. Sleep well, for you will need it. Good day.'

Mary was paraded through the town with hoards of people lining the streets. She hung her head as her escorts pushed people back and deflected various objects that were thrown at her. Finally, after what felt like an eternity to Mary, they arrived at the house and she was shown upstairs to her bedroom. The door closed behind her and the lock clicked as the key turned. She tried the door just to see if it had really been locked, but it held firm. She gazed out of the front window at the crowd that was continuing to grow as people arrived from the court to swell their numbers. She inadvertently ducked as a rotten piece of fruit hit the window, juices splattering across the glass. Throwing herself on her bed, she buried her head in the pillow and tried in vain to shut out the noise of the street.

After some while, Mary rose and went to her bureau. Opening it, she took out some paper, a quill and removed the lid from the inkwell. It was time to prepare her defence. She covered the tip of the quill in ink, then frantically began to write.

Chapter Forty-Three

The following morning, at ten o'clock precisely, Mary was brought in before Mayor John Nelson. He had recently been re-elected to serve his second term as the town's mayor and was feeling buoyed by the publicity that the case had attracted. There were many local townspeople seated in the gallery, along with a large number of strange faces that the mayor didn't recognise, all enthralled by proceedings and keen to get a sight of the accused.

When she entered the room, boos rang around the gallery. Mayor Nelson allowed them to continue until Mary was seated. He then gestured for the crowd to settle down. They duly obliged, keen to see the trial begin.

A number of Justices of the Peace sat alongside him, each armed with their own set of questions for Mary based on the evidence that had been presented to them the previous evening.

Mary sat alone and spread her own papers out on the desk. She made a show of reading them but, in truth, her thoughts prevented her from absorbing any of her scribblings from the night before, as she struggled to comprehend what was happening around her.

As the court fell silent, Mayor Nelson stood to address the defendant. 'Mary Channing, you are charged with petty treason, namely the murder of your husband, Thomas Channing, by systematically poisoning him, first with arsenic, then with mercury. How do you plead?'

Prompted by the magistrate, Mary stood to answer. 'Not guilty, sir.' She sat down again as the gallery behind her erupted into a loud series of catcalls and whistles.

The mayor settled them down again. 'Have you prepared your defence?'

Mary rose once more. 'Yes sir, I have.'

The mayor jotted down her response, an intrigued look on his face. He was keen to hear what Mary had to say for herself. 'So be it.' He looked up and down the lines of justices either side of him. 'Who would like to begin?'

One of them stood, hooking his thumbs into his waistcoat and smiling knowingly at the gallery. 'If it so pleases my Lord, I would like to begin.' The Mayor nodded, and the man turned to address Mary. 'Mrs Channing, why did you kill your husband?'

Mary stood to answer her accuser. 'I did not, sir.'

The justice beamed at her and looked all around. 'You did not? But the evidence surely points to the contrary!' he exclaimed. 'Did you, or did you not, say in a public house within earshot of many others, that you wished your husband of just a few weeks, dead?'

Mary shook her head. 'I don't believe I did, sir. And, if I did, it was surely in jest. What wife has not had cause to say the same about her husband at some point in her marriage?'

'In jest you say?' The justice adopted a serious look, pursing his bottom lip. 'A joke in bad taste, surely. And yet you let it be known that you were not happy with your husband. Why was that?'

'It is true that I was unhappy with my husband, but that was because I was forced into marrying him by my father.

Indeed, it is fair to say that, at first, I did not love my husband, nor indeed like him very much.' The crowd murmured loudly amongst themselves at her response, forcing Mayor Nelson to insist that they calm down and allow Mary to speak. When they had quietened down, she resumed. 'But, as I got to know him, I grew to like him and I am sure that I would have eventually grown to love him.'

'In time you would have grown to love him as your husband.' The justice repeated the sentence for dramatic effect. Another justice stood up, forcing him to reluctantly retake his seat before he could ask another question.

'Isn't it true that you had another lover throughout your marriage to Thomas Channing?' It was more an accusation than a question and Mary knew she had to deny it.

'No, sir. I did not.'

'But you were seen on occasion, particularly in the early days of your marriage to Mr Channing, seen with a number of young men, and one young man in particular. What do you say about that?'

'It is true that I had many friends of my own age prior to my marriage. But as soon as I was betrothed, I saw them no more.'

'So you deny you were seeing other men?'

Mary nodded her head. 'I do.'

Another justice stood to speak. 'Why did you buy poison from Mr Wolmington's apothecary on the Monday prior to your husband's death?'

'Because we had a problem with rats, so I went to buy some ratsbane. When it was discovered they had none in stock, Mr Wolmington's assistant recommended powdered mercury.'

'Powdered mercury? So you admit you purchased it.'

Denial was pointless so Mary nodded once more. 'Yes sir, I do.'

'So how exactly did the dreaded powder end up in your husband's breakfast the following day?' The justice beamed up at the assembled crowd, enjoying his moment in the spotlight.

Mary shrugged. 'I am not sure. My servant made breakfast for him, as was the norm, and he sat down to eat it.'

Richard Channing jumped to his feet. 'That's a lie! You made him breakfast that morning!'

Mary ignored him as the Mayor addressed Channing directly. 'Sir, you will please refrain yourself from such outbursts. Please take your seat and remain there throughout or I will be left with no option other than insist that you leave.'

Red-faced, Channing retook his seat, glowering at Mary.

The justice continued. 'And you did not eat any of this meal, prepared you say, by your servant?'

Mary had realised the evening before when she was preparing her defence that, without Molly and her mystery friend to back her up, she would have to distance herself from the actual poisoning. She had also come up with another idea, one that was bold, perhaps even to the point of madness. But her situation was now beyond desperate and she felt she had no other option. Without Molly, she knew the chances were that she would have to employ it.

'No, sir, I did not. As soon as Thomas had taken a spoonful he complained that he was unable to eat it and asked the servant to dispose of it. Indeed, he even advised me against eating any of it for which I am now thankful. Soon after, my husband fell very ill and I sat at his bedside and nursed him through his discomfort.'

'You nursed your husband through his discomfort? And how exactly did you do that?'

'I comforted him, I bathed him, I wet his head with cold water to help him with his fever, and I disposed of his functions.'

'Did you also give him a glass of wine?'

'Yes sir.' Mary was pleased. Surely the fact that she gave him wine would show how caring she was in his hour of need. 'Actually, I gave him two!'

The justice looked shocked, which perplexed her. 'Two?

You admit to giving him two glasses of wine?'

Mary nodded, suspecting that she had just made a mistake but at a loss as to what it was she had said that was wrong. The justice looked to the gallery and spoke directly at them, although his statement was aimed purely at Mary. 'Two glasses of wine, a wine from a decanter which was also found to have large amounts of mercury in it!' The crowd erupted, while Mary stared at him, eyes and mouth wide open.

'I did not know, sir, I swear it!' She had no idea how the mercury had found its way into the wine, for she had only added it to the rice and milk. She began wondering if her ploy of blaming Molly held more credence than she had originally given it credit for. 'I am telling you, my servant must have done it for she prepared all of his food and served him his drink.'

'But you just said you served him his wine!' The crowd rose to their feet once more.

'I declare to you and all who bear witness, I am innocent of the charges laid before me!' she shouted, trying to make herself heard above the clamour. 'I did not kill my husband. I did not poison my husband. And I will prove it to you by offering to visit my husband's body and touching it. I wish to claim my bier-right!'

A hush descended on the court. Mayor Nelson got to his feet. You want to claim your "bier-right"?' He sounded incredulous. It was a defence he had not heard in a long time.

She nodded her affirmation. 'I do.'

The mayor gathered his justices of the peace around him and they spoke in hushed voices as they discussed their options. Channing leant over to the magistrate and tugged at his robe to attract his attention. 'What's happening?'

The magistrate turned and whispered in his ear. 'She is claiming her bier-right.'

Channing raised an eyebrow. 'Bier-right? What is that?'

'It's an old rule, mired in witchcraft from far less enlightened times. It was believed that the body can still hear and react, even in death. Bier-right, or cruentation, allows the accused to touch the body. Should the corpse bleed, or froth at the mouth, then it is in the presence of the murderer. Should nothing happen, then the accused is presumed innocent.'

'That's ridiculous. How can a body hear and react in death?' Channing was bemused. 'You cannot be serious.'

The magistrate offered a weak smile. 'I'm afraid I am.' He turned back round to face the mayor as he stood to address Mary once more.

'It is an unusual request, but, according to my learned friends either side of me, it is your right. I shall make the necessary arrangements.'

'That is preposterous!' Channing bellowed at the mayor, standing up. The magistrate tried to calm him down, urging him to retake his seat. Channing slapped his hand away and pointed at the mayor. 'I have never heard of such a thing. How can you even contemplate letting her near my son's body? It's absolutely absurd!'

The mayor banged his gavel. 'Mr Channing, please take your seat and be quiet or I will have you removed from the court!'

As the gallery began shouting and whistling at the mayor in support of Richard Channing, the magistrate stood up. Struggling to make himself heard above the furore, he asked if he could approach the bench. The mayor, banging his gavel in an attempt to regain order, gave him permission.

He leant over his desk in order to hear the magistrate speak. 'Sir, I cannot in all honesty countenance this. I have no idea where this young girl has learnt about claiming bier-right, but I believe it is an affront to the court, the victim's family and, in particular, his father who watched him die in such a slow and painful manner. Besides, you must take into consideration the state of the corpse.'

'The state of the corpse? Why is that?' The mayor was

intrigued.

'In the final days of his death, Thomas Channing underwent several procedures in order to purge his body of the poison that afflicted him.'

'Go on.'

'The procedures including pumping his stomach full of water and oil, a mixture designed to rid him of his ailment.'

'What of it?' The mayor was becoming impatient.

'Well now the body is putrefying. Gasses and liquids are filling the body. It is quite likely that by touching the body it may invoke the reaction required of it to condemn the accused under the rules of cruentation. To do so would fly in the face of modern science and the legal system today. It belongs in the dark ages and I fear a mistrial would result should you allow it to happen. Sir, I urge you to reconsider.'

Mayor Nelson sat back, deep in thought. He gestured the justices around him once more and the court hushed as they formed a huddle to hear the magistrate's objection. Finally, after several minutes, they returned to their seats and the mayor addressed Mary. 'Upon further consideration, and in accordance with the wishes of the victim's family, I am afraid it would not be prudent to allow you to see the victim. My understanding is that there is a distinct possibility that you may even be able to provoke a reaction in the body, one that would not be in your favour. I therefore must refuse your right to visit the body.'

The gallery erupted with cheers and more insults and catcalls were hurled at Mary. The mayor banged on his table once more to bring the crowd to heel. Mary looked defiantly at him throughout. Pouting, she glared at the mayor as if challenging him. He glared back and their eyes locked. It was the mayor who felt compelled to pull away. Glancing up and down the line at his panel of justices, he banged his gavel once more. 'We shall continue questioning. Who is next?'

A young man, tall and slender got up. 'Mrs Channing. We

know you purchased the poison at Mr Wolmington's apothecary. We also know how you administered the powder. What I don't understand is why you sat so long at your husband's bedside throughout his ordeal. Was it to ensure he was dying?'

Mary said nothing. She switched her glare from the mayor to her new inquisitor.

'Have you nothing to say?' he enquired. Eliciting no response, he then went on. 'I am also curious as to why you called the physician. Did you have a change of heart? Or did you realise that you had gone too far and were trying to cover your tracks?'

Once again, Mary remained silent, her stare still fixed on the young justice.

'Are you refusing to answer, Mrs Channing?' the mayor asked. Once again, she steadfastly remained quiet. 'Mrs Channing, I asked you a question. Are you refusing to answer any more questions?'

The courtroom held its breath as Mary defiantly remaining silent, glaring at the row of justices sat before her. The mayor's patience ran out. He banged his gavel once more. 'In light of the defendant's refusal to answer any more questions, I declare this pre-trial over. She is to be remanded to the Dorchester county gaol until a date is fixed for her trial. The court is adjourned.'

He gathered up his papers, stood up and promptly made for the exit, followed by all of the justices. Mary felt a lump in her throat as she realized she wasn't going back to her home, but was instead going to be transported to the local prison where any comforts she could have expected would be taken away from her. There was only one avenue left that could deliver her from the inevitable. She placed both of her hands on her belly, then turned to greet the two officers who were to escort her to the prison.

Chapter Forty-Four

The room was full of the overwhelming stench of human excrement and suffering. Men, women and even children were all around, some leaning against walls, some sitting, some laying down, many of them moaning quietly to themselves. The closing of the door behind her was loud and had a finality to it. Mary, fresh faced and young, immediately attracted the unwanted attentions of four men who made their way over to confront her.

'Hello my pretty. What do we have here?' Mary slapped away the hand that pawed at her chest.

'We have a feisty one here lads!' said another, as he made to grab hold of her dress. Mary struck out once more, her fear growing as she realized she was outnumbered and vulnerable.

'Leave her alone!' A fearsome looking woman, toothless and well built, forced herself between them and Mary, pushing the men back.

They growled at her. 'You can't protect her forever,' one said. They loitered, unsure as to what to do. 'You'll have to sleep at some point,' added another.

'Maybe, maybe not. But woe betide you when I wake up

and find you have touched her!' she threatened. As they retreated back to their corner of the cell, she turned to Mary. 'Come over here with me my lovely.' She sat her down in one corner. 'Stay close to me. I'll look after you.'

Mary flashed a grateful smile at her. 'Thank you, Miss...'

'Amelia. And don't thank me, Miss Mary. I know who you are. The cost is a farthing a day. Be sure to arrange it.'

Mary nodded. 'Of course. I will see to it just as soon as I am able.'

'Don't leave it too long. I'd hate to fall asleep and not wake up while something untoward was happening to you.'

Mary suspected Amelia was in cahoots with the men who had challenged her as she entered, but kept her tongue. Now was not the time to rock the boat. First, she must learn everything she could about her new surroundings and its occupants in order to stay alive. She studied her fellow inmates, all of whom looked gaunt, filthy and sick. The damp, squalid conditions were made worse by the complete lack of ventilation. A single ray of light from a small, barred window, cut its way through the darkness.

Mary's fellow inmates all settled down as Mary's protector slid her back down the wet stone wall and took her place beside her. Before long, the only noise was that of the occasional moaning and snoring of those that had the fortune to fall asleep, if only for a short while.

'Mary Channing!' The jailer's pockmarked, grubby face appeared at the small window cut into the thick, wooden door. Mary stood up so she could be seen. 'Come here. You've got visitors.' Mary had no idea who would come to see her, but made her way through the bodies all around her to the door, which was unlocked and pushed open for her to go through. It clanged shut behind her and Mary stood and waited while the jailor slid two large bolts back into their housings and turned the big key in the lock.

'Follow me,' he said gruffly as he made his way down the

dark corridor, his keys jangling on a large iron ring in his hand. Mary scurried after him, passing other cells, the same moans and incoherent mumblings coming from behind the doors.

After going up a steep set of stairs, they both arrived in an ante room. 'Wait here,' the jailor said. Mary did as she was told, curious as to what fate was going to befall her next. She could not contain her surprise as the door suddenly opened and her mother stepped in, closely followed by her father. Mary burst into tears as she fell into her mother's open arms. Her mother also began crying as they tightly hugged each other. Richard Brookes stood to one side, waiting for them to finish. When they finally stepped apart, he too hugged his daughter and she buried her face into his chest, feeling his strength, hoping against hope that he could make everything better, as he had when she was a small girl.

Eventually, he broke her embrace and stood back, still holding Mary's hands. She pulled her right hand free and joined it with her mother's. 'You've got yourself into a right pickle this time, young Mary,' her father said.

Mary couldn't help but laugh out loud. 'I know. I'm sorry. I didn't do it though. Not this time!'

Her father tried to look stern but couldn't. His face softened as he spoke. 'We will do everything we can to help you. We haven't got long but I have come to an agreement with the jailer and you will be kept out of the main cells and placed in a room by yourself, with a bed to lay on.'

'They will also give you better food and you will have an allowance for other things, should you need them,' her mother added. 'If you want anything, just give a message to the jailer and he will pass it on to us.'

'Can you arrange for me to leave here with you and go home?'

Her mother shook her head sadly, a faint smile on her lips. 'Alas no, child. I am afraid that even your father cannot arrange that.'

'Thank you father.' Mary hugged him again. 'Were you in court today?'

Her parents guiltily looked at each other. 'No. We felt it best not to, not with the way people are speaking about you. We feared that should our identities become known, it may have caused upset.' Her father looked at the floor, as if ashamed.

The jailer knocked and opened the door without waiting for a response. 'That's it. Your time is up. I have to take you to your new home, Mrs Channing.' He grinned salaciously and Mary wondered what was in store for her as soon as her parents had left the premises. She hugged them both one last time and shed some more tears before they departed.

Closing the door behind him, the jailor went through his large ring of keys and opened the door behind Mary. 'This way,' he announced. Instead of heading down the stairs, back into the bowels of the prison, he turned left into a small corridor. A number of small rooms stood opposite each other with their doors ajar. They were all identical inside. A flagstone floor, thick stone walls and a single wooden bed with a blanket. Each also had a barred window which let in light, but would not keep out the rain should it come. Beneath the window, there was a small wooden table and chair. They headed about half way down the line of cells before the jailer stopped and stood beside one of them. He held out his arm to show Mary the way. 'This one is yours,' he announced.

She entered the room and stood in the middle. The jailor leant down and picked up a wooden pail. 'Here is your slop bucket. It will be emptied once a day so leave it by the door before you go to sleep at night. You will receive food twice a day. It's nothing special, but it's better than what the others get so don't complain, and at least you won't have to fight anyone off to make sure you get your share. If you need anything else, such as beer or clothes, give me a message and I will make sure it gets to your father. If he is able and willing to pay for it, I will get it for you. You are allowed to accept visitors in your room, should I allow them. If you have need of a man –' he tapped the side of his nose as if sharing a secret '– I have a special room, but I will require advance notice.'

Mary was unsure if the jailor meant he himself was available should she need a man and shuddered at the thought. He closed and locked the door behind him and she heard his feet shuffling on the stone floor as he made his way back to his quarters. She sat on the bed. It was far from comfortable, but it was far better than the squalid damp floor she had found herself sitting on just a short while before. She looked up at the window. The early evening sky was blue and she could hear the birdsong. She sighed. How she longed to be out there flying with them.

Chapter Forty-Five

It was to be more than two months before the case went to court. With the judges operating a circuit across the south of the country, they first had to hear cases in other towns before finally arriving back in Dorchester for the Summer Assize. Mary's case was to be heard in the Old Crown Court, located within the Old Shire Hall Building, in Dorchester in late July of 1705. Mr Justice Price was to preside over proceedings, with Mary's case scheduled to commence at ten o'clock on the morning of Saturday, July the twenty-eighth.

Mary was taken on the short journey from the gaol to the Old Crown Court. Onlookers lined the route, keen to get a glimpse of her. She held her head high, but she looked haggard, her weeks in prison already taking their toll on her. Mary pointedly ignored the taunts and insults thrown at her as she walked the gauntlet of ill-wishers. The mid-morning temperature was already warm and it was clear that it was going to be a long, hot and sultry day. Some of the older women who lined the path pointed at her stomach: Was she with child? Once more, the gossip-mongers were given fuel to add to the fire and rapidly growing legend that was Mary Channing.

Having arrived at the court, Mary was taken through to a small chamber. Nobody spoke to her as she awaited the order to enter the courtroom. She looked nervously around, wishing for it all to be over even though she feared what the verdict would be. Petty treason was a crime worthy of being burnt at the stake in the eyes of the law and Mary was naturally fearful of the consequences should she be found guilty. Eventually, the door to the chamber opened and her name was called. She hesitantly moved forward into the courtroom. A hush fell over the paying crowd sat in the gallery as they all craned their necks to get a good look at her.

Mary was led to the dock, directly facing the witness box. The judge was sat across the room where he had a good view of proceedings. Just below him sat an array of clerks, lawyers and writers who were to note the proceedings down as they happened.

A mirrored reflector, positioned close to her, directed natural sunlight on to her face so the court was able to see every facial expression Mary made while evaluating her testimony. As the sun shone through the open window, her face was illuminated and she looked radiant, causing the suspicions about her condition to go up another level.

With the court assembled, it only remained for Justice Price to make his entrance. He duly entered the courtroom, his scarlet robes lined in ermine and wearing a full-bottomed wig. He cut an imposing figure and his voice was loud, clear and concise.

Price's first job was to select a jury. Comprising of tradesmen, artisans, merchants and gentlemen, the twelve men took their places one by one. Within the hour, they were all sworn in and the indictment was read out, firstly in English then, at Mary's request, in Latin.

With the formalities over, the real business of court began. Mary listened intently as the first witness was called. To her surprise, it was a friend of Thomas's who gave testimony about the visit of Nial to the Channing household a few weeks earlier. Her heart sank as the prosecution's strategy became clear. The prosecutors, Sir John Darnell and Mr Serjeant Hooper, were set to destroy her reputation, one that was already in tatters. As the court were told about how she had behaved with Nial in front of her husband, she sank back in her chair, listening intently to the events that had unfolded while occasionally shaking her head.

Her mood did not improve with the presentation of the next witness. Nial himself appeared in the witness box, clad in his finest tunic and cutting a dashing figure. Mary recalled that night and her shame following their coupling. She wondered what she had ever seen in him and marvelled at how she had been such a headstrong fool beneath her husband's roof. Her concern was growing that Nial would confirm exactly what had happened, even at the expense of his own reputation.

When asked if he had laid with the accused that night, Nial glanced briefly in Mary's direction, the hint of a smile of his face. She refused to look at him, her heart pounding as she waited on his answer. 'I did kiss her before she retired to her bed. But that was all, for I would not go any further.' The answer, while saving his own reputation, did nothing for hers as it suggested she had been willing to go to bed with him, had he consented.

When the prosecution had finished with Nial, Judge Price spoke directly to Mary. 'Do you have any questions of this witness?'

She rose. 'I have, sir.'

The judge gave her the floor and she looked angrily at Nial. 'Sir, I did not kiss you!' she cried. 'Indeed, it was you who forced yourself upon me!'

Judge Price immediately intervened. 'You may question the witness, but now is not the time to give your version of events. I ask you again. Do you have any questions?'

Mary shook her head, her cheeks flushed. 'No sir.' She sat down, feeling dejected. Her mood took a turn for the worse as Gabriel was the next witness to be called. It had been weeks since she had seen him last and her heart fluttered momentarily as he strode purposefully to the witness box. He refused to look at her, instead fixing his eyes on Judge Price.

Sir John stood up and asked him if Mary had ever met him in public following her marriage to Thomas Channing. 'Yes sir,' Gabriel replied.

'And where might that have been?'

'It was at an ale house, although I am unsure which one.'

Sir John checked his notes. 'Could it have been the Antelope?'

Gabriel shook his head. 'Quite possibly, sir. I don't rightly recall.'

Tutting to himself, Sir John turned the page before him. 'No matter. While there, did the accused kiss you?'

'Yes sir.'

'And what did you do?' Sir John looked up at Gabriel, an expectant expression on his face.

'I resisted sir, for she was a married woman!' Gabriel looked pleased with himself.

Once again, Mary was screaming inside. Meanwhile, the murmurs in the public gallery were growing. Sir John went on. 'Quite. Now I believe the accused gave you a gift. Is that true?'

Nodding his head, Gabriel said 'Yes sir, although the gift was not solicited; it was given freely and at first I refused to accept it.'

More lies. Mary shook her head in dismay as she recalled that afternoon at the lodging house. 'And what sort of gift was it?' Sir John's voice cut through her thoughts.

'A pocket watch.'

'A pocket watch.' Sir John spoke directly to the jury who all shook their heads. He let the words hang in the air before going on. 'And can you show us this watch?'

'No, I cannot sir, for she asked for its return soon after.'

'She asked for it back?'

'Yes sir. She sent for it when in prison stating that she needed it to buy favours.'

'I see. Can you describe the watch for us?'

Gabriel screwed up his face, trying to picture it. 'It was a silver timepiece sir, with a silver face and a silver chain.'

'And would you say the watch was an expensive piece?'

'Definitely sir. Far more than I could ever afford.' Gabriel nodded his head enthusiastically.

Sir John consulted his notes, once more. 'And how do you imagine the accused paid for this extravagant gift to you?'

Gabriel shrugged. He knew she had taken the money from Thomas's till at the shop but he didn't want it common knowledge that she had also been paying his gambling debts for him. 'I don't rightly know, sir.'

'So you didn't question her about where she got the money from to purchase such a fine gift?' Sir John sounded stern.

Once again, Gabriel shook his head. 'No, sir. She just presented me with it. Truth be told, I didn't know what to say at the time. Like I said, I told her I could not accept such a fine piece, but she insisted I take it.'

Judge Price then spoke to Mary. 'Mrs Channing, do you have any questions.'

Mary, wallowing in her own misery at Gabriel's betrayal, shook her head without speaking. The Judge persisted. 'Did you give this watch to the witness in jest?'

Mary looked up, questioningly. 'My Lord?'

Sir John also looked up at the judge, wondering what he was getting at. 'The pocket watch. Did you give it to Mister Fletcher in jest, not as a gift. Did you not expect him to return it to you at some point?'

Realisation dawned on Mary. Judge Price was helping her to discredit Gabriel's evidence. 'Yes sir. I only meant for him to look after it for me. As soon as I needed it, I asked for its return. I never expected him to keep it. Mister Fletcher must have misunderstood my intentions when I gave it to him.'

The judge looked at Sir John. 'Do you have any further questions?'

'No my Lord.' Sir John looked chastened. 'I have finished with the witness for now.'

Gabriel was led away as the gallery excitedly discussed the interchange that had just taken place. Mary knew exactly what had just happened. Sir John had just showed her to be a loose woman, one with no morals, who showered her lovers with gifts in return for favours. A woman who should expect no mercy from the court.

Chapter Forty-Six

With the departure of Mary's former beau, the Judge called a halt to proceedings. He banged his gavel on his desk and announced that it was time for lunch. Everyone was to return within the hour for the resumption of the trial.

As Mary was led down to the cellars below, Richard Channing leant over to Sir John and tapped him on the shoulder. 'Splendid work, sir. I think that went well. Would you and your colleague care to join me for lunch?'

Sir John and Serjeant Hooper gathered up their papers and stacked them neatly on the corner of their desk, having determined the order they should be in for when they returned. 'That would be most appreciated Mr Channing. We would love to join you.'

The three men made their way to the tavern opposite the court where they shared a venison pie and discussed the morning's proceedings. 'I feel you gentlemen have set her up nicely with those two damned fellows. I should like to have some time with them alone when all of this is over, particularly that younger fellow, Gabriel! I didn't believe a word of it, especially when they claimed she had not made advances towards them!' Channing wiped his mouth with the back of his hand and drunk heartily from his tankard of ale.

'It is a game of strategy,' explained Serjeant Hooper. 'One whereby we put all of the pieces into place and then go in for the kill. It is certainly a skill, one at which I like to think Sir John and myself excel.'

Sir John pulled a handkerchief from the pocket of his jacket and dabbed at his mouth. He folded it carefully before returning it. 'Mary Channing has been disgraced, both in public and now in the eyes of the law. She will certainly be heading for a fall, one with a rope attached to her neck!' The two lawyers laughed at Sir John's gallows humour.

'But surely she will be for the stake?' Channing said, his eyes narrowing.

'That will probably be the outcome,' confirmed Hooper. 'Especially as she has been charged with petty treason. But the executioner usually strangles them first. After all, we are not complete barbarians!' Again, the two lawyers laughed heartily, attracting the attention of those around them who wondered what they were finding so funny.

'But she deserves to die at the stake,' Channing said, his tone turning more serious. 'For what she has done, she must be made to suffer.'

Sir John shook his head. 'While it is customary to burn women at the stake for their treachery, my learned friend is correct. To publicly burn the wench alive would be to set a dangerous precedent, one that harks back to far more barbaric times. I like to think we, as a society, have moved on since then. But that is to come. First, we have to convince the jury to find her guilty.'

'Mmmm.' Channing sat back in his chair, alone momentarily with his thoughts. As far as he was concerned, the verdict was not in doubt. She would be found guilty and sentenced to death.

And then he wanted her to suffer the way his son had suffered – worse, if possible. The five days it had taken him to die had been long, arduous and excruciatingly painful. He had watched Thomas's life force disappear before his very eyes and he was determined that Mary should feel it as much as his son had. A quick death at the end of a rope was too good for her as far as he was concerned. A faint glint appeared in his eyes. He had friends in high places in Dorchester. All he had to do was find his way to the executioner.

They finished up their meal and Richard left a few coins on the table for the innkeeper. The three men then made their way back to the courtroom, helped on their way by a number of well-wishers.

They parted at the main entrance as Richard headed back to his seat and the two barristers made their way to their chambers to don their gowns and wigs once more. They entered the main courtroom to a spattering of applause as the crowd made it clear whose side they were on.

Mary was then brought up from below and escorted to the dock. She sat down and stared ahead, refusing to acknowledge or even look at those who were goading and insulting her.

Eventually, after several minutes, Judge Price entered the room and a hush fell over the room as everybody settled down. As soon as the judge was settled and had charged his quill, he nodded to the prosecution. Serjeant Hooper got to his feet, his black robes unfurling behind him as he did so. 'I would like to call Amy Clavel to the stand, my Lord.'

Mary wondered what was coming next as Amy arrived at the witness box. She grimaced as she recognized her as the young assistant from Mr Wolmington's shop. *So first they have assassinated my character. Now they wish to prove I poisoned him. Damn you and your friend, Molly!* She thought to herself.

Amy recounted Mary's visit to the shop on the afternoon of the sixteenth of April. Pointing at Mary she said 'She came into the shop and asked me if I had any ratsbane to buy. Upon discovering we had none, I instead offered her mercury and asked if she would prefer to purchase that instead.'

'And what did she say to that?' Hooper asked.

'She asked me if it would do the same job. When I said yes, she said she would have some.' Amy glanced across at Mary, a sorrowful look on her face.

'And how much did she purchase?' Hooper asked.

'A farthing's worth, sir.'

Hooper sighed. 'For the benefit of the jury, can you indicate how much mercury you would buy for a farthing?'

Amy made a circle with her thumb and forefinger. 'About the size of a walnut, I would suggest sir.'

'And did she explain exactly how she intended to use the mercury?' Hooper stood upright, leaning back slightly with his hands on his stomach as he waited for Amy to apply the coup de grace.

'She told me she wanted to poison a rat!' Amy announced triumphantly, smiling at the jury as they all gasped in amazement.

Mary put her head in her hands, shaking it to and fro. Amy gave her one final glance before being given leave to go and departing the witness box.

Hooper then proceeded to call a number of witnesses who had been present in the shop that day, one of whom recalling that Mary had asked if 'he would be her taster.' More uproar ensued as the witness told the court he had responded with 'What, you would give me poison? I had rather you gave me a drachm of innocence!'

Witnesses continued to come and go. From the discovery of the poisoned dog to Mister Wolmington's testimony regarding Mary's visit to the shop shortly before her husband had died asking him to deny she had visited his shop to buy the poison. 'She fell on her knees and asked me for Christ Jesus' sake not to say anything of it.'

Mary spoke up to object to Mister Wolmington's testimony. 'I never said these words, sir. Nor did I kneel before him. If I did, it was only to tie my shoe.'

Having proved beyond doubt that Mary had purchased the poison, Hooper sat himself down and Sir John got to his feet. He announced that the physician who had attended to Thomas was to take the stand. Dressed all in black, the doctor looked pale and ill at ease as he stood before the court.

'Doctor, good day to you, sir,' Sir John began. He gestured around the court with his hands in a theatrical manner. 'Please can you describe to the court the events that led up to you attending to Thomas Channing that day.'

The doctor cleared his throat. 'I received a message from the Channing household requesting my attendance as a matter of urgency,' he began. 'I set off immediately and arrived at the house shortly afterwards.'

'And what did you find upon your arrival there?'

'I found Thomas Channing in bed. His wife was mopping his brow and tending to him.'

'And how would you describe Mister Channing's condition?' Sir John turned a page on his notes then looked up, expectantly.

'Mr Channing was in a state of delirium. He was confused, he was struggling to see and did not respond to questioning. He was experiencing stomach cramps and was continually vomiting. Upon further inspection, his vomit contained blood.'

Sir John referred briefly to his notes. 'And what conclusion did you draw upon finding Mr Channing in this condition?'

'It appeared obvious to me that he had been poisoned' the doctor said bluntly. 'An assumption that I had no reason to doubt, especially after we discovered the dog.'

'The dog? What had happened to the animal?'

'He was found outside in the yard, just a couple of days later, quite dead. It was clear that he had eaten some leftovers of the same meal eaten by Thomas Channing.'

'I see.' Sir John paused for effect. 'So with that in mind, how did you treat Mister Channing?'

'I gave him a concoction of oil and water in order to cleanse his stomach of whatever poison was in his system. It initially appeared to be successful, as there was some improvement in the patient's well-being. I then left for home having told Mrs Channing I would return in the morning to check on her husband.'

'And how did Mrs Channing appear to you?'

The doctor narrowed his eyes. 'She appeared to be concerned for the welfare of her husband. She promised to look after him in my absence and to send message if his condition worsened.'

Mary stood up. 'Who sent message to you in the first place, doctor?'

'I believe it was you, Mrs Channing?'

'Thank you.' Mary sat down again.

Undeterred, Sir John continued with his questioning. 'Did you return again in the morning?'

The doctor nodded. 'I did.'

'And what did you find?'

'Unfortunately Mr Channing's condition had worsened. I tried treating him over the course of the next few days, but he did not respond. The poison had seized his lungs and I informed his father that death was inevitable.'

'How long after that did it take for him to pass?'

'I arrived on the Wednesday.' The doctor did a quick calculation in his head. 'By Saturday his pulse had quickened and he died that evening with a hacking cough, like a rotten sheep.'

Sir John referred back to his notes, turning two pages over before finding what he was looking for. 'I understand you carried out the autopsy. How soon was that after Mr Channing's death?'

'It was the following afternoon, on the Sunday. Mr

Channing's father, Richard Channing, insisted the body be opened.'

'And what did you discover upon opening the body?'

The doctor pulled a face. 'It was not pretty. The bottom of his stomach, lungs and parts of his liver were black. There were also a large number of black spots in his guts.'

There was a gasp in the gallery and Sir John allowed them to fully absorb the information before resuming. 'What do you believe caused the discolouration to the victim's innards?'

'I believe it to be caused by poison. The symptoms described, such as vomiting, delirium and loss of eyesight are all indicative of imbibing mercury. There were also signs of arsenic poisoning, although this had not proved fatal.'

'Arsenic?' Sir John sounded surprised. He had not known of this and there was no mention in his notes.

'Yes. His fingernails in particular indicated he had been taking arsenic over a period of weeks. While this may have been for medicinal purposes, it is likely the build up in his body would have caused some damage in due course.'

'Was this mentioned in the autopsy report?'

'No.' The doctor shook his head.

Sir John raised an eyebrow. 'Why not?'

'Because, while the presence of arsenic could possibly have resulted in the death of Mister Channing in the longer term, it was not the cause of death in this instance. The purpose of the autopsy was to establish the precise cause of death.'

'But you believe he was being systematically poisoned prior to this event?'

'It is probable.' The doctor shrugged. 'But it is not for me to speculate.'

Mary was as surprised as everyone else by this. If Thomas had been taking arsenic for medication, surely she would have known about it. She racked her brains, thinking back over the course of the last few weeks of their time together. She recalled the problems he was having with his stomach and the frequent calls of nature he had to endure. She herself hadn't been affected so hadn't taken too much notice of it, thinking it was just part of his weak demeanour. But the more she thought about it, the more she suspected what had been going on under her nose. Molly had prepared all of their meals, until that fateful day when she herself had made him breakfast. And Molly had insisted on giving him those corn cakes every night, which he loved, but she herself had avoided. Had Molly been lacing his corn cakes with arsenic? Had she been so upset with him and his advantageous actions towards her that she had taken her revenge?

Damn Molly! No wonder she had disappeared. She probably thought it was she who had killed him!

Chapter Forty-Seven

It had taken several minutes for order to be restored to the courtroom as the gallery pounced on the doctor's testimony. No sooner had Judge Price returned everyone to their seats than he called time on the day's proceedings and it erupted again.

The crowd burst on to the streets, pouring into the taverns of Dorchester to discuss the events of the day. Among their number was a young man by the name of Samuel Turner. Dressed smartly in a waistcoat with matching breeches, his white shirt was rolled up at the sleeves and he carried with him a fine leather bag, draped over his shoulder.

He headed towards his lodgings, passing a number of taverns along the way, revelling in the excitement of the crowd. Arriving at his lodgings, he made straight for his room and the small table that was located in the far corner, beneath a small window.

Sweating from the balmy heat that suffocated the room, he opened the window as far as it would go and placed his bag on the table. Samuel then unbuckled the straps on his bag and removed several sheets of paper. They contained a number of notes that he had made throughout the day at the court. Placing them in order, he set a blank sheet of paper to one side, took out a piece of square graphite wrapped in yarn, and began writing, frequently referring to his notes.

A short while later, he had completed his essay. He read it back to himself, occasionally making minor amendments. When he was finally satisfied with the contents, he stood to peer out of the window. A man sat on a large, brown horse was waiting patiently in the street outside. He rolled the paper into a tube, fastened it with twine, then rushed out of his room, down the stairs, and into the street. 'Are you Tom?' he enquired.

'Yes.' The rider responded, leaning forward to grab the paper tube. Settling himself back in his saddle, the horseman placed the tube into his saddle bag. 'Is that all?' he asked. Samuel nodded then slapped the horse on the flank. It took off at speed, heading for the City of London, the home of the newly formed daily newspaper, the Daily Courant.

Samuel smiled to himself and put his hand in his pocket. He pulled out two copper coins. 'This calls for a celebration,' he said out loud as he tossed the coins in the air and caught them again. In two days time, on Monday morning, the trial of Mary Channing would be the headline news in London.

Chapter Forty-Eight

Mary was returned to her cell at the County Gaol later on that evening, long after the crowds had dispersed, ignoring the calls and pleas from the other inmates for news as she passed their cells. Tired, hungry and frustrated at how the day's proceedings had unfolded, on arrival at her cell she sat on the bed to eat the cold, greasy gruel that was awaiting her.

Before she was finished, the jailer arrived at the door. 'Mary Channing. You have a visitor!' he called through the small hatch, before inserting the key, turning it and pushing open the door.

Mary sighed, set the inedible gruel to one side and rose wearily as Gabriel stepped into the cell. 'I don't want to see him,' Mary told the jailer immediately.

'No, Mary, wait.' Gabriel implored her, his hands outstretched before him.

The jailer stood in the doorway, blocking them both in the small cell. 'Well?'

Mary hesitated. Her curiosity was piqued. What on earth did Gabriel want? 'I'll see him,' she said, begrudgingly. As soon as the door was closed, she flung herself at Gabriel, hitting him with a flurry of punches to his arms and chest while kicking out at his shins. Gabriel retreated to the wall, trying to grab hold of her arms as he did so. Finally, he managed to get hold of her. Pinning her arms to her side, he pushed her backwards towards the bed. Feeling it behind her, she suddenly felt overcome with tiredness and sat down, a sullen look on her face. Panting heavily, Gabriel pulled up the chair from the table and sat before her.

Without looking up, she said 'Why are you here? Have you come to gloat?'

'No.' He clasped his hands in front of him, his elbows on his knees, leaning forward. 'I came to apologise.'

'What for?'

'For what I said today in court. For not helping you sooner. For not asking for your hand in marriage. For all the wrongs I have done unto you. I am truly sorry.'

Mary shrugged her shoulders. 'Why are you sorry? I've done this to myself. I've allowed it to happen. I've been stupid and selfish and immature. Why should you care, anyway?'

'Don't be like that Mary. You know I used to love you. I would have done anything for you. But what you did was wrong. It doesn't matter how much I loved you. I can't cover you for that.'

'You used to love me,' she repeated glumly. 'But not anymore. You know I would have done anything for you.'

Gabriel fell silent for a moment. 'We are from different sides of the street. Your father would never have allowed us to be together. Besides, you were always off having too much fun. If it hadn't been me, it would have been someone else. And, I suspect it sometimes was.'

Now it was Mary's turn to fall quiet. 'Why did you lie?' she eventually asked.

'When?'

'Today, in court. Why did you say those things?'

'I had to. You know I did. I could have said a whole lot

more as well – and they wanted me to – but I didn't.'

'Like what?' Mary looked up, her eyes flashing.

'About you wanting him dead. About you wanting me to kill him for you.' He stopped, not wanting to cause her more distress. His voice softened. 'Look, you know what they're like. Richard Channing visited the owner of the mill where my father works. He hates you. He wants you to burn at the stake for what you did. The mill owner told my father that if I didn't do as I was told and tell them what they wanted to hear, he would give me a whipping and we would all be thrown out onto the street.'

'I loved you,' Mary said quietly. 'Why couldn't they have just let us be? We weren't doing anything wrong.'

'There was plenty wrong with it, Mary. You know that.' He fell quiet, letting her gather her thoughts. 'Did you do it, Mary?'

She didn't respond. She felt overcome with fatigue. And now she was also feeling emotional. She just wanted to go to sleep and never wake up. Gabriel persisted. 'I need to know, for my own piece of mind.'

'Yes.'

Gabriel's eyes narrowed. 'How? Was it like they said?'

'No. It wasn't like they said. I didn't know what the powder would do. And it wasn't meant for him, it was for me. He wasn't even supposed to eat it.'

'You were going to poison yourself?' Gabriel was incredulous. 'Was it over me?'

Mary shook her head and even gave a small laugh. 'I think you flatter yourself! No, it wasn't over you. Believe it or not, I had long forgotten about you.'

'So why then?'

'Because I was with…' she stopped herself. Then slowly and deliberately she began speaking again. 'I was having problems with my stomach. Women's problems. I spoke with Molly about them and she had a friend who was supposed to help. She told me to use ratsbane but the apothecary didn't have any. So they gave me mercury instead. I didn't know it would have that effect, I swear.

'Anyway, I asked Molly to ask her friend if the mercury could be used and she said it would be fine. So I cooked myself some breakfast and added the powder, only for Thomas to come down and eat it before I could have any. Before I knew it, he was being ill so I threw the rest of it away.'

'So where is Molly and her friend?'

Mary burst into tears. 'I don't know. She disappeared the morning Thomas fell ill. I haven't seen her since.' She looked up. 'Can you find her for me? Bring her here so she can explain everything?'

'I wouldn't know where to start, Mary.'

Crestfallen, Mary stared at the floor again. 'I think you had better leave,' she announced, standing up. Gabriel stood too and replaced the chair under the table. He moved to hug her but she shied away, putting her hands up to deter him. 'Please, don't. You need to go.'

He nodded before banging on the door. They both heard the jailer's shuffling footsteps approaching. 'Can I come and see you again?' Gabriel asked before the door opened.

'If you want.' Mary just wanted to go back to her cell now.

The door opened and Gabriel stepped outside, the jailer closing and locking the door behind him. Mary laid herself down on the bed, curled herself up into a ball and was asleep within minutes.

Gabriel followed the jailer to the prison gates. The jailer held out his hand and Gabriel dropped a penny into it. 'I'll be back tomorrow,' he said.

'Aye,' the jailer said, seeing Gabriel out of the gate and locking it behind him. 'You know where to find me.'

Gabriel smiled to himself as he made his way down the street and into the nearest inn. As he entered, he looked down the row of snugs until he saw the man he was looking for. He slid into his seat and lifted the tankard that was awaiting him.

'Did you get to see her?' Samuel Turner had his pencil at the ready and a clean sheet of paper in front of him.

'I did.'

'What did she say?'

Gabriel began recounting the conversation he'd had with Mary and Samuel began scribbling furiously, keen not to miss anything out. When he'd finished, he hailed the landlord over. 'Another two ales please.' He watched the man make his way back behind the bar and pull two tankards down from the beam above him. 'Do you believe her? About the servant girl Molly and this mystery woman having a hand in it?'

Gabriel shook his head. 'I don't know. But I don't see why she would make it up. She said was going to take the poison for herself. Why would she do that if she knew what she was taking?'

'So who is she? This woman?'

The man returned with their beers. Gabriel waited for him to leave before answering. 'I don't know. But I do know that Mary is keen to find her. She wanted me to do it for her.'

'Well, that makes two of us. See what else you can find out about her and I'll do some digging my end. In the meantime, I want you to go back and see Mary every night and see what she has for me.'

'Fine by me. Just as long as you're paying, I'm happy to do it.'

Samuel knocked back his drink and slammed the tankard back on the table. 'I will meet you here at the same time tomorrow. Until then, see what you can find out about this servant girl and her friend.' He strode out into the street feeling excited. The Mary Channing trial was to be the news story of the year, if not the decade! And now he had the inside line on exactly what Mary Channing was thinking as she went through it.

Chapter Forty-Nine

With Sunday being a day of rest, the trial wasn't due to restart until the following morning. Gabriel visited Mary on Sunday afternoon to see what else she could tell him about the mysterious woman, whom she believed had caused her to inadvertently poison her husband. Much as she tried, Mary was unable to give him any more information other than she believed she had stayed at the lodging house on the corner of East High Street, opposite the grocer shop owned by the Channings.

Having paid the jailer for Mary to remain in the single cell for another night, he made his way back to the mill. He ran into Samuel on the way and passed on what little he had got from Mary. He promised to return to the prison the following evening to get a reaction from her following on from the day's court proceedings.

Following his conversation with Gabriel, Samuel set off on his way out of the town, to a small hamlet located to the east. He had discovered where Molly had lived prior to arriving in Dorchester and was setting off on foot to find her former home.

The warm weather of the previous few days was still holding

firm and he carried his jacket over his shoulder as he strode down the lane, shirt sleeves rolled up, enjoying the sunshine, the warm breeze and the birdsong. He took in large gulps of the country air, revelling in its sweet aroma. It was certainly a far cry from Little Britain in the City of London where he worked for the paper. Launched just four years earlier, the Daily Courant was the nation's first daily news sheet, priding itself on its reporting of current and foreign affairs. Samuel had only recently joined the small band of staff and was anxious to make a name for himself as quickly as possible.

The Mary Channing case had first come to his attention when he had run into two stagecoach drivers who had made the journey from Exeter to London, stopping overnight in Dorchester on the way. The pre-trial had just taken place and the talk was of her attempt to claim bier-right, leading to speculation among the chattering classes that she was a witch – as if murdering her husband of just three months wasn't bad enough!

He tentatively approached the paper's owner, Mr Buckley, with a view to going to Dorchester to cover the trial itself. Buckley was initially dismissive, stating that the case didn't really fall into the paper's remit. But, as the taverns and inns of London began gossiping about the case, Buckley changed his mind, believing there was obviously a market for carrying updates on such salacious behaviour. And so it was that Samuel had found himself headed out of the maelstrom that was London in July, just in time to escape the heat and mayhem of the capital.

After a long walk, Samuel finally arrived at the outskirts of a small village and approached the first house he came to. Knocking on the door of the cob cottage, he stood back and waited for someone to open the door. Within a short while, it creaked open and a young girl opened the door. 'Hello,' said Samuel. 'I am looking for the house where a girl called Molly used to live.'

Without speaking, the girl disappeared back inside the

house leaving Samuel standing on the doorstep. He peered inside the dark interior, which felt cool. He withdrew quickly as the young girl reappeared with a man whom Samuel assumed to be her father as he had the same colour hair, round face and blue eyes. Samuel held out his hand to shake it, but the man just looked at him, keeping his own hands by his sides. 'How can I help you?' he said, his accent thick.

'I was wondering if you know Molly? She used to live around here.'

The man scratched his head. 'Molly? I do know of her. Why?'

'I was wondering where she lived.'

'She hasn't been around here for ages. She left to go and work in town.'

'Oh, I see. Are her parents still here?'

The man nodded. 'Yes.' He pointed at a tiny worker's cottage further down the road. 'They live over there.'

Before Samuel could thank him, he had closed the door shut. 'Charming. Manners of an ox,' he said to the closed door, before turning on his heel and setting off towards the cottage.

He arrived at a small gate, opened it and marched toward the door, his heels crunching on the neatly kept path as he went. Inside a dog barked and he stopped, looking around cautiously. He and dogs had never got on and he had a fear of them after being bitten by one a few years earlier. Having established that one wasn't going to be flying around the corner anytime soon, he approached the door. He raised his knuckle to announce his arrival and it opened on cue. A tall, slim woman with long grey hair stood before him. 'What do you want?' she said rudely.

Thomas held out his hand. Once again it was ignored. Feeling slightly flummoxed, he stammered slightly. 'I-I-I'm looking for M-M-M-Molly.' It was an affliction he'd endured as a child. Strangely, he hadn't suffered with it for some time but the way she was looking at him unnerved him.

'Why?'

'Can I c-c-come in?'

'No. Why are you looking for Molly?'

'I wish to speak with her.'

'Well she isn't here.' The woman went to close the door and Samuel stuck his foot in it to prevent her from doing so. She glared at him.

'M-m-my name is S-S-Samuel.' He swallowed hard. He didn't understand why he was suddenly feeling so nervous. Swallowing again, he steeled himself. 'Is Molly your d-d-daughter?'

The woman nodded, but said nothing, her hand still on the door ready to push it closed.

'I was wondering if you have seen her recently.'

'No. We haven't seen her since she went to work for young Mister Channing.'

'I guess you have heard what has happened to Mister Channing.'

The woman nodded once more. 'Everybody has. Why? What's it got to do with our Molly?'

'Probably nothing. But I was hoping to ask her if she knew what had happened.'

'Well she isn't here, so you can't.' She moved to close the door again.

'Wait! Have you any idea where she is?'

Molly's mother looked at his foot, forcing him to withdraw it from the threshold. 'No. Like I told them officers that came here before, I haven't heard from her at all. Last I heard, she'd gone to London on the coach, not that she had the decency to tell me and John.'

'John?'

'Her father.'

'Did she ever m-m-mention having a f-friend?'

'No. Molly didn't have no friends. She kept herself to

herself and her nose out of everybody else's business.'

The dig wasn't lost on Samuel. 'Oh, I see. Well thank you anyway. You've b-b-b-been a great help.'

'Have I? I doubt that!' She closed the door firmly, leaving Samuel to contemplate a long walk back to Dorchester. On the plus side, he now knew that Molly had gone to London. He would stop off and have a drink at the George where he could talk to the coach drivers who frequented the bar. With any luck, one of them would remember picking Molly up and would know exactly where she had gone.

Chapter Fifty

The court rose as Judge Price entered the room, respectfully returning to their seats only after he had sat down. He briefly glanced at his papers before calling the court into session. He addressed the prosecution, asking them if they had any further witnesses to bring before the court. Sir John rose to tell the Judge that they had no further witnesses.

Judge Price then turned to Mary. 'Mrs Channing, it now falls to you to conduct your defence. Please would you call your first witness.'

Mary stood up. 'Certainly sir. My first witness is Annie White.'

Annie was brought up to the witness box. Looking middle aged and withdrawn, she had to be told several times to speak up as she confirmed her name. Once she was sworn in, Mary stood to speak. 'Miss White, what is your profession?'

'I am a hatter.'

'So you make hats for a living?' Mary had studied the techniques of Sir John and Serjeant Hooper and had decided to adopt their tone and style.'

231

'Yes. That's right.'

'What do you know of mercury powder?'

'We use it in the manufacture of a number of hats. It is used to smooth down the felt. But it has to be used sparingly as it can have some side effects – ones which affect the mind.'

'Affect the mind?'

'Yes. It can cause you to go mad.' She looked at the gallery. 'This is why we say "mad as a hatter".' She smiled.

'And you think it is caused by the mercury?'

'Yes, I do. Although the owner of the shop where I work won't have it. He reckons it don't do you any harm. But I know it is the mercury. It can't be anything else.'

The gallery began murmuring. It was a well-known occupational hazard for hatters and the phrase was in common use.

Mary nodded as well. 'Do many people die from their exposure to mercury?'

'Yes. We've had a fair few at our place.' Annie looked at the judge who was observing her, taking in every word. 'Usually, after the madness, comes the illness and then death. It can take days or it may take months. But it always gets you in the end.'

'And do they eat the mercury?' Mary was getting to the point of her argument.

Annie shook her head, smiling. 'No, of course not.'

'So how does the mercury get into their system.'

'Through touch and through breathing in the powder I would imagine.' Excited whispering could be heard coming from the gallery. Sir John and Serjeant Hooper conferred with each other.

Mary glanced at them, feeling confident. 'So tell me, what do you know about the death of Mister Channing?'

Annie looked nervous again. 'Not much. Only that I heard he was handling the mercury before he fell ill.'

'So you are saying that it is possible he didn't eat the

mercury. Instead, he held it in his hands and this is the most probable cause of his death.'

'I reckon so. You don't have to eat it to fall ill, not in my experience.'

Mary looked triumphant. 'Thank you Annie.' She took her seat.

The judge looked across at the two barristers. 'Any questions, gentlemen?'

Serjeant Hooper slowly stood up while Sir John reclined in his chair, his arms crossed, a smug look on his face. 'Yes my Lord.' He addressed Annie while looking down at his notes. 'Have you ever worked in an apothecary?'

Annie shook her head. 'No sir.'

'And do you still work as a hatter?'

'No sir.'

Hooper looked up. 'No? Why is that?'

Annie looked at Mary, then looked down at the floor, shamefaced. 'I lost my job.'

'You lost your job.' Serjeant Hooper looked at the jury before returning his attentions to her. 'And why did you lose your job?'

'It was a misunderstanding. I didn't do it!' Annie exclaimed.

'Do what exactly?'

Annie lowered her voice again. 'Take the money.'

'That's right.' Hooper was smirking. 'You were accused of stealing some money from your employer. Tell me, what happened after you were caught with the money?'

'I was sent to the County Gaol.'

Hooper looked down at his notes again, making a show of finding the right piece of information. 'That's correct. You were sent to the County Gaol, right here in Dorchester. For three months. Tell me, when did you get out?'

'Not long ago.' Annie looked at Mary again, shaking her head.

'Let me remind you exactly when you were released.' He put his finger on his paper as if emphasizing what he was about to say was true. 'July the tenth. Just under three weeks ago, in fact.' Annie said nothing so Hooper continued. 'Is that where you first met Mrs Channing? In Dorchester County Gaol?'

Annie glanced at Mary again. 'Yes.'

'And is that where you first spoke about the effects of mercury on members of your, erm, profession.' He put extra emphasis on the last word, his tone one of disdain.

'We may have spoken about it. I can't remember.'

Hooper looked up at Judge Price while still talking to Annie. 'I put it to you that it is where you first spoke to Mrs Channing about the effects of mercury and that she, seizing upon an opportunity to discredit the doctor who treated and diagnosed the cause of death of Mister Channing, concocted this cock and bull story about how the victim accidentally killed himself by handling the mercury – the same mercury that Mrs Channing herself admits that she purchased! What say you now?' He looked triumphant.

'That's not how it was,' Annie said, her voice small once more.

'So how was it, exactly?'

Annie said nothing, glancing nervously around the court room before putting her head down and staring at the floor.

'No further questions, my Lord.' Hooper sat down, looking pleased with himself.

Disheartened, Annie was led from the court.

Mary called a number of other witnesses throughout the rest of the session, all of whom provided alternative explanations for how Mr Channing may have come to be poisoned, but the damage was done. When there was no one left to call, the Judge congratulated Mary on her professional and spirited defence before summing up for the jury.

'Mary Channing has been accused of the most heinous

of crimes, that of petty treason, by poisoning her husband of just thirteen weeks. Before considering your verdict, you must take into account three things. Firstly, that Thomas Channing did indeed die by poisoning. Secondly, that the poison was administered with the knowledge and contrivance of the accused. And thirdly, and perhaps most importantly, that it had been administered in the expectation of causing the death of Thomas Channing.'

With that, the judge retired to his chambers while the jury retired to a large room to consider their verdict. Inside the courtroom, the gallery drew their own conclusions and wagers were struck while Mary Channing was left to contemplate her future, still sat in the dock.

Chapter Fifty-One

The jury of twelve men took just half an hour to return to the courtroom to give their decision. The judge took his seat before them, told Mary to stand, and asked them to deliver their verdict.

'Guilty!' the chairman of the jury announced loudly, a sneer on his lined face.

The gallery erupted while Mary remained standing, bolt upright, her faced fixed in a look of stoic defiance. She gripped on to the iron bar in front of her, her knuckles turning white with the effort. Inside, her stomach was churning. Even though she had resigned herself to being found guilty, the words of the judge regarding her vigorous defence had given her some cause for hope. Judge Price looked sad as he lifted up the piece of black cloth before him and placed it on top of his powdered wig.

'Mary Channing. You have been found guilty of the charges laid before you, that of petty treason, specifically that of murdering your husband by poisoning him. I therefore have no other option than to sentence you to death. You will be taken from this place and burnt at the stake.' The crowd gasped, with a few women screaming out 'No!'

The judge waited for the commotion to subside before continuing. 'Do you have anything to say?' He looked gravely at Mary who was still gripping on to the bar to support herself.

She looked around the court, hoping to see her parents or even Gabriel, but she couldn't spot a friendly face anywhere. She looked back at the judge, then down at her stomach. Raising her head, she spoke loudly. 'Yes sir. I would like to plead the belly!'

Once again there was uproar as the crowd began shouting and catcalling. The judge banged hard with his gavel as he struggled to regain order. Finally, after several minutes, calm was restored and the judge looked sternly at Mary. 'You wish to plead the belly?'

'Yes, sir. For I am with child.' She placed her hands on her stomach for good effect. Only that morning she believed she had felt the baby inside her for the first time, although it could have just been nervous apprehension in advance of the day's events.

'Very well.' The judge conferred briefly with his assistant and called the two barristers to approach the bench. 'Gentlemen,' he said. 'I have no alternative than to delay the carrying out of sentence.'

Sir John responded. 'My Lord. But of course. Could I respectfully request that the necessary checks be carried out?' The pleading of the belly was a constant thorn in the side of the prosecution, with women regularly claiming they were with child when, in fact, they were merely delaying the carrying out of their sentence while hoping to receive a pardon.

Judge Price nodded. 'I will arrange for a jury of matrons to examine her. I will then let you know of their findings. If the child inside her has not yet quickened, then sentence may yet be carried out without delay. I will order the Sheriff to make the necessary arrangements for the examination and decide accordingly.'

Both barristers bowed, before returning to their table to

gather up their papers. Judge Price addressed Mary. 'I will offer you a stay of execution while the facts of your condition are confirmed. The sheriff will organise for a jury of matrons to meet with you just as soon as it can be arranged.'

Richard Channing, who had been observing the proceedings with a degree of satisfaction until Mary had pleaded the belly jumped to his feet. The magistrate pulled him back down again. 'Shush, he implored. Please remain quiet and let justice be served. She will be examined and, should she be with child, she will be reprieved only until she has given birth. If she is lying, then the sentence will be carried out immediately.'

'But what if she is carrying my son's child – my grandchild?' Richard looked flabbergasted.

'Then the necessary arrangements will be made for the child to be handed over to you as soon as it is born, should you wish to receive it.'

Channing looked across at Mary who had been observing him. She quickly turned away from his gaze. He shouted across to her. 'You shall have my son's child and I shall take it from you. You will never get to hold it. You will never get to know it. And I shall bring it up as my own in memory of my son!' He shook his fist at her for good measure as she was escorted past him, down the stairs and outside where she was shackled. She then began the short walk back to her prison cell with the officers either side of her. As she once again ran the gauntlet of the angry mob that lined the street, she afforded herself the faintest of smiles. She had cheated the executioner – at least for now.

Chapter Fifty-Two

'Is it mine?'

Mary was lost in her thoughts. If she told Gabriel the child was his, then he would no doubt tell the world and maybe even lay claim to it. Her fate as an adulteress who had then proceeded to kill her husband would be sealed. There was no need to mention that Nial could also be the father. Mary's only real option was to tell Gabriel that it was Thomas's child.

'Mary, I need to know. Is it mine?'

She smiled sadly at him. There was a time, not that long ago, when he was her world. While her father may have put paid to her dreams of marrying him, the events of the last few weeks had proven that Gabriel would never have been right for her. He couldn't have provided for her, not to the same level she had been brought up to expect. He would have quickly spent the dowry on offer for marrying her. And then, when it was all gone, he would have turned to her to obtain more money. Gabriel was weak, immature and prone to fits of anger if he could not get his own way. And he could never have tamed her. Mary knew she would have soon tired of him. She shook her head.

'No, the child is not yours.'

Gabriel looked as if he was about to burst into tears and raised a fist to strike her. He hesitated as she glared up at him, her eyes suddenly full of fire. Lowering his arm, he retreated to the wall behind him, his eyes welling up with tears.

'What did you expect, Gabriel?' Mary spoke softly. 'You made it perfectly clear that we could not have a future together. I can see that now and I was a fool for ever believing otherwise.'

Gabriel nodded, reconciling himself to what he knew was true. 'I'm sorry Mary. You are right. So the child is by Thomas?'

'You need to ask?' Mary was tired of lying.

'I don't believe you.'

Mary sighed. 'It doesn't really matter what you believe anymore. But for my sake, and perhaps even that of your own, it would be best if you kept that thought to yourself. As far as I am concerned, the child is Thomas's.'

There was a knock on the door. The jailer pushed it open. 'They are ready for you.'

Mary followed him out of the door. The jailer put his arm across Gabriel's chest as he made to follow. 'Not you.'

He directed her to a cell along the corridor. Larger than the one used for her own confinement, twelve women of varying ages were awaiting her inside. The jailer stepped in behind her, only to be told in no uncertain terms that he was not welcome and that he was to leave. He closed the door but remained at the window, a lustful look on his face. Unable to force him to leave, one of the matrons removed her apron and held it up to the small hatch to prevent him from seeing. Eventually, realizing that he would be unable to witness proceedings, the jailer shuffled off back along the corridor to his quarters.

After checking to make sure the jailer had gone, the women turned to face Mary. 'Please undress,' one of them told her. Realising that there was no dignity to be preserved in the procedure, Mary removed her dress, leaving her standing in just a chemise and petticoat. Four of the women squeezed at her breasts and her stomach, making mutterings as they did so.

'When did you last have your bleed?' one of them asked.

Mary had worked it out beforehand. 'I have missed five cycles.'

Two of the women looked at each other. 'I should have thought you would be bigger by now should that be true.'

Mary shrugged. 'Perhaps my time here has stunted the baby's growth,' she offered by way of explanation.

'Perhaps.' A fifth woman stepped forward. 'Lay down on the bed.'

Mary did as she was told. There was more squeezing of her stomach and they raised her chemise to examine her more closely. 'It is certainly swollen,' one of the women said. 'And her breasts feel full.' Her chemise was pulled down to reveal them. 'There is a browning too,' said another, pointing at her nipples. Mary felt as if she were a cow being sold at auction. But her ordeal was not yet over. Her legs were spread and one by one they peered up her petticoat, prodding at her. 'She is no longer a virgin,' one offered, causing some bawdy laughter. 'I would hope not!' another cackled 'for she was married! What kind of man would not exercise his rights on his wedding night, especially with this pretty one!'

More cackling ensued. Pulling her petticoat back down over her knees, they beckoned for Mary to get to her feet and get dressed. 'Have you felt it yet, inside you? one asked. Mary nodded. 'Only this very morning,' she replied. They conferred briefly before agreeing that Mary was definitely with child.

They gathered together at the door, their examination over. 'You may yet delay your fate, young lady. Jailer!'

The jailer returned, a glint in his eye, giving Mary cause to wonder if he had actually been able to watch her humiliating examination. She pushed it to the back of her mind for it no longer mattered. If he had a mind to, he could do whatever he wanted to her in prison and there was no longer anyone who would be prepared to stand up for her.

Chapter Fifty-Three

Samuel Turner unfurled the news sheet and studied his handiwork with a degree of satisfaction. Mary's trial was the lead story on the front of the Daily Courant, which had just been delivered by the messenger. The man was still sat on horseback, awaiting payment.

He tossed the messenger a coin, then handed him another tightly rolled paper tube. The messenger pocketed the money before placing the tube in his pouch and setting off again at speed, back towards London. Sitting down at a table placed outside in the garden, Samuel read the piece again, fascinated at seeing his own name and words in print.

He knew that the story was going to run for at least another two days. Tomorrow's edition would carry the events of that day's trial, with the sentencing forming the headline. He had left out the sensational news about Mary being with child. That would be the story for the following day and he was looking forward to his meeting with Gabriel when he hoped to learn the identity of the father. The Daily Courant prided itself on only reporting the facts, so he would have to present it as such, not as mere speculation. Not that the good people of London would care much about who the father really was, for they would happily form their own opinions. But they would have to wait for his next exclusive.

Samuel knew that by day three the story would have run its course and would be relegated to a small paragraph at the foot of the page. But no matter, for he had arrived in Fleet Street!

He checked his pocket watch. It was time for him to make his way up the hill to the Antelope where he had arranged to meet with Gabriel. He didn't particularly like the young man. He was full of his own bravado, boastful of his relationship with Mary and his exploits. While Samuel had no real feelings either way as to Mary Channing, he was quickly coming to the opinion that Gabriel had undoubtedly helped bring about her downfall.

He neatly creased and folded up his copy of the Courant then placed it in his pocket. He set off at a pace, keen to taste his first ale of the day. The sun was on its downward trend and was like a giant orange fireball in the sky. Judging by the sunset, the next day would bring more of the hot, balmy weather.

As he opened the door to the Antelope, he was hit by a wall of noise. The bar was full, everybody crammed in, shoulder to shoulder. He pushed his way through the crowd, apologising as he moved through the mass of bodies, knocking drinks and banging elbows. He finally managed to force his way to the bar and tried in vain to catch the attention of the serving girl who was struggling to keep up with demand. All around everybody was discussing the trial, the sentence of death that had been passed and, of course, the final shocking twist when Mary had declared she was with child.

After what seemed an age, the girl finally paused in front of him and asked what he wanted to drink. He ordered two ales and she quickly poured them from the barrel on the stand behind her. Dropping two pennies on the counter, he picked up the beers and worked out the best route back through the crowd before finding his way to the table where he expected Gabriel to be waiting for him.

After more banging of elbows and spilling of drinks, he arrived at his destination. Gabriel was sitting there, staring into his tankard, looking glum. Samuel sat down opposite him, pushing a fresh ale across the table. 'Penny for your thoughts?'

Gabriel ignored him, instead picking up the fresh tankard of ale. He drank thirstily, before slamming down the vessel and wiping his mouth on his sleeve. He stared out of the window as Samuel studied him. Eventually, Gabriel turned to face him. 'I can't believe it,' he said.

Samuel waited, still saying nothing.

Gabriel took another slug of ale. He slammed the tankard down on the table again. 'I really thought it was mine. All the things she said to me. She lied. She lied to me all along. All the time she said she only wanted me, she was laying with him.'

Samuel stayed silent but he his attention was at its height. 'Him?'

'Yes. Him!' Gabriel fell silent again.

'I see.' Samuel was already rewriting the headline in his head. 'So who, exactly, is him?'

'Her husband. Thomas Channing. I mean, how could she?'

Samuel was intrigued. 'Why would she fall with child by her husband and then murder him?' he asked.

Gabriel shrugged his shoulders. 'I dunno. Maybe because she wanted it all, but without him. Don't ask me. I've never understood women.'

Samuel suddenly realized what Gabriel had said earlier. 'You thought it was yours?'

'Yes.' Gabriel nodded, absent-mindedly, staring out of the window again.

'So you had relations with her.' It was a statement more than a question.

Gabriel suddenly realized what he had said. He tried to

backtrack. 'No. I just thought that she wanted a child with me. We had talked about it. But she wanted Thomas out of the way first.'

This was something that hadn't come out of the trial. 'So she told you she wanted him dead?'

'Yes.'

'Did she tell you how she was going to do it?'

'No.'

'Did she ask you to do it for her?'

Gabriel hesitated once more, knowing that he had already said too much. The last thing he wanted was to implicate himself in Thomas Channing's death. He leaned forward, lowering his voice so nobody could hear him, although with the volume of noise going on around, it would have been highly unlikely. 'Look, I don't want any of this coming out, right?'

Samuel nodded. 'That's fine. Tell me what happened.' He gave Gabriel his most concerned look as reassurance.

'She asked me to kill him. I said no, of course. But she kept going on about it. Then she started giving me gifts, such as the pocket watch. I never asked for it. She also kept giving me money. She was stealing it from Thomas. And then she asked me once more if I would kill him so we could be together.'

'So what did you say the second time?'

'I said no, of course! I'm no murderer!'

'I see.' This was confirmation as far as Samuel was concerned that Mary Channing had deliberately set out to kill her husband. 'Meanwhile, you were having relations with her.'

'Yes. We used to meet up whenever we could. She couldn't get enough of me,' Gabriel said, boastfully. 'Which is why I thought the child was mine. There was this one instance when we got carried away and...' Gabriel drifted away, sitting back and staring once more out the window.

'You don't believe her, do you? About Thomas being the father.'

'No. She despised him. She ridiculed him, saying he was deformed and that she would never lie with him. I am sure that the child is mine. It has to be!'

Samuel smiled to himself. So Mary Channing really was an adulteress as well as a murderess. And it was obvious that, as far as Gabriel was concerned, he was the father of Mary's unborn child. Samuel had no reason to disbelieve him. Mary was lying about Thomas Channing being the father. After all, she had declared that she despised him! What Gabriel had just told him was pure gold. His editor would love this! As would the readers of the Daily Courant.

Chapter Fifty-Four

On the Friday following the end of the trial, the jailer came to Mary's cell and announced that she had a visitor. When the door opened, Mary was surprised by her mother coming into the cell. Bursting into tears, she collapsed into her mother's arms. Her mother held her for a while before squeezing her arms and pushing her back. 'How are you?' she asked.

Mary gave a small laugh. 'Isn't that obvious?'

Her mother grinned. 'I suppose so. A silly question really. I'm sorry.' She paused, briefly. 'Are you really with child?'

Mary nodded. 'Yes.'

'Is it…?'

Mary nodded again. 'Thomas's? Yes.' She knew she had caused her parents enough harm without adding to their burden of having an illegitimate child in the family as well.

Her mother looked relieved. 'I see. Good. That's something. I suppose.'

An awkward silence fell between them. Eventually Mrs Brookes spoke. 'Your father is doing everything he can to help you.'

'Is he? I would have thought he would wish he was well

251

rid of me.'

'Yes, well. That's as maybe, but you are still our daughter. He has written to Queen Anne asking her to grant a pardon in your case. At the very least she may commute your sentence, especially as you are now with child.'

Mary's face brightened. 'Really? The Queen?'

'Yes. We also believe – although, of course, he will not confirm it – that you impressed Judge Price with your defence. He may well be moved to grant a circuit pardon.'

Mary raised an eyebrow. 'What's that?'

'I'm not really sure, but according to your father at the end of each circuit, the judge can put forward those he feels worthy of a second chance. Apparently, you made quite an impression on him and he is not entirely convinced of your guilt.'

Mary wasn't so sure. She remembered his harsh eyes, grey and unfeeling that seemed to bore into her, as if reading her very soul. But, then again, he had encouraged her and guided her through her defence, so maybe he did have a heart. 'So you think there may be a chance at redemption? Even for someone like me?'

Her mother pulled her close and hugged her again. 'Of course! You are just a girl. Young and impetuous, a little bit silly and prone to fall in love. But that is only normal. And you come from a respectable family so there is every chance that Judge Price, or the Queen herself, may be moved to look favourably upon your case. Particularly as you are with child, and especially if that child is Thomas's. How can they not look kindly upon you?' She pushed her back slightly again to look into her eyes. 'Mr Hutchins has also resolved to help you after speaking with your father.'

'Who is Mr Hutchins?' Mary was bemused.

'Mr Hutchins! The Reverend, here at the jail! Have you not been to see him at all since you have been here?' Mrs Brookes tutted her annoyance.

'Oh, him. Yes, on occasion. But I didn't know his name.

Why would he help me?'

'He has said he wants to save your soul and that you are worthy of spiritual redemption. But you must assist him in this.'

'How am I to do that?'

'You must attend his services at every opportunity. He has also offered to provide personal tuition on the ways of the Holy Lord. You must promise to make yourself available to him whenever he requests it. Do you understand child?'

Mary did understand. She now remembered who Mr Hutchins was and his reputation within the walls of the prison were little better than that of the jailer himself, particularly when it came to young women. Still, if it meant she could receive a pardon, it would be worth it. 'Yes, mother. I will try my best.'

'Good. Because your life depends on it. Now I must leave soon. Your father will continue to pay for your new chamber to stay in while we await news of your pardon. Please do everything you can to assist with his endeavours. Now give me a hug.'

They embraced one more time before her mother pulled apart and knocked on the door. The jailer opened it immediately and Mary fancied he had been listening at the door throughout.

Mary waited patiently for his return. Within a few minutes, he arrived to take her back to her new cell. There, on the table, were a number of religious books along with a note from the Reverend John Hutchins to read every one of them and await his visit later that evening. She shuddered, fearing that she knew exactly what was going to happen to her.

Chapter Fifty-Five

Richard Channing was incandescent with rage. His wife watched him as he paced up and down the room, ranting and raving. She remained silent, knowing that to say something could see him turn on her.

'A pardon? From the Queen? How dare they? Who do they think they are, that their daughter can kill my son and then get off scot free, on account of her carrying his child? It's completely preposterous!'

The news had reached him just minutes before, brought by messenger from Sir John Darnell. The barrister had thought it prudent to let Mr Channing know before he learnt it through gossip or read it in The Dorchester and Sherborne Journal.

Channing slapped the back of his hand on the piece of parchment, causing his wife to jump. 'There is even talk of the judge recommending her for clemency, so taken was he with her at the trial. How could he?' He sank into a chair, suddenly overcome with exhaustion, putting his fingers to his temple and rubbing it. 'My head feels as if it will burst,' he grumbled.

Mrs Channing felt now was the time to speak up. 'So what

are you going to do about it?'

'What do you mean, "do about it"?' He didn't look up.

'If you feel so strongly about it and you honestly believe she could receive a pardon, then you need to start thinking about what you can do about it. Before it goes too far.'

Channing leant forward on the chair. With his elbows on his knees, he straightened the parchment between his hands and read it once more. He rose as he read, and began walking back and forth once more. 'You are right. I need to act fast.' His face brightened as he began to think. 'I shall raise my own petition. I am far better connected than that upstart Brookes. I shall go to the Queen myself and demand a fair representation of the case be provided to her, one that doesn't paint over the truth and demands clemency on account of the Brookes girl being with child.'

Mrs Channing smiled. 'That's more like it. You should be able to nip this in the bud and demand that justice is served for our son.'

With his face returning to something like its normal colour, Channing bent over and kissed his wife on the forehead. 'Thank you. You have made me see sense and given me cause to act quickly to right this wrong.' He yelled for his manservant. 'Ready my horse at once!' He turned back to his wife, a grin on his face. 'I shall go to see the magistrate immediately and then I will set off for London. Once I am there I shall easily be able to garner enough support to ensure Mary Brookes gets exactly what she deserves!'

Chapter Fifty-Six

Samuel Buckley sidestepped the horse and carriage that was heading to West Smithfield and continued on his own short journey to his office in Little Britain. A horse was tethered just outside the door to the railing, its flank heavy with sweat. He smiled to himself, knowing that it had carried the messenger with the next report from young Samuel Tyler, with further news of the Channing trial. While he considered himself above news stories such as this, his newspaper had seen sales soar and businesses enquiring as to the availability of advertising space. In short, Mary Channing was good for business.

He took the stairs two at time, finding the messenger in his office. He snatched the paper tube and tossed the horseman a coin before waving him away. He rounded his large desk and sat down behind it, unfurling the paper and putting weights on each corner to hold it flat. Taking a magnifying glass from his drawer, he leant over and began reading young Tyler's prose. Noting the remarks about the disappearing maid and her mystery friend, he quickly got to the end. "GUILTY!" His face sported a big grin as he sat back, picturing the headline.

MARY CHANNING TO BE BURNT AT THE STAKE

Dipping his quill into the inkwell set in his desk, he scribbled a few notes in the margins of Tyler's report before summoning the clerk from the room next door. 'Take this at once to the setters and tell them it is to be the lead in tomorrow's issue.' His own story, about the Treaty ratifying the Union between England and Scotland, would be reduced to a single paragraph near the bottom of the page.

Once the clerk had gone, he rose and went to the walnut cabinet that sat in the far corner. Picking up the decanter, he poured himself a large brandy and toasted Mary Channing. He had no idea who she was, or where she had come from, but her fate was sealed and it was going to make him an even richer man.

He finished his drink and decided to take lunch at his club in nearby Aldersgate. He would return to the print-works afterwards to see how the publication of the newspaper was going and check its contents for errors before giving the printer permission to proceed. He also needed to see how much paper they had in stock. With demand far in excess of supply, he was keen to increase the amount being printed.

As he entered the cool and dark interior of the club, he could hear lots of murmurings in the main room. He removed his hat and gave it to the doorman, along with his cane. He entered the room and noted his usual table was available by the large window overlooking the garden to the rear of the property. Making his way to it, he saw a group of men surrounding a short, stocky individual, who was looking quite flustered.

He ignored them as they concluded their business with the gentleman and returned to their various tables. Buckley gave his order to the servant who scurried off to the kitchen to prepare it. As he sat back, the man he had noticed in the centre of the small mêlée approached him. 'Sir, may I speak with you briefly?'

Buckley nodded. 'Certainly, sir. '

The man pulled out the chair beside Buckley. 'May I?'

'You may indeed. What is it you wish to discuss?'

The gentleman sat down and presented a piece of parchment, unrolling it and setting it down on the table. 'My name is Richard Channing and I am seeking to raise a petition to put before the Queen.'

Buckley could not believe his luck. 'I believe I have heard of you. My sincere condolences for your loss.'

'Thank you, Mister…?'

'Buckley.' He held out his hand and Channing pumped it eagerly. 'Samuel Buckley. Now how can I be of service?'

Channing ran his hand across the paper. 'As I said, I am seeking to raise a petition to put before the Queen and I am hoping you will support it.'

Buckley cast his eyes over it, noting a number of names, many of which he recognized as being men of influence and power. 'And what are you hoping to achieve with this petition?'

'Well, as you have heard, my son was poisoned by his wife of just thirteen weeks. Her father, a man by the name of Brookes, is presently trying to obtain a pardon for his daughter from the Queen.'

'I see.' Buckley steepled his fingers in front of him. 'And the reason for your petition?'

'My wish is to see that she is not pardoned and that her sentence is carried out as soon as possible.'

Buckley smiled. This would add to his story, sell more newspapers and see more advertisers flock to him. 'Of course. It would be my pleasure. Now tell me, where do I sign?'

Chapter Fifty-Seven

The tall, lithe figure of Reverend Hutchins, Clergyman of Dorchester Gaol, arrived at the door to Mary's cell. 'I shall be a while, so do not hurry back.'

The jailer smirked. 'Of course not, sir. Take as much time as you want.' He turned the key in the lock and opened the door, stepping aside so that Hutchins could enter. He closed the door behind him and peaked through the window. He noted with an element of glee that Mary looked alarmed at the sight of her visitor.

As the jailer's footsteps faded, Hutchins approached Mary who rose from her bed. He picked up one of the books he had left on the table. 'Have you been reading any of the books I left for you?'

Mary shook her head. 'I have not yet had an opportunity, sir.'

'I see.' A sneer appeared on his face. 'If you are to find spiritual redemption, you must do exactly as I tell you. I am disappointed that you have not yet begun your lessons.' He suddenly struck Mary with the back of his hand, catching her full on the cheek. She fell backwards, clutching at her face.

'Now sit up straight, and let us begin.' Mary did as she was told, her cheek smarting. She rubbed it in an effort to soothe the pain. Hutchins opened the book he was holding and scanned it, seeking the right passage. 'Ah, yes. This is the one. *Holy Living and Holy Dying*. This book will provide you with instruction on leading a virtuous life. It will also give you the instruments required to prepare for a blessed death, should you fail to reach the standard required for me to intervene on your behalf. Now, read this passage while I pray for you and give you your first lesson in morality.' He handed her the book and knelt before her, his hands on her knees, his head bowed.

Mary looked down at the pages, her legs trembling slightly. She began 'But so have I seen a Rose newly springing from the clefts of its hood, and at first...' She felt his hands move down her legs to the hem of her dress. '... it was fair, as the Morning, and full with the dew of Heaven, as a Lamb's fleece...' she gasped slightly as she felt his hands go up under her dress, touching her skin, lightly stroking her calves. She instinctively clamped her knees together.

'Continue,' Hutchins murmured, his head down, his eyes shut and his breathing heavy. He continued to gently stroke the backs of her legs. Mary closed her eyes briefly before opening them once more, forcing herself to read on.

'... but when a ruder breath had forced open its virgin modesty, and dismantled its too youthful –' she gasped out loud as she felt his hands between her knees, roughly forcing her legs apart. She tried to close them again, but he would not let her.

'Stay still girl,' he instructed, his head still bowed, not looking at her, his hands now moving over her thighs, lightly rubbing them up and down. 'Now, go on. Read the passage through until you reach the end, without stopping.'

She tried to block out all feelings as she felt his hands roaming under her dress, moving further up the inside of her thighs, forcing her legs yet wider. She looked for the point where she had finished on the page. 'Youthful and unripe retirements, it began to put on a darkness, and to incline its softness, and the symptoms of a sickly age...' Mary flinched as she felt his fingers probing inside her, her back straightening, trying desperately to blank out what was happening to her. She quickened her reading. 'It bowed the head, and broke its stalk and, at night, having lost some of its leaves, and all of its beauty, it fell into the portion of weeds and outworn faces.'

Hutchins suddenly groaned and slumped to the ground before her, removing his hands from beneath her dress and returning to his groin where he clasped them together, as if in prayer. She leapt to her feet and stood by the door as he remained kneeling, his head bowed and his eyes closed. Tremors appeared to be running intermittently through his body. She regarded him from afar as he continued shaking and mumbling to himself. Finally, he gathered his composure and stood up. Mary saw the stain on the front of his frock and felt disgusted with herself.

Without looking at her, Hutchins gestured for her to retake her position on the bed. 'I fear you have a long way to go, child. Your responses are not those of a woman of virtue and I cannot recommend you to God if you do not control yourself and your urges.'

Mary knew it was pointless arguing with him. To do so would only cause him to strike her again. He reached up and drew another book from the table. He opened it, flicking through the pages, looking for a relevant passage. Handing the book to her, Mary sat back down on the bed. Feeling miserable, she steadied herself. As she did so, Hutchins closed his eyes and bowed his head once more, reaching up under her dress. Mary felt his hands on her knees again. She closed her eyes, counted to ten, opened them and began reading.

Chapter Fifty-Eight

The sound of the choir singing subsided, to be replaced by the muffled exultations of the Archbishop. Richard Brookes hung around outside the Chapel Royal in the grounds of St James's Palace waiting for the morning service to be over. Finally, the doors were flung open by two footmen, resplendent in gold and red, and Queen Anne herself came into view from within.

The small crowd cheered and waved as she gracefully descended the steps into the cold, autumnal morning. Her handmaids followed, holding her dress up at the rear to prevent it from getting wet and muddy as she made her way back to the Palace.

'My lady! My Queen! Please! I must speak with you!' Brookes shouted as she passed by. Undaunted, Brookes pushed back through the crowd and ran to get ahead of the Queen. Reappearing further down the line, he frantically waved his sheet of paper at her. She ignored him at first and the two footmen tried to stand between him and their monarch as he appeared at the front of the assembled crowd once more. 'My Queen! I beg of you, please!' The desperation in his voice was all too apparent.

The Queen stopped, half turned and stared at him. She motioned to one of her handmaids to go to him and ask what it was he wanted. 'My daughter is to be executed but she is with child' he said, hurriedly. 'I beg of the Queen to show mercy.' The handmaid returned to the Queen and whispered urgently in her ear. She looked at Brookes, sizing him up and down. Smartly dressed, with polished boots, he didn't look like the father of a girl who had been sentenced to death. She said something back to the handmaid who quickly returned to Brookes. The Queen continued on her way with her entourage, completing the short walk to St James's Palace.

'Will she receive me?' Brookes pleaded as the young girl arrived in front of him. Nearby onlookers crowded in to hear her answer.

'She will. I am to take you to the Palace where you will await her.'

Brookes was allowed to step out of the crowd into the thoroughfare and followed the young girl as she hurried back to the Palace. With her dress reaching the floor, it was as if she was gliding along. Brookes, even with his athletic build and long legs, struggled to keep up with her.

They swept into the courtyard and he was shown to a side door. A modest room awaited him and he was told to be seated. A guard stood by the door into the main residence with a pike in his hand. He pointedly ignored Brookes who was trying to gather his thoughts.

It had been his wife's idea to approach the Queen in person. As friends and associates turned their backs on him and as his business interests began waning, the family was becoming increasingly desperate and frustrated at the lack of progress. Their finances were also coming under pressure, to the point where they were contemplating sending Mary back into the general prison population as they could no longer afford the bribes and the fees the jailer was charging for Mary's cell and extra food.

After what felt like an age, the door opened and the handmaid appeared. 'You may come now.' She turned smartly on her heel and he had to sprint to catch her up. He followed her down a long corridor, overlooking a perfectly manicured courtyard with a fountain in the middle. Finally, they both arrived at a large, formidable oak door with iron studs. Two guards stood outside, one either side. Without acknowledging them, the maid pushed through and ushered him in.

Queen Anne was sat before him. She had changed into another dress and had wrapped a blue, ermine trimmed gown around her. Her long brown hair had been plaited at the back and hung down over her left shoulder. Her face was masculine, yet attractive. Brookes didn't quite know what to do, never having been in front of royalty before, let alone the Queen of England. He shuffled to a point before her and bowed, not looking up, waiting for instruction.

After a brief silence, the Queen spoke. 'What is your name?'

Brookes stood up straight but continued to look down at the floor, fearing what would happen if he dared to look her in the eye. 'Richard Brookes, my lady.'

'And the name of your daughter?'

'Mary Brookes, my lady.'

'I see. Is she not also known as Mary Channing?'

Brookes stiffened. The Queen had heard of her. Perhaps she had received his petition after all. 'That is correct my lady.'

'I understand that she poisoned her husband.'

'She was found guilty of poisoning him, my lady, and has been sentenced to death.'

'I see.' The Queen pulled her gown closer to her shoulders and held it tight at her throat. The air was chilly in the large room and the fire had not been lit as her presence had not been expected in it. 'So why would you have me grant a pardon in this instance?'

Brookes had rehearsed his speech many times and he hoped his memory would not fail him as the nerves took over. 'Mary is but a child, my lady. It was a marriage of my making, a decision I bitterly regret now for her husband was not right for her.'

The Queen held up her hand. 'Did her husband beat her?'

'Not to my knowledge, my lady. I believe her husband was an honourable man.'

'So why did she poison him.'

'I am not sure that she did, my lady.'

Queen Anne raised an eyebrow. 'But a jury of her peers found her guilty.'

'I know my lady. But her servant girl disappeared on the morning of his death and I have cause to believe that maybe it was she who did it, perhaps with the aid of an accomplice.'

'Why would the servant girl have cause to poison her master?'

'Because he was being brutal with her.'

She pursed her lips. 'Brutal?'

'Yes my lady.'

'And yet you say you believed the husband to be an honourable man.'

Brookes felt as if he had tripped himself up. This was not how he had rehearsed it in his mind. 'I did say that my lady. And I believe he was honourable with my daughter. But my understanding is that he was not honourable with his servant.'

'But you have no proof.'

Brookes stared hard at the ground again. 'No. But I know my daughter and I am convinced she would not have done this. She is a kind and virtuous girl. She may not have loved her husband, but she is carrying his child.'

The Queen conferred briefly with one of her advisers who was stood just behind her chair, to her side. He nodded before scurrying away. She returned her gaze to Brookes, her face unsmiling. 'You say she was virtuous.'

Brookes nodded. 'Yes my lady.'

'And you say she is carrying his child.'

'That's correct my lady.'

The adviser returned holding a sheet of paper in his hand. He handed it to the Queen who slowly read it, absorbing its contents. Looking stern, she handed it back to the adviser. 'Who is Gabriel?'

Brookes was taken aback. 'I don't know my lady. I do not know of anybody called Gabriel.'

'He is a miller's son, close to Dorchester. Are you sure you have no knowledge of him?'

Puzzled, Brookes looked up at the Queen for the first time. 'I can assure you, my lady, I have never heard of nor met this Gabriel.'

'But I have reason to believe your daughter has.'

'My lady?'

'This young man named Gabriel. I believe your daughter has knowledge of him. Indeed, your assertion that she is a lady of virtue would appear to be false, as it is now clear that she had more than a passing association with him. Consequently, I see no reason to give a pardon to your daughter.'

A confused look grew on Richard Brookes' face. 'But my lady, you seem to be blessed with more facts than I. Please, do tell, who is this Gabriel of whom you speak?'

Queen Anne stood up as if to leave. 'According to this morning's Daily Courant, he is the father of your grandchild.'

Brookes stood in stunned silence as the Queen left the chamber followed by her adviser. The handmaid approached and touched him gently on the elbow. 'Mr Brookes. Come. It's this way.'

He was shown the way back to the side entrance where he was met by a guard who escorted him to a small iron gate set in the wall. The gate clanged behind him as he stepped out into the traffic. The rain began to fall as he slowly walked back into town. On the way, he came across a seller with a hand full of newspaper sheets. 'Is that the Daily Courant?' he asked. The seller handed him a copy and Brookes handed him a halfpenny. The headline hit him like a slap in the face.

MARY CHANNING TO HAVE BASTARD CHILD

Brookes was flabbergasted. He had always known that his daughter was headstrong and carefree. He had hoped that marriage would calm her down and put an end to her errant ways. Indeed, he had hoped that her new husband would be able to clip Mary's wings and control her. But it wasn't just the fault of Thomas Channing. As her father, he was also to blame. The long trips away on business had provided his daughter with every opportunity to behave like a wild child. And his choice of husband for her had been her undoing, for Thomas Channing had proved to be too weak and unworthy of her. Brookes screwed up the paper and clutched it in his hand. He hung his head in shame. Now he knew for sure what his daughter had done. And he also knew that no amount of petitioning, pleading or religious servitude would be enough to undo the damage that had been done. Her fate was now sealed. His daughter was to burn at the stake.

Chapter Fifty-Nine

S amuel Tyler packed up the last of his belongings and dropped them into his leather bag. Slinging it over his shoulder, he had one last look around the room to ensure he hadn't left anything behind, donned his tricorn and left.

Mrs Caudle was waiting at the foot of the stairs with the bread and cheese she had cut for him, bundled in linen and secured with twine. 'Thank you, Mrs Caudle. It has been a pleasure.' Tyler took the food from her and she opened the door. The long spell of fine weather had finally broken and rain was now threatening, with dark clouds gathering on the horizon. He surveyed them suspiciously, sniffing at the dampness in the air, before exiting the door.

'Good day, Mr Tyler. God speed.' Mrs Caudle smiled sweetly at him as she shut the door behind him, then headed back to the scullery to continue cleaning and scrubbing the bedsheets in readiness for her next guest.

Tyler sauntered along the road towards the George where he was to catch his stagecoach back to London. He would be home by the evening and he was looking forward to catching up with his friends, along with the hustle and bustle that made the capital so different to the sleepy backwater that was Dorchester. He smiled to himself and pondered as to what his reception would be. His reports had made the lead story on the Daily Courant for three days running and he had undoubtedly saved the best until last. Indeed, his final piece had apparently caused a sensation, with scandal at its heart to set the tittle-tattle tongues of London wagging at speed.

He passed the large building where the trial had been held and paused a while, reflecting on his achievement and the adulation he would surely receive upon his return to the capital to take his place once more among the reporting fraternity. He puffed up his chest with pride, clicked his heels together and proceeded on his way. He briefly checked his pocket watch. The coach was due to leave on the hour which should give him enough time to get a brandy with which to toast Dorchester and Mary Channing before he left, probably never to return. Her demise had led to his success and it was the least he could do to raise a glass to her.

He arrived at the George to find the horses being hitched to the front of the coach. He dropped his bag off with the drivers before going inside to pay for his one-way journey back to London. Having paid the fare, he headed into the bar and ordered himself a brandy.

'I thought I might find you here.' Gabriel's Dorset accent was distinctive, as was his voice. Tyler smiled and turned to offer him a drink. Before he could speak, Gabriel's fist smashed into his face, knocking him backwards into the bar. As he slid down to the floor, more punches rained down on his head to the point where he felt he would black out. He heard shouts as the landlord rushed from behind the bar to restrain Gabriel. Kicks to his ribs and legs followed as Gabriel was dragged backwards by the landlord.

Tyler blinked rapidly, trying desperately to regain his

senses. He tasted blood in his mouth and lifted his hand to touch his face. He could feel the blood trickling from his nose. His lip was already swelling and his ear felt tender as well. He winced as he tried to stand, his ribs sending a sharp pain coursing through his body. He opened his eyes and the room gradually came back into focus. Meanwhile the ringing in his ears subsided and the shouts of Gabriel and the landlord became clearer.

'Get off me! Leave me alone!'

'Leave it Gabriel! He's not worth it!'

'I'm going to kill him!'

'Not here you're not. Now calm down.' The landlord had him in a bear hug, holding him from behind, his strong arms lifting Gabriel off the floor as he struggled to break free.

Rising slowly to his feet, Tyler winced as he gingerly felt his ribs. He pulled a handkerchief from his pocket and put it to his mouth. Pulling it away he surveyed the dark red blood on it in wonderment. He had never been hit in the face before and he was feeling very close to tears.

Gabriel stopped struggling and the landlord released his vice like grip on him, remaining close by just in case he launched himself at the young man again. 'Do you know what you have done?' Gabriel demanded as he glowered at Tyler.

Tyler dabbed his mouth with the handkerchief but didn't respond.

'I'll tell you what you have done. You have just condemned her to death.' Gabriel was regaining his self-control and his voice, while trembling, was returning to a normal level.

'I did not condemn her. She was already condemned.' Tyler spat the words out, his lips feeling twice their normal size.

Gabriel went to go for Tyler again but the landlord was ready, grabbing him firmly by the arm. 'Gabriel!' he warned. 'Enough!'

Gabriel shrugged off the hand that was holding his elbow and stood down, but his fists were still clenched and he continued to stare menacingly at Tyler, his eyes full of hate and fury. 'I told you that I was the father in confidence. You promised me that you would not print that. You promised!' His outburst over, Gabriel relaxed and unclenched his fists. He lowered his voice. 'How could you? You might as well have lit the bonfire yourself for now she is without hope. I hope you burn in hell!' Gabriel gave him one final look and lurched forward at him, causing Tyler to retreat and hunch down, in front of the bar. Gabriel stopped and stood over him as the placed his large hand on his shoulder, squeezing it tightly. 'Don't worry.' Gabriel said to the landlord. 'He's not worth it.' He went to leave, then half turned and spat in Tyler's face. 'May you rot in hell. Should you ever come back here, I will kill you. Understood?'

Tyler nodded weakly, holding the handkerchief to his mouth. He watched Gabriel leave and turned back to the bar, leaning on it for support. He went to grab his brandy but the landlord picked it up. 'I don't think so. You aren't welcome here anymore. I think it's time you left.'

He made his way outside, still holding his ribs. Both drivers looked at him suspiciously. 'What happened to you?' one of them eventually said.

'Somebody just hit me.'

The drivers smirked. 'Why would they do that then? You been talking when you should have been listening?' They both laughed out loud.

Tyler tried smiling but his split lip wouldn't let him. 'No, not quite. Writing more like.'

'Writing?' The London accent was unmistakeable.

'Yes. I am a writer for the Daily Courant.'

'Why are you down here then?' Both drivers had their interest piqued.

'I have been following the Mary Channing case.'

One of the drivers went to the front of the horses to ensure they were correctly hitched up. The other pulled a sheet out of his pocket. 'This was you, was it?' He held out that morning's edition of the Daily Courant, the one that revealed Gabriel as being the true father of Mary's unborn child.

Tyler nodded, a little unsure now as to what reaction he was going to receive. Earlier that day he had been triumphant, believing everyone would thank him for his fine piece of detective work. Now he was feeling wary. The driver opened the door to the stagecoach. 'Come on, in you get. We're leaving in a minute. You're the only one on today, from the looks of it.'

Tyler climbed inside, the driver supporting his elbow as he helped him in. He closed the door behind him, then leant in through the window. 'Tis a funny business, that one. Are you sure she did it?'

'What?' asked Tyler. 'Poisoned her husband. I would have thought so.'

The driver looked lost in thought. 'Mmmm, maybe. I'm not so sure.'

'Why's that?' Tyler thought this fellow must have taken leave of his senses. Of course Mary Channing had poisoned her husband.

'It's just that we had two women a little while back now that seemed to know a lot about it. They were talking in the coach.' He stopped and shouted to his colleague. 'Here, Robert, what was the name of that young girl we had the other week. The one that had worked for that Channing girl.'

'Dunno!' came back the response.

'Molly?' Tyler offered.

'Yes, Molly that's her.'

Tyler raised an eyebrow. It was about the only thing on his face he could move without feeling pain. 'And you said she had someone with her?'

'Yes, that's right. She was with an older woman. Quite well to do. They made quite an odd couple.'

'And what was her name.'

'Not sure. Molly kept referring to her as Miss something.'

'Wasn't it Liza, or Liz?' the other driver offered.

The driver shook his head. 'Maybe, maybe not. I'm not sure.'

'And why do you remember them so clearly.'

The driver pushed back from the window of the door. 'Because this lady was telling Molly about the effects mercury had on the body. And the young girl was laughing. It struck me at the time that it seemed to be a strange conversation for two women to be having.'

The coach set off, with Tyler deep in thought. So there had been a mystery woman. And it was she who had spirited Molly away. On the very morning of Thomas Channing's death. The realization dawned on him and he put his face in his hands. 'Oh God! What have I done?'

Chapter Sixty

The jailer arrived at the door to Mary's cell. 'Get up. You're leaving.'

Mary was suddenly fearful. 'Where are we going?'

The jailer chuckled. 'You'll soon see.'

She exited the cell, giving it a longing look as he closed and locked the door. The sermons with Reverend Hutchins had increased in frequency and she wondered what he had in store for her next. She looked down at her belly, which was swelling in size by the day. He hadn't raped her yet but she was expecting it and she was afraid for what it might do to her unborn baby. It was the only thing keeping her alive at the moment and to lose it would bring a swift end to her own life, as well as that of the child she was carrying.

She followed him back down the stairs to the depths of the prison and believed she was being returned to the main cell. The stench down here was even worse than she remembered it, while the moans and groans of the incarcerated bore testament to the squalid, inhuman conditions in which they were all being kept.

'Has my father not paid you?' she asked as the continued

onward. The jailer said nothing, shuffling along at his usual half pace. Time was unimportant down here, for there was plenty of it to go round.

He passed by the main cell that had been her home for several months. She paused, half expecting him to stop, then had to hurry to catch him up again. Instead, he halted outside another door, chose one of his many keys from the large ring hanging from his breeches, slid it in and turned it. Pushing the door open wide he said 'In here.'

Mary hesitated as she peered into the gloom. The walls were damp and covered in mould. Old straw barely covered the stone floor and the small window, set high in the thick wall, shed little light through its bars. She stepped inside and, as her eyes slowly adjusted to the darkness, she saw two pairs of eyes looking at her. The door banged shut behind her and she turned quickly and grabbed hold of the bars to the small window set within. 'My father? I asked if he has paid you?'

The jailer answered gruffly. 'What do you think?'

'I am sure he will,' Mary pleaded. 'Please, send word. He is a man of honour. I know he will not sanction this!'

As he shuffled away she turned and sank to her knees, holding her stomach. Even if she could withstand the advances of Reverend Hutchins, she did not know if the baby would survive these conditions. Her food rations would be reduced, her health would suffer and she would surely die when the winter months set in.

'What brings you here child?' A voice suddenly came out of the darkness. Mary tried hard to focus, relying on her peripheral vision to see. A woman was sitting with her back to the wall, legs out in front of her. It appeared to be the driest wall in the cell. Mary made her way over to her.

'I think they have brought me here to die.'

The woman cackled, before falling into a coughing fit. Eventually she stopped coughing and regained her composure.

'Oh should it be that easy, for it is the only escape from here. You must be with child?'

Mary nodded, then realized the woman probably couldn't see her. 'Yes.'

'Welcome to our exclusive little club. We are all with child in here. You have come to the birthing room. How much longer do you have.'

'Just a few weeks. How many of us are in here?'

'Only the three of us, including you. My name is Annie. And she is Mabel. Say hello, Mabel.'

A small voice called across the cell. 'Hello.'

Annie went on. 'What is your name?'

'Mary.'

'Not Mary Channing?' the woman suddenly sounded quite animated and Mary wondered if she was safe.

'Yes. Why?'

She cackled again. 'Mary Channing, as I live a breathe. Mabel, we have someone of notoriety amongst us!'

The other woman crawled over. Mary could see she didn't have long to go as her stomach dragged on the floor. She wondered how long she had been there. Her hair and face were filthy and her clothes had been reduced to rags. She felt her arrive at her side.

'Hello Mary. Pleased to make your acquaintance.' She held out a hand, small and bony. Mary guessed her age to be not much older than her own, but she looked like an old woman with her hair already showing signs of gray. She held out her hand and then quickly withdrew it, wiping it on her dress. Mabel didn't seem to notice, let alone take offence.

'You are quite famous, Mary Channing.' Annie said. 'I heard you killed your husband because he beat you once too often!'

Mary didn't feel disposed to tell her any different. 'I did.'

'I hope he died a long and painful death.' Annie appeared

in the dim ray of light that was trying its hardest to illuminate the cell. She too didn't have long to go before she gave birth, and looked older than her years.

'He did.'

Cackling again, Annie suddenly lapsed into another coughing fit. Mary instinctively put her arms around her and supported her as she went on all fours, the coughs racking through her tiny body. Mary was shocked to find Annie was all skin and bone. Every ounce of goodness left in her had gone to nourish her as yet unborn child. Mary gulped. The horror of what was to become of her suddenly hit her. She would remain here until her child was born, barely surviving and wasting away. And then, when it was over, they would end her misery. Even being burnt at the stake seemed better than this vision of hell that had been dreamt up for her.

Chapter Sixty-One

'Please my darling, I beg of you.' Elizabeth Brookes was on her knees before her husband who was sat in his wing back chair. She clasped his hands in hers, imploring him to restore their daughter to the cell in which she had been kept. Elizabeth had visited Mary upon receiving word from the jailer that she wished to speak with her father. With Richard Brookes refusing to go to the gaol, she had gone herself and had been in shock at the conditions in which her daughter had suddenly found herself being placed.

Brookes shook his head, sadly. 'Dearest Elizabeth, I cannot.'

'But she is your only daughter!' She buried her face in his lap and he stroked her hair as she sobbed. She looked up again, tears streaming down her face. 'Please Richard. Do it for me. I know how much she has hurt you, but you did not see where they have confined her. It isn't even fit for pigs.'

'You do not understand, my love,' Richard held her face in his hands. 'Mary has ruined me. I – we – are close to losing everything. Society is turning its back on us. Even if I wanted to, I couldn't. I simply cannot afford it.' He raised her face to his and kissed her gently on her forehead. 'While we all believed the child to be by Thomas Channing, there was hope. Reverend Hutchins said her lessons were going well and she was showing contrition. Even the efforts of Richard Channing were losing momentum as public opinion turned in her favour. But now...' He leant back in his chair, his eyes filling with tears. 'The news of Mary's adultery has put paid to everything. Nobody will support her now. Her fate is no longer within my control. It is in God's hands.'

Elizabeth withdrew her hands from her husband's lap and dabbed at her eyes with her handkerchief. 'Are we really ruined?'

'Very nearly. The costs of keeping Mary in prison have been steadily rising. The jailer's fees are extortionate. There is no end to that man's lack of decency. And the favours I have paid for in an effort to secure Mary's pardon have cost us dear. Our creditors are withdrawing their terms and my business interests in Honiton and Exeter are suffering. Damn that newspaper. And damn that Gabriel!' He balled his fist and punched it into his other hand, making Elizabeth start.

'What are we to do?' Elizabeth looked around the room, suddenly fearing that she herself could be joining her daughter in prison as a debtor.

Brookes stood up and began pacing the room. 'I will assign the running of the businesses in Exeter and Honiton to our sons. Richard, Caleb and William can go to Exeter and Joshua, Ebeneezer and Thomas will go to Honiton. By distancing myself, it may help satisfy our creditors and bring in new customers. We can sell the land we own towards Hampshire to the farmer who works it. He has offered to buy it many times and I shall offer him favourable terms to secure a quick sale. I shall also go to speak to the bank in London to see if I can extend my credit with them.'

'Do you think they will?'

'I am not sure. I would like to think that, once Mary has gone, everything will calm down and return to normal again. All we have to do is hang on in there until then.'

Elizabeth recoiled. 'Things will be better when she has gone? How can you be so callous!' She stood up, a defiant look in her eyes, challenging her husband. 'She is my daughter. I cannot turn my back on her! I will never turn my back on her!'

'Forgive me. I am sorry my love but, for the sake of everyone associated with this family, I have to. To openly support her after what she has done will be to bring dire consequences upon all of us, and I simply cannot allow that to happen!' Brookes stepped forward to hold his wife and look her firmly in the eye. 'I know you love her. And so do I. But we cannot go on like this. Visit her as often as you like. Take her food if you are able. Be there for her. Be there for the birth of the child. But I can no longer go. I have to do the right thing by our sons. Mary is no longer my concern. Our sons – and their future – must come first!'

With that, Brookes marched out of the room. Elizabeth knew better than to chase him and try to change his mind, for it was obviously made up. In her heart she knew he was right. Mary had brought shame upon herself and her family through her refusal to conform and behave as society saw fit. Her high spirits as a child, particularly with six brothers, had been amusing when she had been younger. However, as she had turned into a young woman, it had spiralled out of control, to a point where even her father could no longer impose his sense of order upon her.

Wiping her face, Elizabeth straightened her hair and readjusted her clothing. Once she had composed herself, she went down to the kitchen. The cook was preparing some venison stew. A large joint of salted meat was hanging by a hook from the oak beam and Elizabeth took a sharp knife to it. Slicing off a large piece, she picked up some vegetables and placed the goods on the table. She then retrieved a clay pot and spooned some of the stew into it before placing everything carefully into a large, wicker basket.

After covering the goods with a piece of cloth, Elizabeth went back upstairs. Gathering her bonnet and shawl, she looked around for sight of her husband. There was no sign of him and she fancied he had gone riding, something he often did when he needed to clear his head and calm his temper.

With nobody around to stop her, Elizabeth picked up the basket, headed out of the door, down the drive and onward into Dorchester to see Mary and inform her of her father's decision to withdraw all forms of support.

Chapter Sixty-Two

Mary absent-mindedly scratched at the lice that were crawling over her. She could hardly sleep for the continual itching that blighted her body. Had there been enough light for her to see by, she would have witnessed for herself the bites and splotchy skin that covered her.

Annie was moaning to herself in the corner. Her waters had broken early in the morning and the puddle beneath where she was sat had not yet dried, such was the high level of dampness in the cell. Mary sensed it would not be much longer before the child arrived. She had tried to attract the attention of the jailer to bring help but without success, not even a yell from him to hold her tongue and be quiet!

The intensity and frequency of Annie's cries suddenly increased and she yelled out as she was gripped by a contraction. Mary called over to her other cell-mate. 'Mabel, I think Annie is close now. Do you know what to do?'

She heard a forced laugh through the darkness. 'Why would I know what to do? I have never had a child before.'

'Me neither.' Mary sat back, holding her hands to her ears,

trying to block out the noise. Had she not done so, she would have heard the approaching footsteps. The draft caused by the door opening alerted her to someone coming in. 'Mother!' She wearily got to her feet, supporting her ever-growing belly, her joints stiff and sore.

It only took Elizabeth a second to realise that Annie had gone into labour. As the door closed behind her, she called out to the jailer. 'This girl is giving birth. Bring somebody, quickly.'

The jailer laughed at her through the window. 'It's nature. The girl will be fine. It happens all the time.' He turned the key in the lock. 'I'll be back in an hour to let you out.'

Elizabeth handed the basket of food to Mary before getting down on her knees beside Annie. She felt her forehead, which was hot to the touch in spite of the cold chill that gripped the room. 'Mary, give me the cloth on top of the basket.' Mary did as she was told, ignoring the basket's contents and instead going to her mother to hand over the cloth. 'Do you have any fresh water in here?' Elizabeth asked. Mary nodded, heading for the pail in the corner. She returned with it, setting it down beside her mother. Elizabeth put the cloth in the water, squeezed it to remove the excess, then held it to Annie's forehead. The girl groaned as she felt its coldness.

'Is she going to be all right?' Mary asked in a hushed voice.

Elizabeth gestured for her to go the other side of Annie. 'Hold her hand, let her know you are there for her. I shall do the same. All we can do now is just wait.'

Annie was gripped by another contraction, this one longer than the last. 'How long has she been like this?' Elizabeth asked.

'A fair while. But they are coming quicker now.'

Elizabeth felt between Annie's legs, raising up her skirts. She was appalled at how thin the girl was. 'She is opening. It won't be long.'

Annie screamed again, panting rapidly as she tried to ease her discomfort. Elizabeth reassured her. 'Hush child, you are nearly there.' Annie grunted as she felt herself pushing, holding her breath as she did so. Mary felt her squeezing her hand with all her might as she began forcing her baby out. Elizabeth shifted to get a better look at what was happening. 'I can see the head! The baby is coming! Push again Annie!'

Annie pushed once more, screaming at the top of her lungs as the baby's head broke through, swiftly followed by its small body. Elizabeth grabbed it in her hands and cleared the mucus from its mouth. The baby remained silent, before bursting into a low, growling cry. 'It's a boy!' Elizabeth announced. She looked around for a cloth to wrap it in. There wasn't one. The only cloth she had was the one she had soaked in water to cool Annie's forehead down. She picked up some of the straw that was around them and wiped the baby clean as best she could.

Mary watched in awe as the child continued bawling, not knowing what to do. Elizabeth handed the boy to her and Mary held it to her bosom. The child tried sucking upon contact with her skin, so Mary put her little finger into its mouth. He fell into contentment as he began sucking on it. Elizabeth took the food out of the basket and ripped out the cloth that lined it. 'Here, wrap him up,' she said to Mary, handing it to her.

When Mary had finished swathing the small child into the cloth, she handed him to Annie. Annie's eyes were glazed over, seemingly unable to comprehend what was happening. Meanwhile, Elizabeth was busying herself between her legs with the cold, wet cloth. 'Just one more push, Annie. Please, for me.' Annie closed her eyes and made a conscious effort. 'Well done! That's it. It's all over.' Elizabeth removed the afterbirth and cleaned her up with the wet cloth.

Annie looked at the boy laying on her chest, but was still not really understanding what had happened. Mary suddenly realized how young Annie really was beneath all of that grime on her face. She couldn't have been much older than sixteen. 'Are you all right?' she asked. Annie said nothing, still panting.

The baby began crying again and Elizabeth appeared at her side once more. 'Try and feed him, Annie, there's a good girl.'

Mary passed the baby to her mother, then unbuttoned the front of Annie's dress. Meanwhile Elizabeth held the child to her breast. It sucked noisily before becoming agitated. Elizabeth removed the baby and it began screaming again. She studied Annie's nipple and gently squeezed it between her fingers. Nothing came out. She did the same with the other breast, but again couldn't get it to lactate.

'What's wrong mother?' Mary looked at her mother, concern crossing her face.

'She has no milk.'

'Is there nothing we can do?'

Elizabeth shook her head, a sad look on her face. 'She needs a wet nurse but she won't get one in here... unless...' she looked at Mabel who had not moved, watching the spectacle unfold from afar. 'Mabel?'

'What?' Mabel responded, sullenly.

'Do you have milk in your breasts?'

Mabel drew her knees up to her chest and wrapped her arms round her legs. 'No.'

Elizabeth looked at Mary. 'What about you?'

'No, not yet.'

Footsteps were approaching from afar. The jailer was returning. Her hour was up. 'Quick, take this food. Share it with Annie. It's possible she may start giving milk with some nourishment inside her.'

Mary looked at her, her eyes wide open. 'And if she doesn't?'

Elizabeth looked sadly at Annie. 'Then the baby will die.'

Chapter Sixty-Three

The grain mill came into view as Richard Channing reached the top of the hill. He reined in his horse, and the steed went up on its hind legs, whinnying as it was brought to a sudden halt. Richard looked down upon the sandstone building, seeking out signs of life. Smoke was coming from a fire within a small building that was located a short distance from the main mill. A youth appeared, a grain sack balanced across his right shoulder. He was naked to the waist, his skin and breeches covered in the dust of the ground grain. He humped it off his shoulder into a two-wheeled cart that had been balanced on a tree stump, then heaved it on top of the dozen or so filled sacks already on it before positioning it neatly on top.

He slapped his hands together and clouds of dust appeared in the early evening sunlight. He then marched back into the mill, presumably to collect another sack.

Channing dug his heels into the horse's flank and it galloped at speed down the hill, arriving quickly in the yard. He leapt off, landing on both feet, and tethered the horse to the wheel of the cart.

Gabriel reappeared with another sack across his shoulder. He hesitated when he saw the stranger stood by the cart. 'My father isn't here at the moment. He will be back shortly,' he said.

'Is your name Gabriel?' Channing stood with his legs apart. His riding crop was in one hand and he smacked it menacingly into the gloved palm of his other hand.

A look of fear crossed Gabriel's face. 'Who wants to know?' he said, warily.

'Richard Channing.'

Gabriel dropped the sack behind him, letting it fall. He looked around for the pitchfork. He spotted it, just inside the mill door. Channing followed his gaze and saw what he was looking at. 'I wouldn't if I were you, boy.' He took a pace forward to emphasise the point. Gabriel quickly sized up the distance between himself and Channing and leapt to his left, towards the mill door.

Channing was on him just as he reached the doorway, grabbing the waist of his breeches as Gabriel reached out in vain for the pitchfork. He lost his balance and fell into the dirt as Channing yanked him backwards. Channing stood over him, slapping the riding crop into his gloved hand again, a malicious sneer on his face.

'I am going to teach you a lesson, boy. A lesson that you will never forget.' He raised up the riding crop.

'No!' Gabriel screamed in pain as the crop viciously struck the top of his arm. He curled up into a ball, trying in desperation to escape the stinging blows that Channing was raining down on him, welt marks appearing over his arms and his torso as he rolled around on the ground. Frustrated at being unable to land a clear blow, Channing began kicking at him, launching his riding boots into Gabriel's ribs and his legs. The young man was screaming at the top of his lungs. 'Father! Help me! Father!'

Exhausted, Channing stepped back. He bent over, his hands on his knees, gasping for breath. As he recovered, Gabriel peeked through the fingers of his hands to see where his assailant was. He screamed once more as Channing stood up and launched another attack, kicking and whipping indiscriminately, moving up and down and around Gabriel's body as he sought to land a clean shot.

Channing paused for breath once more, his face red and sweating from the effort of attacking the young man on the ground before him. He collapsed as a block of wood landed square across his shoulders, putting Channing flat on his face. He tried to get to his knees but another blow knocked him back down. Exhausted, he lay there, his chest burning with exertion and his back smarting with pain.

'Are you hurt son?'

Channing looked up to see an older man crouching next to Gabriel, holding the boy's head and gently stroking his hair. Gabriel was sobbing quietly as his father consoled him. The man looked across at Channing, who was now resting on his knees, still panting heavily. 'What is the meaning of this?' he demanded, his voice quiet but firm.

With his wide shoulders and strong arms, Channing knew he would be beaten should he challenge the man. Channing pushed himself up and got slowly to his feet, dusting himself down and rubbing at his shoulders where he had been struck. He bent forward to pick up his riding crop.

'Leave that where it is.' Gabriel's father glared angrily at him. 'I asked you a question. What is the meaning of this?'

Channing regained his composure. 'Your son has caused irreparable damage to my family's name and my reputation. I demand satisfaction.'

Gabriel stiffened and his father tightened his grip on him. 'I think you have already had satisfaction, sir. If you require any more, then you will have to take it up with me.'

'Do you know who I am?'

Gabriel's father nodded solemnly. 'I have a good idea of

exactly who you are, sir.'

'Then you should know better than to get in my way. Move away and let me have at the boy.'

Gabriel's father pushed Gabriel away, laying his head gently on the ground where he remained curled up, sobbing quietly.

'I'm afraid I cannot do that sir.'

'Move away, damn you!' Channing pointed at him with his finger.

Gabriel's father picked up the piece of blockwood, planted one end on the ground and leant on it. 'I said no. If you are looking for a fight, then I will be your man.'

'I could have you turned out of your home for this insolence!' Channing pumped up his chest.

Gabriel's father looked sternly at Channing. 'I'm sure you can sir. But I will not let you do any more harm to my son.'

'Do you know what he's done?'

'I have a fair idea. But he is a young man. He will learn. And what you have done to him today will help him with that. But I will not step aside. If you want satisfaction, then you'll have to have it with me.'

Channing was defeated. He knew he was no match for the miller. His face was pained.

'I am truly sorry for the wrong my son has done you.' Confident that Channing would not launch into another attack, Gabriel's father let the blockwood fall to the floor. He went over to Gabriel and gently lifted him to his feet. He began leading him away, back home for his mother to take care of him. He stopped, his arm around Gabriel's shoulder, and spoke once more to Channing. 'I am sorry you could not protect your son. But I will do everything in my power to protect mine. If I see you around here again I shall finish what I started and see you delivered to hell.'

As he carried Gabriel back home, Channing called out after him. 'I shall put you and your family out on the streets, if it's the last thing I do. Mark my words, for you have not heard the end of this!'

He untethered his horse and mounted it, still rubbing at his shoulders. He considered chasing the two men down with his horse, but decided against it. Spinning the animal round, he headed back up the hill for home.

Chapter Sixty-Four

Elizabeth and Mary sat side-by-side, staring at Annie. The baby had died two days ago but the young mother had refused to let it go, convinced the boy was still alive.

'What will happen to my baby?' Mary asked in a small voice.

'You shall be the child's mother. It will be loved and cared for by you.' Elizabeth put her arm around Mary and pulled her tight.

'He won't though, will he? I will not be here to look after him.'

'You are having a boy, are you?' Elizabeth tried to change the subject.

'I believe so. Although I wouldn't mind a girl.' She snuggled into her mother, delighting in her warmth. She always felt so cold these days, as if the damp were seeping deep into her bones. As the winter months began to close in, Mary found that her teeth were always chattering and she would shiver uncontrollably all night long, making it impossible to sleep.

'I wish I'd had more daughters.' Elizabeth drifted off into

her own thoughts, remembering Mary as a small girl, growing up. 'The boys were always off with their father. I seldom got to see them, especially as they got older.'

'How are my brothers?' Mary sounded wistful.

'They are fine. Father has sent them to the west country to care for the businesses. I believe they are doing quite well. There is talk of them returning for Christmas. I for one cannot wait to have them in the house again. It seems so quiet without having them around.'

Mary fell silent and Elizabeth wondered if perhaps she should have remained quiet about Christmas. It had always been such a happy time in the house and she recalled the celebrations they had all enjoyed the previous year, when Mary was still living with them, just a few weeks before she married Thomas and set off on the road that had led her to this dark, damp, prison cell.

'Will you take care of him?' Mary looked up at her mother and Elizabeth marvelled at how young and innocent her daughter looked. She nodded.

'Of course I will.'

'You won't let the Channings have him, will you?' Mary obviously wasn't aware that it was now public knowledge that the child was not Thomas Channing's.

'Of course not. He will be born a Brookes, and he will be raised as a Brookes.'

'Promise?'

Elizabeth nodded once more. 'I promise.' She leant over and picked up the basket. Inside she had some cheese and pickles. She broke some cheese off and handed it to her daughter. Annie looked over at them but made no effort to move closer and join them. Elizabeth had already resolved not to share the food with Mary's inmates, if only to ensure Mary was able to give birth to a healthy baby. Besides, it was obvious to her that Annie was very close to death and Mabel would not be too far behind. It was as if Mabel, too, had given up. Having seen Annie give birth to a baby who could not survive the night, it was small wonder Mabel did not want to consider the ordeal that was due to befall her.

Mary picked at the cheese, chewing it slowly. Elizabeth offered her some bread, but she shook her head. 'Please Mary, you must eat for the sake of your baby.' Mary relented and broke a bit of her cheese off, putting it on the crust and popping it in her mouth. Elizabeth noticed a gap in her front teeth and wondered if she had lost one. It would not surprise her if she had. She decided against asking her for fear of upsetting her.

Annie began moaning in her fuddled sleep. Elizabeth went over to her and touched her forehead. She was burning up. 'She has the fever,' she called over to Mary.

Mary sat upright. 'What fever?'

'Childbed fever.'

'What's that?'

Elizabeth returned to Mary's side. 'It's what happens when you give birth sometimes. It cannot be helped.'

Mary looked alarmed. 'Will I catch it?'

'No.' Elizabeth shook her head. 'It is not contagious. But it would probably be best to stay away from her, just in case.'

Mary ate the rest of her food in silence, watching Annie toss and turn, groaning as she did, unaware of her surroundings. As the jailer returned, Elizabeth gently retrieved the lifeless body of the infant from Annie, handing the tiny corpse to the jailer. 'Be sure to give him a decent burial.'

The jailer took the boy as if it were a rag doll, holding the child by its arm. 'What will you pay me for it?'

Looking disgusted, Elizabeth nodded farewell to her daughter as she began the long climb back up the steps to the outside world. The jailer tossed the body across the corridor like a rag doll, then turned to lock the cell door. He winked at Mary through the barred window as he did so. 'Not long 'til it's your turn my lovely.'

Chapter Sixty-Five

Mary awoke from a fitful sleep as the first rays of light landed on her face through the iron bars, set deep into the thick, stone wall. She immediately looked to her side for her newborn baby, but the child wasn't there. She stared at the small bed of straw she had created on the flagstone floor and clutched at her stomach as she recalled the events of the night.

The jailer's wife had assisted her as the baby was born in the small hours. Her waters had broken late the previous evening and the contractions had started soon after. It had taken several hours to attract the jailer's attention, her agonized screams failing to raise him. Eventually he had arrived, his stomach full of gruel and mind fuggy with ale.

He peered through the small window in amusement and then laughed out loud. 'Tis time witch. Nothing to stop you meeting the devil now.'

He shuffled off to get his wife. Elizabeth Brookes had arranged and paid for her to assist with the birth a few days earlier, knowing full well what was in store for her daughter should she not be around to help her.

The jailer and his wife arrived and he worked his way slowly through his large ring of keys before finally getting the right one, much to his wife's annoyance. She chastised him as he closed the door behind him, locking it as he left. Not that Mary would be going anywhere. She was doubled up in pain, sweat stinging her eyes as the moment came upon her.

With a final, loud scream, the baby had arrived. Mary collapsed back against the cell wall, exhausted while the jailer's wife cleaned the baby off with a handful of straw, before handing her to Mary. 'She's beautiful, child. Here, hold her.'

'Her?' Mary had been convinced the child would be a boy. She gazed down on her baby in wonderment. Her daughter was perfect. The food her mother had been supplying had given both Mary and her newborn daughter a fighting chance.

Mary held her to her breast as she sucked away, the sensation bonding mother and child. Before long, the infant was asleep and Mary spoke quietly to her as she dozed in her arms.

'I've got to call my husband and take her away with me,' the old woman spoke harshly, without a shred of sympathy.

'Please,' Mary pleaded. 'Just a few minutes.'

The old woman looked at her for a few moments, before reluctantly relenting. 'I'll rest here a while before shouting him. What are you going to call her?'

'I don't know. I haven't thought about it. I thought it was going to be a boy and was going to call him Thomas.'

The old woman squinted her eyes. 'Thomas? After the father? Assuming he is the father! Have you no shame?'

'Not any more,' said Mary in a hushed voice, rocking the baby back and forth in her arms.

The woman grunted. 'It doesn't really matter. But you need to think of a name quickly. The Reverend will want her baptised as soon as possible.' She squatted over the wooden pail in the corner of the cell and relieved herself before heading to the wall and seating herself down. It was where Mabel had sat as her life had slowly ebbed away. She'd never even had the chance to give birth.

As tiredness overtook her, Mary lay on her side and placed her daughter beside her on the gathered straw, the baby's head nestling in the crook of her arm. She was vaguely aware of the cell door being opened and had murmured as the child was lifted from her, but fatigue saw to it that she was unable to resist. Now, as the first grey light of dawn began pushing out the gloom of the night, the chill of the cell was seeping once more into Mary's bones. She sobbed quietly to herself, her arms wrapped around her knees as she gently rocked backwards and forwards. The giving of life would result in the taking of hers, for now she no longer had a reason to live. She knew that they would soon come for her and that her own, short life would soon be over. Mary knew it would bring blessed relief, but the fear of death and the thought of the pain she would have to endure was overpowering. She sincerely believed that God would be merciful. But the manner in which she would meet him would not.

Her mother arrived later that morning. 'Mary! What has happened?'

Mary had fallen into a troubled sleep again and awoke with a start. She looked to her side and began crying in anguish. 'My baby! They've taken my baby!'

Elizabeth went to the cell door and banged on it. The jailer, who had not yet made ten strides, reluctantly turned on his heel. 'Yes madam?'

'Where is my daughter's baby?' she demanded.

'With my wife, madam, waiting for you. You are to take it away with you.'

'Bring the child at once.' Elizabeth ignored the jailer's heavy sigh as he disappeared back up the corridor. She heard him cursing as he went but ignored it, instead returning to Mary and taking her in her arms. 'Are you well? Did you get help with the birth?'

Mary's sobbing had subsided as her mother had taken charge. She nodded. 'Yes. The old woman helped me.'

'Good.' Elizabeth desperately wanted to ask more, but left her daughter to her own thoughts as they awaited the return of the child. She wondered if it were a boy or a girl, but decided it did not matter. She would find out soon enough.

The jailer returned with his wife who had the baby in her arms. As soon as the door was opened, Elizabeth took the child and rushed her to Mary. The infant murmured as Mary placed her on her breast and began sucking hungrily, before drifting off to sleep. Meanwhile, Elizabeth lifted the cloth and peered at the tiny little body. 'A girl!'

Mary smiled softly. 'Yes. A girl.' She yawned and her eyes drooped as she struggled to fight off the sleep that she so desperately needed. Finally, she succumbed, falling into a deep slumber. Elizabeth watched over them awhile as they both slept together. As the sun rose higher, weak shards of light forced their way through the small cell window. The jailer returned after an hour to let Elizabeth out. She passed him some coins. 'I will be back tomorrow. In the meantime, the child is to remain with her mother. I trust you will look after both of them for me.'

The jailer smiled as he shook the coins in the palm of his hand. 'Certainly madam. Anything you say.'

Chapter Sixty-Six

L ent Assize for the district of Dorchester began on Friday, the eighth of March, 1706. Judge Price took his seat to preside over proceedings once more and studied the list of names before him. The name close to the top of the sheet of parchment was familiar to him. Mary Channing.

He looked around the courtroom. Normally, such an event would not attract much attention but there were already plenty of people seated, with yet more coming in. The infamy of Mrs Channing had not faded in the interim months. He wondered how she had fared over the winter.

Downstairs, Mary was sat awaiting her fate. She hadn't wanted to go, knowing that the proceedings would only confirm what she already knew in her own heart. Her father's attempts to once again gain her a pardon had faltered. In the eyes of the courts, she was already dead.

Her mother held out her arms. 'It is time. I should go.'

Mary kissed her baby gently on the forehead as her mother removed the child from her arms. 'Goodbye, my sweet,' Mary called out as her mother left the room. Mary stood up from the bench as an officer took her arm to lead her up into the court.

The gallery gave a collective gasp as she took her place at the dock. She looked nothing like the defiant, attractive young woman who had stood before them the previous summer. Instead, a waif-like figure appeared, painfully thin, rags for clothes, her hair thinning and lacklustre. The filth and grime of her prison cell was ingrained on her face and her lifeless eyes appeared disinterested in what was going on around.

Judge Price was as shocked as everyone else, but maintained his composure. He recalled the horrific events surrounding the death of Thomas Channing and steeled himself. This was Mary's last hope. He was the last thing standing between her and her fate. Regardless of what he personally thought about her plight, it was his job to see justice served.

He brought the gavel down loudly on the lectern. The crack barely shook Mary out of her malaise. 'Mary Channing,' he began, his voice clear and authoritative. 'You have been brought once more before me to see if you can give the court just reason why the sentence handed down on you last July should not be passed. What do you say?'

Mary barely looked at him. 'I had a baby girl.'

'So I understand.' He looked around at the gallery. 'Ordinarily I would offer my congratulations, but I don't see how that would help you in this matter.' A few members of the gallery sniggered at his feeble attempt at humour. He returned his gaze to Mary. 'I will ask you once more. Can you give the court any just reason for not carrying out the sentence of last July?'

'I am innocent.' Mary seemed to suddenly take stock of her situation and gathered up what little strength she had left.

'That was not the finding of this court. Do you have anything new to add to your defence that may cause us to reconsider?'

Mary looked deflated. 'My lord, I swear I am as innocent as the child unborn. I have nothing further to add.'

Judge Price looked disappointed. 'I am afraid that this is

not a sufficient plea. I therefore order you to prepare for death. You have insisted you are innocent of the crime of petty treason throughout your trial. But this is not the findings of this court. I have no choice than to now give the order to carry out your sentence. You are soon to meet with God. Now is the time to confess your sins and admit your guilt. Only then will you be able to find peace.'

Mary shook her head. She raised her voice for the benefit of all in court. 'I am innocent. I shall meet with my God, knowing this to be true. Indeed, I look forward to it for only then will I truly be at peace.'

As the judge banged his gavel for the final time, Mary was led away. Richard Channing was sat, unnoticed by Mary, just behind her to her left. He nodded his head enthusiastically as he watched her leave, resisting the urge to call after her and applaud the judge's final verdict.

Meanwhile, in the gallery, Samuel Tyler finished scribbling the words of the judge on his piece of paper. In his heart, he had hoped for a final reprieve. If anybody had been studying him, they would have noticed a solitary tear roll down his cheek, before being quickly wiped away with the sleeve of his coat.

Chapter Sixty-Seven

Richard Brookes held his granddaughter in his arms for the first time. The decision had finally been taken between Mary and her mother that the child would not return with her to the awful conditions in her cell. Instead, while Mary was to ready herself for her execution, her daughter was to take her first steps towards life away from her mother.

She gurgled as he gently stroked her cheek. Elizabeth readied the lukewarm bath she had prepared, testing it with her elbow before reaching out for the child. Brookes handed the baby over and Elizabeth gently placed her in the water, supporting the back of her head. It was the first time the child had been properly bathed and, as she splashed around with her feet and hands, Elizabeth rubbed a soft sponge over her, gently removing every last piece of grit and grime from her granddaughter's young body in an effort to cleanse her of the past three and a half months.

Brookes sat down beside her, spooning small handfuls of water over her, studying her intently. 'She's beautiful, isn't she?'

Elizabeth agreed. 'Yes.'

Initially Brookes had been reticent about taking the child

on. The question over the child's parentage had lingered and he was concerned about the fallout, particularly with regards to what other people would say and think. But Elizabeth was adamant. 'She is a Brookes!' she admonished, wagging her finger at him as he suggested the baby be given to the parish to be cared for. He had never seen her so defiant and wondered if that was where Mary had got it from, along with her stubbornness.

'But the child is a bastard!' he argued, before quickly retreating under a volley of blows.

'She is not a bastard!' she countered. 'She is to be our child. We shall raise her as our own. To hell with what people think. Besides, I made a promise to Mary.'

Brookes held up his hands in defeat, a broad smile on his face. 'Fine, I accept it. I won't hand the child over to the parish. We shall keep her and raise her as our own.' And so it was that Elizabeth Brookes came home from the court with their granddaughter. Brookes himself had not gone to the court, fearing that he would not be able to control himself when he saw Mary, while feeling guilt and remorse for being unable to help her anymore.

Now, as he looked down on the baby, he knew there was no doubt that the child would be raised as his own. She reminded him of Mary and he remembered how he had felt when Mary herself had been born. Six sons had more than satisfied his desire for an heir. Now he had a daughter, one who would grow to be the apple of his eye. Mary would soon be leaving him, but Brookes knew that he was already falling for the little girl that was gurgling happily away in the bath while blowing bubbles at him. He also resolved that he would not allow himself to make the same mistakes that had resulted in Mary ending up in such dire straits.

Brookes cooed at the infant as Elizabeth removed the last smudges of dirt from her tiny feet and lifted her up. Brookes passed his wife the linen sheet with which to dry the child and watched contentedly as Elizabeth gently wiped her dry before dressing her. When she had finished, Elizabeth handed the infant back to Brookes then pulled at the chord to ring the bell in the servants' quarters. The wet nurse appeared. 'Take her up now. Feed her and put her to bed. I will be up shortly to check on her.'

The woman lifted the baby from Brookes' arms and he sat back as he watched the nurse leave, cradling the baby confidently. Elizabeth went over to the cabinet and filled two small crystal glasses with port. She handed him one of the glasses and took the seat opposite her husband. They sipped in silence before Richard spoke. 'What are we to call her?'

'Mary wanted her baptised as Grace.'

'Grace? That's a nice name. And yet I sense you are not keen on it.'

'No.' Elizabeth shook her head. 'I think there is only one name for the child.'

Brookes balanced his glass on the edge of his chair, holding on to it by its stem. 'And what is that?'

'She shall be called Mary.'

Chapter Sixty-Eight

The clergies gathered in the ornate dining room at Reverend Hutchins' grand house in Dorchester. The Bishop of Bristol stood at the head of the table and outlined the reason for their impromptu meeting, even though no explanation was required. 'Firstly, I would like to thank you all for coming here today. You are, I am sure, all aware of the Mary Channing trial, which is why I have called this gathering.'

The room all nodded as one while casting their eyes upon each other. Having confirmed that everyone was settled, the Bishop went on. 'Our host, Reverend Hutchins, is the Ordinary at Dorchester County prison. He has been giving Mrs Channing lessons and teaching her in the ways of our Lord, Jesus Christ. Yesterday, her death sentence was confirmed and she has now requested that she be baptised.'

Conversation immediately struck up around the table and the Bishop patiently waited for it to die down. When silence finally fell, he resumed. 'Our purpose today is to determine if the Channing girl is worthy of baptism in light of the sequence of events that have caused us to arrive at this point.' He sat down, squeezing his large frame snugly into the carver chair.

'She refuses to confess her crime, yet she has asked to be baptised. The two are incompatible.' Reverend Smythe stood up, his cherubic cheeks a pinkish red. 'I cannot reconcile her heinous crime with the ways of our Lord. Without confession, how can she be absolved of her sins?'

Reverend Porter rose next. 'And yet, gentlemen, she has asked to be baptised. Regardless of her intentions, are we to refuse her such a thing? What would God think of us if we did not permit a child – one that is to meet with him far sooner than ourselves – to be baptised in the name of our Lord, Jesus Christ?'

There were more murmurings and mutterings around the table. Porter held up his hand to quiet them, then went on. 'I believe it is right that we should grant her wish. God will surely see through her when she kneels before him and judge her accordingly.'

A young man got to his feet. The Reverend Samuel Conant was the newly installed Rector at Holy Trinity and St Peter's and he cut a dashing figure with his coat cut in the latest fashion. 'We must be aware of the message that a baptism of Mrs Channing will send out. On the one hand, we don't want the Church to appear weak, granting the key to the Kingdom of God at the drop of a hat. On the other hand, the Church must be seen as being merciful. I am sure my parishioners would see her baptism as a merciful act, one that allows her to be judged by the Lord and not by man.'

'Hear, hear!' Reverend Black got to his feet. 'I think Reverend Conant is correct. Who are we to judge? Mrs Channing will pay for her crimes with her life. Have we, as men, not done enough to her? There is much sympathy for her, especially among the ladies of my parish. Her age is in her favour, for they consider her young and naïve. The situation surrounding her forced marriage to a man she did not care for is also being met with sympathy. And her steadfast refusal to admit her guilt, in spite of the dire consequences, has led many to question if she really did it.'

Porter stood once more. 'I agree. I have followed the case and it would appear the evidence, while strong, is purely circumstantial. There is the question of the missing servant girl and this other woman who, as yet, remains unidentified. We may also be at risk of making a martyr of her, particularly in the eyes of those women who have suffered greatly at the hands of their husbands.'

Smythe appeared to be going redder by the second as his agitation grew. He pushed his chair back and slammed his fists on the table. 'Gentlemen! Surely we cannot pander to the will of the chattering classes? The woman murdered her husband, while with child by another man! This is not the behaviour of somebody who fears God! This is the behaviour of a wanton woman with little or no concern for anybody other than herself! She does not deserve our help in this matter. I, for one, cannot acquiesce to her demand to be baptised.'

The room lapsed once more into heated debate, forcing the Bishop to stand and motion for everyone to settle down again. What say you, Mr Hutchins? You have been guiding her in recent weeks and have a better knowledge of the girl than everyone else gathered here.'

Hutchins got to his feet and looked around the table at his colleagues. He sighed as he considered his words. 'Mr Black is correct. There is much sympathy for her and as time has gone on, there is also perhaps less desire to see her put to death among many in the parish. We should perhaps be wary of upsetting them further by denying her request for a baptism and should consider any potential backlash.'

The gathered men looked at each other, nodding. Hutchins went on. 'That said, however, having met with her on numerous occasions, I personally feel she is unrepentant. She is compliant in most things, yet I would say she has resisted God's will, being a reluctant participant in my teachings. She is saying and doing what she thinks is required in order to save her neck. I myself remain unconvinced that she has truly given herself to God and I cannot think of any valid reason why she should be baptised.'

Several of his colleagues nodded in agreement as he retook his seat. Conant got up to plead Mary's case once more. 'With respect to Mr Hutchins, she is young and not without support. Surely it is for God to decide, not us. As my friend Reverend Black has already said, there are many doubters out there who feel she may indeed be innocent. I for one feel it would be a mistake to deny her this request.'

He sat down, his cheeks flushed from his efforts. With nobody else standing to express their thoughts, the Bishop of Bristol pushed himself up out of his chair. 'I believe we have all had our say. It therefore falls upon us to put it to the vote. I shall abstain from the decision unless required to give a casting vote. All those that believe she should be baptised, raise your hands.' A show of hands went up. 'Now for all those against the baptism, raise your hands.' He did a quick count and was relieved to find a decision had been reached without need for him to vote himself. 'The ayes have it on a count of five to three. Reverend Hutchins, I leave it to you to make the necessary arrangements and carry out the baptism. But you had better be quick. The day of her execution has been set for the twenty first of March, so you only have a few days.'

Hutchins slowly got to his feet. 'As you wish, your Lordship. But I want it to be noted that I am against this decision. Having spent a many hours with Mary Channing, I believe to baptise her is a mistake and that she will not repent her sins. Nor, as far as I am concerned, will she ever be allowed to enter the Kingdom of God.'

Chapter Sixty-Nine

Richard Channing arrived at the small stone cottage just outside Maumbury Rings. He dismounted his steed and knocked on the door. There was no answer. He led his horse round to the back of the cottage where there was a trough full of water. The horse drank as he looked around for the man who resided in the cottage.

The wind whipped up and he pulled his collar tight to his neck. Spring was around the corner as witnessed by the many snowdrops that had sprung up amongst the grass around him, but the icy chill of winter was still clinging on.

He strained his ears and fancied he could hear occasional banging noises off in the distance, being carried on the wind. He jumped on his horse again and set off up the winding path that had been weathered due to years of use. As he turned the corner, he saw the gallows and involuntarily shivered. Long enough to hang up to eight people at a time, the oak beam was supported at each end by two uprights. They were to the west end of the old Roman amphitheatre, a scene of more barbaric times Channing thought to himself, without feeling any sense of irony. The original amphitheatre had all but disappeared, with the largest stones being taken to build cottages and outbuildings located close by. Nature was doing its best to erase the rest of the structure, but the foundations were still visible for all to see. Its location, close to Weymouth Road, was far enough away from Dorchester to be out of sight, while close enough for those to make their way to it on foot whenever public executions were carried out.

The man Channing was looking for was lifting a large square oak beam into the deep hole he had meticulously dug out for it the previous day. Large set and balding, he looked up as Channing approached. Having lowered the beam into place, he placed a number of stones into the hole, packing them tightly against the wood to hold it upright. When he was finally satisfied the beam would remain where he had positioned it without the need for any further support, he stood up and wiped his hands on the front of his woollen smock.

'Mr Woods?' Channing pulled up his horse in front of him and leant forward on his saddle.

'Yes?'

'It is my understanding that you are the executioner.'

The man narrowed his eyes. 'What of it?' he said, cautiously. Few people knew his name or his occupation, which is how he preferred it.

Channing smiled. 'Don't worry, it's nothing sinister. It is just that I would like to request a favour of you, one that I know you will find financially beneficial.'

Wood's face hardened. 'I am sorry sir, but I fear you may have misjudged me. My job is to carry out executions, not grant "pardons".'

'No, it's nothing like that. I do not wish for you to let somebody escape, nor indeed to ease their suffering. On the contrary, I am hoping you will turn the event into a spectacle.'

'Sir, I am not into spectacles, either.'

Channing reached into his pocket and withdrew a leather pouch. He shook it so the man could hear the contents jangling inside. 'This purse contains several guineas. I would like you to have them.'

The man stepped forward with his hand outstretched, but Channing quickly withdrew the pouch, clutching it to his chest. The horse took a couple of backward steps and Channing had to steady the animal before encouraging it forward again.

Woods stopped, looking up at Channing, his head inclined slightly to one side. 'So what would you have me do to earn such a purse?'

'That's the spirit.' Channing grinned. 'It is my understanding that you will be carrying out the executions on Thursday.'

'That is correct.'

'One of them is to be the woman Mary Channing.'

'Is it?' The executioner rarely knew the names of those he was to execute. They were just brought to him and he did his job. It was up to the prison to sort out who they were and to tell him how they wanted him to dispatch them.

'Yes, it is. I hear that you will have three executions to carry out that day. She will be the only woman executed, and she will also be the only one to be burnt at the stake, so it will be easy for you to identify her.'

Woods shrugged. 'If you say so.'

'I do say so.'

'So what would you have me do?' His eyes narrowed. Normally requests came from the family who either wanted a speedy and merciful death, or help with their escape. To date, he hadn't entered into agreement with any of them.

'Mary Channing is to be burnt at the stake for she has been found guilty of petty treason.'

Woods shrugged. 'What of it?'

'I have heard that the executioner can, on occasion, aid with delivering a merciful death, either by ensuring they are dead before they are tied to the stake, or by rendering them senseless while on the stake before the flames can take them.'

'That's right.' Woods himself would place a cord around the neck of the convicted as the flames were lit and pull it tight before the flames could consume the body. 'Is that what you want?'

Channing laughed. 'No. I do not wish you to ease her suffering or deliver her quickly to death. On the contrary, I wish you to ensure she feels the kiss of the fire right up until the end.'

Now it was the executioner's turn to laugh. 'You want me to see to it that she is very much alive throughout her ordeal?'

'Yes. I do. She deserves nothing less.' Channing tossed the pouch in the palm of his hand once more, holding it out before him like a prize. 'So what do you say?'

Woods grinned. 'I think I can oblige the gentleman this one small favour.'

Channings tossed the purse to him. 'Excellent. I would also like to request one more thing of you.'

Woods caught the purse one handed. 'Sir?'

'The wood you will be using for the fire.'

'What of it?'

'Make sure it is nice and green. We don't want it to be over too quickly now, do we.'

Chapter Seventy

The morning of March the twenty-first, 1706 was wet, grey and miserable. Mary tearfully bid her mother and daughter farewell and was led to another cell, located just inside the entrance to the prison. There was already a gathering of people in the room, including her father who hugged her as soon as she entered. It had been a while since he had seen her and he could not believe how thin and gaunt she had become. Her eyes were hollow and lifeless. 'My dearest Mary. What have they done to you?'

Mary smiled weakly. 'They have all but done the executioner's work for him. If it were not for today, I would surely perish sooner rather than later.' Brookes grabbed her hand and took her to one corner of the cell where a long wooden bench had been placed. He sat her down and took his place beside her, a protective arm around her shoulder.

She glanced around nervously. Two other men were in the cell surrounded by family, well-wishers and do-gooders. One was sobbing silently to himself while Reverend Hutchins read a passage from the Bible to him. The other looked defiant, staring

at everyone as if challenging them to carry out the sentence that
had been passed on him.

Brookes watched the Reverend as he delivered his sermon.
'How was your baptism?' he asked Mary.

'I never received it.' She looked up at him and Brookes
could see the anguish in her eyes.

'You never received it? I thought it had been agreed that
you were to be baptised.'

She shook her head. 'The Reverend Hutchins told me that
he was unable to find the time to fit me into his busy schedule,
what with three executions to prepare for and his parish work to
do.'

Brookes made to stand, but Mary dragged him back down
onto the bench. 'It does not matter now, father. I know I am
innocent and that God will be merciful. It is of no consequence.'

'I shall flog him myself when this is over!' Brookes fumed.

Now it was Mary's turn to comfort him. 'You will do no
such thing. He will answer for his sins himself one day, and
believe me, there are many of them.'

Brookes looked quizzically at Mary's face, but she would
not expand on what she had said. Instead, she lapsed into silence
as he talked about her about how well her brothers were doing
in the business and how much they all adored their new little
"sister". She did not know that her mother had renamed her
Mary and Brookes felt it prudent not to say anything for fear
of upsetting her. Before long, he too fell silent as he ran out of
things to say in order to distract her from her thoughts.

'Joseph Carter?' The Under Sheriff entered the cell,
accompanied by the jailer and two officers. The man who had
been sobbing suddenly became hysterical as the officers moved
to secure him. He cursed and struggled as they attached shackles
to his ankles and wrists. His wife tried to placate him as he
attempted to pull away from their grip. She held his face in her
hands, kissing it all over before he was finally yanked away from

her. He was half carried, half dragged from the cell as his legs refused to move.

Mary heard the cheers and catcalls go up outside as the crowd caught sight of him being loaded onto the back of the horse cart. The noise continued as the two officers returned.

'Daniel Marks.' The Under Sheriff addressed the second man who stood up slowly, calmly holding his hands out in front of him. The two officers applied the shackles as he spoke to the Under Sheriff. 'You're making a mistake. I am innocent.'

'That's not what it says here,' the Under Sheriff responded. 'You have been found guilty of bigamy. Take it up with your maker when you see him – assuming he lets you in.' He nodded to the two officers to lead him away.

Yet more cheers could be heard as he entered the courtyard of the prison and was lifted up onto the back of the cart. With both men secured, the driver flicked the reins and the horse set off at a plodding pace through the streets towards Maumbury Rings. Mary could hear the noise of the crowd getting fainter as the cart continued on its way and wondered why she wasn't on it. Had there been a last minute reprieve? She allowed her hopes to rise. Perhaps her father's efforts had paid off after all. She looked up expectantly as the Under Sheriff arrived in front of her. He pulled out his pocket watch and squinted at it. 'It is almost time for lunch. I'm afraid you'll just have to wait Mrs Channing. But fear not. We will get to you in due course.'

'How dare you! Have you no pity?' Brookes jumped to his feet but Mary pulled at his hand once more. 'Father, it is to be expected. Please sit down.'

Brookes reluctantly took his seat again as the Under Sheriff departed, along with the jailer and the family members of the other two prisoners. The only person that remained behind in the cell was Hutchins. He made his way over to them. 'Hello Mary.' He knelt before her and she flinched, drawing her legs up on to the bench and forcing her knees together. Even with her father next to her she didn't feel safe. She gripped his arm tightly with both hands, pulling herself closer to him.

'Get him away from me!' Mary's eyes were wide open with fear.

'Mary, what is wrong?' Brookes could see the distress on his daughter's face.

'Just keep him away from me!'

'But Mary, he is going to bless you.'

'No!' she screamed. 'Get him out of here!'

Brookes stood up and pulled the Reverend to his feet by his collar. 'What have you done to her?' he hissed.

Hutchins sneered at him. 'Nothing.'

'Why did you not baptise her?'

'But I did.'

'You, sir, are a liar!' Brookes raised his hand and Hutchins flinched, falling away backwards before he could be struck.

'Jailer!' Hutchins yelled at the top of his voice. 'Help me! Get me out of here! This man has gone quite mad!'

The jailer arrived promptly and opened the door to the cell. Hutchins fell out and scrambled across the floor to the wall opposite. He steadied himself and regained his composure before giving Mary one last smirk. 'May you rot in hell, for that is all you deserve.'

Mary was trembling as her father took her in his arms and tried his best to console her. Then the tears came. 'I'm sorry father, for everything I have done to you. I never meant for this to happen.'

Brookes was close to tears himself. 'Hush, child. It is not your fault. I was never there for you and I should have been. I should never have forced you into that marriage with Thomas. I should have listened to you and your mother. If I had, none of this would ever have happened. Please, I beg of you, forgive me.'

They both hugged and fell into silence once more, holding

each other, saying nothing.

A few hours later, they heard a large number of footsteps approaching. The jailer arrived with his entourage. He opened the door and the Under Sheriff stepped inside. 'Mary Channing.' He motioned the two officers to come in with the shackles. 'Stand up. It is time.'

Chapter Seventy-One

The crowd lined both sides of the streets. Had Mary looked from her elevated view on the back of the cart, she would have seen them stretch to the horizon, as far as the eye could see. Instead, she kept her head down and her eyes closed, quietly praying to herself and blocking out the raucous noise of the people that lined the road either side of her.

The early evening sun appeared as a large white globe through the thin, grey cloud. A light drizzle was being swirled back and forth in the wind, unsure of which direction to take. The Under Sheriff led the way on his horse, a proud look on his face, taking in the spectacle of the crowds. This was by far the biggest execution he had overseen and he was intent on ensuring it went off without a hitch.

Richard Channing rode alongside him, keen to see justice done, smiling at the onlookers as he passed them by, occasionally waving and calling out greetings as he recognised faces in the crowd. Richard Brookes rode his horse to the rear of the small convoy, feeling utterly miserable. The occasional piece of rotten fruit hit him, but he ignored it, refusing to rise to the goading of the onlookers.

They continued up East High Street and Mary took a long look at her old house where she had lived with Thomas for those few, short weeks. She wondered what had ever happened to Molly and half hoped to see her at the gate, but the garden was empty and the windows of the house were shuttered. A hundred yards further on and the apothecary shop appeared on her left. Mr Wolmington was stood outside and Amy Clavell turned away and put her head to his chest, sobbing as the cart passed by. Next, Thomas's grocer shop came into view, boarded up and devoid of any activity. Outside stood a handful of people, all of them stony faced, saying nothing, just watching in solemn silence as Mary's slowly passed them by.

The cart turned left into Bow and the lane narrowed, forcing people either side to squeeze close to each other or move along as the cart made its way through them. The small entourage were now at the outskirts of Dorchester and the houses began to give way to heath and farmland. Mary knew there was not much further to go and began shaking uncontrollably, a mixture of fear and cold as the light rain began soaking through the thin material of her tattered dress, chilling her to the bone and causing her teeth to chatter uncontrollably.

People were now running at speed towards Maumbury Rings, keen to get there before Mary arrived to secure a good position from which to watch proceedings unfold. Mary watched them go, feeling sadness and shame that so many were there to witness her final moments. Channing half turned on his horse to see Mary looking at him. He winked at her, a sadistic grin on his face, before digging his heels into the horse's flank to speed it up. It broke into a trot and he too left them behind in order to take up his vantage point from where he would be able to see everything at close hand.

As they rounded the corner, the Rings came into view. People were everywhere, pointing at Mary as the cart plodded slowly towards them. For the first time, Mary could see the large gallows. The two men who had shared her cell earlier that morning were both hanging lifeless from its long beam, their hands tied behind their backs, left there for all to see. Mary gave an involuntary whimper at the sight. Perhaps for the first time, the horrific reality of what was about to happen struck her. There would be no escape, no last minute reprieve and no mercy. The sick feeling of dread in her stomach exploded as the full horror of what was about to befall her hit home. Mary frantically pulled at the shackles, trying to break free while appealing to her father to come and help her. He shook his head sadly, close to tears, knowing that the worse was yet to come. He so wanted to turn the horse around and head for home so he could not witness what was about to happen, but resisted. He knew he had to try and be there for her.

The cart drew to a halt before the gallows. A welcoming committee consisting of the local clergy and dignitaries were stood in a half circle with Reverend Hutchins taking up position in front of them. He was reading from the Bible and they were chanting their responses to his prayer. The driver jumped down from the front of the cart and climbed wearily up into the back. Taking a key from his jacket pocket, he undid the padlocks that had secured Mary's shackles to the cart and let them fall. 'I'm sorry Miss Mary. May God have mercy on your soul,' he whispered as he helped her down into the arms of the two officers who were awaiting her.

They dragged Mary to Reverend Hutchins and forced her down on her knees before him. He placed his hand on her forehead and began praying for her soul. The assembled clergy gathered around her in a circle, joining in with the prayer, hiding her from the view of the large crowd who had all fallen silent.

Mary looked around with frightened eyes and saw Channing standing just outside the circle. She became even more distressed. 'Please, remove that man. I cannot bear the sight of him!' She began struggling and the two officers had difficulty holding her down as she rocked backwards and forwards, trying in vain to get to her feet.

'Hold still, child!' Hutchins admonished her, but to no avail. He turned to see the object of her angst and approached him. 'Mr Channing. It may be better for all if you removed yourself.'

Channing looked affronted. 'Sir, I have been awaiting this day for close to twelve months. I will do no such thing!'

'Please Mr Channing, I beg of you. For the sake of everyone else here, just keep out of sight, at least while we hear her confession.' Hutchins placed his hand on his Bible and held it out before him. 'As soon as it is over, you can return.'

Channing reluctantly gave in. 'I would like to have heard her confession, although I expect you will be wasting your breath. For the sake of expediency, I shall remove myself, at least for now.'

As soon as Channing disappeared from view, Mary settled down. Hutchins placed his hand on her head and looked down upon her. She looked up at him, unseeing. 'Mary, it is time for you to confess your sins. What say you?'

Mary said nothing, a haunted look in her eyes. Hutchins tried again. 'Mary, it is time. Preserve your soul and confess or forever hold your peace.'

'I am innocent.' Mary's voice was small, but those around her could still hear. Her father turned away, unable to watch any more as she was lifted up and led to the stake. The large square post rose up from the assembled logs and faggots that the executioner had arranged earlier that morning. A brazier was set to one side, full of white hot charcoal. An unlit torch was stood to one side, the swaddling covered in thick, black tar.

The two officers lifted her up on to the platform and turned her round to face the crowd. A deathly hush fell as the executioner roughly pulled her hands behind her back and connected the shackles on her wrists to the metal rings on either side of the stake. She held her head up high and gazed out upon the crowd, which stretched as far as she could see. The faces were blurred as her eyes welled up. 'I am innocent!' she called out but nobody responded. She turned to her left and saw a solitary figure heading back up the track towards Dorchester. 'Goodbye father,' she whispered, grateful that he would not be there to witness her final moments.

With her wrists chained to the beam behind her, the officers retreated to a safe distance. Having finished securing her, the executioner jumped down from the platform. Channing caught his attention as the man went to the brazier and picked up the torch. The executioner nodded to him as he stuck the tarred end into the charcoal, stirring it up. Embers rose up into the now darkening sky as the torch burst into flame. He twisted it a few times to make sure it was fully alight, before holding it up above his head for all to see.

The crowd murmured excitedly and jostled as they moved forward as one, pushed from those behind, eager to see what was going on. The executioner checked the direction of the gusting breeze, before marching purposefully to the pile of wood arranged in front of Mary. He began running the torch along its front. The faggots caught easily, as did the seasoned wood on top of it. He had been good to his word, however. The green wood was located in the centre of the woodpile, directly beneath Mary. It would not catch quickly and she would feel the intense heat of the fire long before the flames would begin licking at her.

As the smoke started billowing up into the grey sky, he tossed the torch into the heart of the assembled logs and pulled a length of cord from waistband of his breeches. Rolling it around both of his hands, he flexed it in front of him to ensure he had a good grip. He marched to the rear of the fire and leapt up, catching hold of the beam to steady himself as he did so. He glanced over to Channing once more and caught his eye to let him know he would be true to his word. He let go of one end of the cord and threw it around Mary's chest, catching it the other side. Gripping it tightly, he pulled it up to her neck and leant backwards.

The smoke was rising up around her and Mary was already struggling to breathe. She began coughing, her weak body shuddering as she did so. Her eyes were smarting as the smoke filled them, causing her to blink rapidly. The combination of smoke and tears in her eyes meant she could see nothing, although she could hear the cheers and gasps of the crowd as the fire began to rise up before her. From afar it looked as if Mary was being engulfed, but there was still a good gap between her and the flames that were flicking like a serpent's tongue through the gaps in the wood. Thick, acrid smoke was now spreading up from between her feet as the green wood below began heating up, the fire within them struggling to fully burst into life. She could feel the heat on her face and beneath her feet. The warmth of the fire spread rapidly up through her body and was not unpleasant, drying her from the light rain that had soaked her through. She closed her eyes and imagined she was stood in front of the large inglenook fireplace in her father's kitchen on a winter's day, the cook fussing around behind her, the smell and crackling of burning wood mixing with that of the food on the stove. She felt warm inside as she felt an inner calm, the sensation taking her back to another time, far away from this place.

She felt the touch of the cord on her neck. She began to struggle as it was pulled tighter, compressing her throat, restricting her airway. Shaking her head from side to side, she felt herself slipping from consciousness while desperately gasping to fill her lungs with the smoke filled air.

Her head slumped forward as she finally lapsed into unconsciousness. The executioner relaxed his grip while appearing to the casual onlooker that he was still pulling the cord tight. 'Sorry child,' he whispered as he satisfied himself that she had merely fainted and was not dead.

As he leapt down away from the flames that were now beginning to catch the logs beneath him, the Under Sheriff met him, handing him his purse. 'It is done?' he enquired.

The executioner grunted at him. 'It is done.' He walked quickly to where he had left his coat, picking it up and putting it on. Channing made to approach him but he held up his hand, stopping him dead in his tracks. The executioner merely nodded at him, turned down the collar on his coat and walked back up the small stone path to his cottage. He entered, closing the door firmly behind him and drawing the bolts across inside. His work was done and he had no desire to witness the outcome.

Chapter Seventy-Two

The onlookers watched in morbid fascination as the flames grew higher. Mary was obscured from view as thick swirls of smoke gathered around her. Slowly, the green wood began catching light from beneath, heating the wood above it, releasing yet more thick smoke.

'Tis green wood!' one man suddenly shouted. The word spread back through the crowd as realization dawned. This would not be over quickly.

'Oh dear God!' One old woman crossed herself quickly. 'The poor girl.'

'Don't fret.' her husband reassured her. 'She will be dead already.'

'Really? How so?' The old woman was puzzled. 'I thought it was the fire that was to consume her!'

'No. The executioner has already delivered her. She will suffer no longer, poor thing.'

The smoke cleared as a sharp gust of wind blew it away. Spurred on by the sudden draft, the green wood finally caught, the flames bursting into life and leaping skyward as the wind died down once more. The tattered bottom of Mary's dress smouldered, then caught light. Mary stirred, slowly coming to. The warm feeling she remembered from earlier was now growing increasingly uncomfortable. She went to pull away from the source of the heat, but found her hands and feet tied. Unable to comprehend what was going on, she tried to raise her feet as the soles felt as if they were resting on hot coals. She opened her eyes and screamed as the flames danced in front of her face. Looking down, she saw the skin on her feet bubbling, the bones within becoming visible as her flesh melted away like molten wax. The pain registered in Mary's brain as she regained full consciousness and she began screaming at the top of her voice like an animal caught in a trap.

The two officers looked at each other. 'He didn't do for her!' the older man yelled. 'Where is he?' They looked around but were unable to see the executioner anywhere. 'Quickly! Do something!'

'Like what, exactly?' the younger man replied, dumbstruck and unable to move as he watched the flesh on Mary's legs melt away in front of him, the fabric of her dress burning quickly, revealing her thin, blackening body beneath.

The crowd was becoming distressed. Shouts were being hurled at the two officers as both men and women pleaded with them to end Mary's suffering. People were turning away, picking up their small children and holding their faces to their chests while covering their ears so they could neither see nor hear Mary's agonised screams.

The older officer reached into his pocket and pulled out his handkerchief. He ran behind the burning pyre and jumped upon it, even though the flames were all around and the heat was unbearable. He reached around and grabbed Mary's face with one hand. It felt like hot wax to the touch. Her lips and ears had already disappeared and it was all he could do not to jump away in horror. He shoved the handkerchief into her mouth in an attempt to stifle her chilling screams, before jumping off once more.

'Quickly, find a musket or a sword!' he called out to his colleague.

The younger man ran to the crowd, yelling out for a weapon. A gentleman with a tricorn produced a sword and he snatched it, running back to his older colleague. They both looked at up the flames, knowing it was not safe to enter but knowing they had to put an end to Mary's misery. Realising it would be impossible to get close enough to her to put the sword through her, the older man turned around. 'Does anyone have a musket?' he yelled at the top of his voice, trying desperately to be heard over Mary's blood curdling screams and the hissing of the fire.

'Stop right there!' Channing appeared before them. 'Return that sword to its owner and stand down. There is nothing you can do for her now.'

The older man hesitated, brandishing the sword in front of him. Channing remained unmoved, staring at him coldly. 'I ordered you to return that sword immediately.' He glanced across at the Under Sheriff who had a look of horror on his face as he watched the drama unfold. Mary's screams were cutting through him and he wished the whole, horrific event would be over 'Sir!' Channing barked at him. 'Tell your men to stand down and return to their positions.'

The Under Sheriff nodded his assent, then turned away. He had seen enough. He too, headed for the path and joined the hundreds of people hurrying out of the Rings.

'Look!' A youth near the front pointed up at Mary. Her hair had caught fire and her eyes were just two, dark, black holes. Her screams were subsiding as the fire consumed her body and her head suddenly slumped forward down onto her chest.

The old woman crossed her chest again and fell into her husband. 'Poor girl.' she sobbed as he held her tight.

'Come on, we've seen enough' he said as he led her away,

refusing to look at Mary as he quickly passed her by.

The flames were now at their zenith and molten flesh was dripping off Mary's lifeless body, revealing the skeleton beneath. Those that remained looked on, fascinated, unable to pull their eyes away while others held handkerchiefs over their noses and mouths as both the smoke and the smell of cooking flesh hit them.

Mary's suffering was finally over. Many stayed until the end, some praying, others crying, a few consoling each other. The grand spectacle that had been promised by the authorities had failed to deliver. The barbarity of her death had shocked and appalled in equal measure with few of those present ever wanting to attend a burning again.

The only person who remained throughout was Richard Channing. Justice had been served, although he felt strangely hollow inside. The hatred he had carried for Mary Brookes had gone. All that was left was sorrow – for his son, for his family and now, inexplicably, for Mary herself.

Chapter Seventy-Three

The fire burned long into the night. A few sat in groups watching it die down until there was nothing left to see. Mary's body had been reduced to ashes.

Come morning, the smouldering embers still occasionally flickered into flames as the fire, too, tried desperately to hang on to life. As the sun rose, the sky was clear of cloud, the drizzle of the previous evening giving way to blue skies. A pair of skylarks sang as they wound their way up into the thin air over the Rings, climbing as high as they could fly before falling rapidly back to earth to start again.

Richard Brookes returned on horseback just after midday. He paused at the top of the path, looking down upon the remains of the fire. He sniffed at the air. The unmistakeable aroma of burnt wood filled his nose. He spurred his horse to move forward once more and they slowly made their way carefully down the path, passing the executioner's house without Brookes giving it so much as a glance.

He reached the outer ring of ash, a mixture of white and black, remnants of charred wood amongst it. He dismounted, leaving the horse to wander off to the rocks that circled the boundary, where the grass was longest. Lowering its head, the animal began pulling at the long strands, chewing contentedly in the spring sunshine.

Brookes pulled his cane from his belt and wandered cautiously to the rear of where the pyre had been. The tall oak beam, squared as if made for a ship, stood proud. Blackened and still warm to the touch, it remained surprisingly unharmed by the ravages of the fire. The chains that had held his daughter firm were still connected to it, the empty shackles hanging limply to each side.

He poked his cane at the charred remains at the foot of the post. Spotting what looked like small fragments of bone, he took a small clay pot from the bag hanging at his side and bent down. With his gloves on, he gently picked it up with forefinger and thumb and studied it closely before dropping it into the pot. He continued a while, squatting on his haunches, seeking out bone from wood, gathering them up.

When he could see no more, Brookes stiffly stood up, placed the cork lid back on the pot and tapped the top of it with the end of his cane until it fitted snugly. Testing it briefly to make sure the lid would not come off, he put it back in his bag and pulled the drawstring tight on it.

He walked back to his horse and gathered the reins. He walked it back out of the Rings. When he reached the road, he mounted it and settled into the saddle. Without looking back, he headed slowly towards home, lost in his thoughts, letting the horse travel at its own pace.

Brookes came upon a small roadside stall selling small bouquets of spring flowers. He stopped to pick up a bunch of bluebells, sniffing them before giving the young girl a sixpenny to pay for them. She fumbled for a farthing for change, but he waved it away, patting her gently on the head before climbing back on his horse, the flowers held in one hand as he picked up the reins in the other. He paused. 'Do you have any bulbs as well?'

'Yes sir, but only daffodils.' The girl picked up a small bag and he reached down to grab them from her. Tossing her another sixpence, he slowly continued on his way, head held high, refusing to engage with passers-by who stopped and stared at him before going about their business, talking in hushed voices as they scurried off.

Arriving at his house, he rode the horse straight to the stables where he dismounted and handed the reins to the stable boy, telling him to brush the horse down and return it to its stall. He picked up a small garden fork before heading down to the bottom meadow with the bluebells and the bulbs. Two beagles joined him, their tongues hanging out as they went on an unexpected walk with their master.

The meadow grass was getting tall and he removed his glove and held out the down-turned palm of his hand as he walked through it, enjoying the slight tickling sensation as he went. The crows squawked in the trees to the bottom of the meadow where the woodland began. A brook ran alongside its border, the water clear and gurgling as it rushed over the stones beneath it. It was one of many that criss-crossed the many fields he owned, and he fancied it was these that had given rise to the family name, for the Brookes had resided on this land for three generations now.

He reached his destination. A mature chestnut tree stood tall alongside a small wooden bridge. He put the flowers down at the base of the tree and removed the bag from his shoulder, setting it down beside him. Taking the fork, he began digging at the soft, peaty soil. It came away easily and the hole quickly took shape. When it was elbow deep, he stopped and put the fork to one side. Reaching for the bag, he took out the pot and removed the lid. He picked out the pieces of charred bone one by one, carefully placing them at the bottom of the hole. When the pot was empty, Brookes gently scraped the soil back into the hole, covering the bones.

Opening the small sack, he took the small daffodil bulbs and began pushing them into the loose soil. Once they were all in, he used his hand to scrape the rest of the soil over them and pressed it all down firmly with his palm.

When he was finished, he sat back under the tree and gazed at the spot for a while. The brook alongside him bubbled and babbled and the crows continued squawking as the sun began setting behind the trees. He noted with a faint smile that they were just beginning to sprout their summer covering of leaves. The long, cruel and turbulent winter was nearly done.

His thoughts wandered back to happier times, when Mary was a small girl. He recalled her playing in the water here, jumping off the small bridge he had constructed with the help of her two eldest brothers, so she could cross it to go and pick flowers in the woods and go hunting for butterflies and stag beetles. When she was older, they would catch sticklebacks and minnows together with a makeshift net that the cook had made out of sackcloth. He smiled to himself as he ran through his memories of Mary as a young girl. They were simpler, happier days.

As the sun began dipping down behind the horizon, a chill whipped around him. He fancied it was Mary's soul, leaving the ground and ascending the invisible steps to a far better place. He hoped Saint Peter and God would be merciful and that his parents would be there to greet her. He stiffly pushed himself up off the ground. It was time to head back for supper before he was missed. He brushed remnants of soil from his breeches and his hands. He returned the empty pot to his bag and slung it over his shoulder. 'Goodbye, Mary. I promised I'd bring you home. You're safe now.'

He walked slowly back up to the house, the last warmth of the sun on his neck, the two dogs following closely at his heels. As he approached, he could hear the baby crying. He smiled to himself as he let himself in through the back door and heard his wife shouting to the wet-nurse to pick the infant up from her cradle to begin her feed.

He hung his bag up on a hook on the back of the door, picked up a bucket of water and placed it on the table. He smelt the aroma of stew wafting through from the kitchen as he washed his hands. Drying them on a linen cloth, he went though to the front room. The wet-nurse had just finished feeding they baby and was about to place her back in her cot. 'I'll take her,' he said, letting the woman place Mary gently in his arms.

He made his way to the large bay window overlooking the front lawn. He sat down gently in his rocking chair. Mary was just going off to sleep and he placed her, face down, onto his chest, carefully supporting her head as he did so. He began rocking the chair backwards and forwards as Mary dozed contentedly on him. Before long, he too was fast asleep.

If you have enjoyed this book, please visit our website at:

https://hainesgritton.com

and sign up to our newsletter to receive information about other existing and upcoming titles.

Printed in Great Britain
by Amazon